Once Dishonored

Mary Jo Putney is the *New York Times* and *USA Today* bestselling author of more than sixty novels and novellas. A ten-time finalist for the Romance Writers of America RITA® award, she has won the honor twice and is on the RWA Honor Roll for bestselling authors. In 2013 she was awarded the RWA Nora Roberts Lifetime Achievement Award. Though most of her books have been historical romance, she has also published contemporary romances, historical fantasy, and young adult paranormal historicals. She lives in Maryland with her nearest and dearest, both two and four-footed. Visit her at MaryJoPutney.com.

Also by Mary Jo Putney

Rogues Redeemed

Once
DISHONORED

ROGUES REDEEMED

MARY JO
PUTNEY

CANELO

First published in the United States in 2020 by Kensington Publishing Corp.

This edition published in the United Kingdom in 2021 by

Canelo
Unit 9, 5th Floor
Cargo Works, 1-2 Hatfields
London, SE1 9PG
United Kingdom

A CIP catalogue record for this book is available from the British Library.

Print ISBN 978 1 80032 580 7
Ebook ISBN 978 1 80032 579 1

Look for more great books at www.canelo.co

Printed and bound in Great Britain by Clays Ltd, Elcograf S.p.A.

1

Chapter 1

London, March 1816

Lucas Mandeville hesitated at the entrance to the ballroom and thought of cannonballs crushing masts and setting sails ablaze. Bellowing sailors and hand-to-hand combat with pistols and cutlasses. In his Royal Navy days, he'd fought his share of sea battles with the French, had almost died in one. And he'd rather be on a burning deck than in this ballroom.

But he'd made a private pledge to do his best to reestablish himself in the world he'd been born into despite the number of people who would give him the cut direct, or worse. He cast his mind back to his one youthful season in London, when he was an eager young midshipman. He'd enjoyed the balls and dancing and flirting with pretty girls. Surely he could do that again.

Lucas arranged his face into a calm he didn't feel and stepped into the ballroom. His hosts, Lord and Lady Clanton, greeted him. The lady offered him a friendly smile. Her husband's expression tightened but he didn't spit in Lucas's face. He managed a civil nod and said, "Foxton," though he didn't offer his hand. Probably his wife had told him to behave because Lucas had a title, a substantial fortune, and the Clantons had two unmarried daughters.

Lucas greeted his hosts politely, then joined the throng. He'd attended some social occasions with his cousins Simon and Suzanne Duval, but those had been smaller groups whose guests were carefully chosen to be tolerant of Lucas. The people he'd met at those events were the sort who accepted that between the absolutes of white and black there could be many shades of gray.

Lucas inhabited that gray territory.

He greeted several people he'd met at Duval House and they returned his greetings amiably. So far, so good.

He eyed the dancers, his foot tapping. His dancing had been very rusty, but Suzanne had given him lessons before hosting a small dining and dancing party where he could practice. His missteps had been laughingly forgiven by his partners. By the end of the evening, he was able to hold his own on the dance floor.

Now it was time to put his regained skills into practice. He asked a married woman he'd met at his cousins' home to dance. She accepted and they both enjoyed it. Then another dance with another woman he'd met at the Duvals'.

The long dance ended and his partner thanked him with a smile before returning to her husband. He was looking around for another partner when a collective gasp of shock rippled across the ballroom.

He turned and saw a woman in black stride through the crowd. Her raised head and erect posture made him think of queens. Cleopatra facing the ruler of the Roman Empire. Elizabeth the Great rallying her troops against the might of the Spanish Armada.

Mary Queen of Scots advancing to the scaffold.

Dead silence fell and the music faltered and stopped. Then the whispering began. "How dare that female show her face here!" a woman hissed. "A divorcée! An adulteress!"

"They say Lady Denshire lay with four of her husband's friends," another woman whispered avidly.

The first voice said, "Only three. My husband was there when they testified in court!"

"Scandalous!" another woman said with fascinated horror. "An utter disgrace!" The whispering continued as the guests melted away, leaving the woman in black alone in the middle of the dance floor.

The dim lighting showed that Lady Denshire was graceful with dark chestnut hair and her head raised high. In the lift of her chin, Lucas saw pride, anger, defiance, and terror. She was a female version of himself, in fact, and he saw her posture change as defiance was assaulted by fear and humiliation.

She slowly turned, her gaze sweeping over the retreating guests as if looking for a friendly face. She was beautiful and haunted and desperately alone.

On impulse, he crossed the empty ballroom and smiled at the woman in black. "I'm Foxton, Lady Denshire. Though we haven't been formally introduced, will you join me for a waltz?" On that last word he shot a commanding glance at the musicians. The leader nodded in relief to have some direction and the quartet struck up a waltz.

She froze, looking like a deer ready to take flight. "Why do you want to dance with me? I am a pariah."

"I'm something of a pariah myself," he said peaceably, "and I was not put on this earth to cast stones." He extended his hand again. "Waltz with me."

Chapter 2

Kendra looked into the man's eyes and saw only kindness. She took his hand, desperately grateful that he was offering support in a whirlpool of condemnation. As they began to waltz, she felt the warmth of his grip through her kidskin gloves and realized that her hands were ice cold.

Whatever had possessed her to come to this ball? Because she wanted justice, but she would not find it here. She concentrated on the steps of the waltz, not needing the further humiliation of stumbling over her partner's feet.

"I just realized that we have been formally introduced," Foxton said. "Many years ago. I was Lucas Mandeville and unless my eyes deceive me, you were Kendra Douglas then."

She raised her gaze and really looked at her partner. Blond hair, strong, regular features, and the expression of a haunted saint. It took time to recognize that this man had once been a lively young midshipman she'd flirted with in her first season.

He looked like a man who had traveled long, hard roads between then and now. Or rather sailed stormy seas since he'd been a Royal Navy officer. "The last time we danced together was the night before you left for Plymouth to join your ship."

He nodded. "You wore a very pretty gown with a lot of blue embroidery that made your eyes look like sapphires."

She'd forgotten that herself. Mr. Mandeville had been too young and too excited by his new career to be husband material, but she'd liked him and wished him well. "You have a good memory. You were dashing and charming and I was sorry when you departed to join your ship."

"I liked to think of myself as dashing, but mostly I was just young. It was a very long time ago," he said quietly.

"For both of us," she said, her voice taut. "I gather you've inherited your grandfather's title. Is being a lord enough to keep you from being tarnished by dancing with a scandalous woman like me?"

"I may be even more scandalous than you." He gave her a slow, wry smile. "Shall we tarnish each other ?"

She'd liked the young midshipman then, and she liked the haunted lord now. Her tension ebbed, but she had to ask, "Do you know the crimes I have been accused of?"

He shrugged. "I heard some gossipy whispers when you entered the room, but that is rumor, not knowledge."

She was glad he appreciated the difference. "Do you know what it's like to stand accused and not be able to defend yourself?"

"Actually, I do," he said thoughtfully. "My circumstances were not identical, but there are similarities."

What could have made Lucas Mandeville a pariah? Cheating at cards? Never. Cowardice under fire? She supposed that any man in battle might succumb to terror, especially if young, but it was hard to imagine that of him.

Reminding herself that she had barely known him all those years ago and didn't know him at all now, she decided it was pointless to speculate. Better to relax and enjoy this dance in the arms of a compassionate stranger.

The music ended and her partner stepped away from her. "Have you had enough of this ball?"

She sighed. Her anger and defiance had burned out, leaving emptiness. "I have. I'll find no justice here."

"Justice can be elusive," he said dryly. "If you're ready to leave, I'll escort you to your home."

Her eyes narrowed. "Are you interested in learning just how scandalous I am?"

"Not at all." He smiled a little. "My cousin once told me that I'm an incurable knight errant. You are probably too angry now to want friendship, but you look like you could use an ally or at least a fair-minded listener."

She turned his words over in her mind. An ally would be welcome, though she wasn't sure she could trust that much. But a fair-minded listener would be welcome because she had a desperate need to tell her story to someone who might believe her. "You're right about that, though whether you can be such a person remains to be seen. I'm staying nearby and I don't need an escort, but you may accompany me if you wish."

"I'm trying to prove that I'm still a gentleman, so I do wish it," he explained. "Night streets can be dangerous for a woman alone."

The music was starting for another waltz and couples moved onto the dance floor, leaving a wary space around Kendra and her partner. Foxton took her arm and escorted her to the sidelines where their hostess was saying good-bye to other departing guests.

Lady Clanton's mouth tightened when Kendra approached. "I hadn't realized you were still on my guest list, Lady Denshire."

Kendra had wondered why she'd received an invitation. "I'm sorry I've brought notoriety to your doorstep, Lady Clanton."

The other woman's face eased into wry humor. "I should probably thank you. Notoriety enhances a social event." She turned away to speak to another guest.

Foxton accompanied her to the vestibule, where an efficient footman produced Kendra's black cloak and Foxton's hat. After she donned the cloak, she took her escort's arm and they descended to street level. He asked, "Where do you live? You said it was nearby."

"Thorsay House. It's just off St. James, only three blocks away." Kendra was surprised by how relaxed she felt on his arm. Was it because they had a prior acquaintance, or because he didn't judge, leer, or despise her? Perhaps both.

Foxton walked like the military officer he'd been: upright, quietly alert to their surroundings, and clearly not an easy victim. She wasn't afraid of a short walk at night in this part of London, but it was no bad thing to have a capable male escort.

"Thorsay," he said thoughtfully. "Named for the group of Scottish islands between Orkney and Shetland?"

"Yes, all three of the archipelagos are more Norse than Celtic, though they're part of Scotland now. Thorsay House belongs to the laird of the islands, and he allows Thorsayians to use it as a sort of boardinghouse when in London. My grandmother was from Thorsay, first cousin to the laird. I spent summers there so I qualify as Thorsayian." The relaxed, accepting nature of Thorsay House had been a sanctuary in the hell her life had become. "I was grateful to be welcomed at the house when I needed a new home."

"You were forced out of your marital home?" Foxton asked quietly.

"Yes." Her voice was stony. That had been the worst day of her life, a raging firestorm whose details blurred in her mind. What she remembered was pain and loss.

Neither of them spoke as they walked the short blocks to Thorsay House. At the bottom of the steps, she paused to pull her key from her reticule.

She was going to offer a polite thank-you for Foxton's escort when he caught her gaze and said soberly, "Your life has been shattered, Kendra Douglas. Rage and grief are inevitable and likely necessary. But at some point you need to step beyond the anger toward your future. What is possible? What matters most to you, and how can you take the first steps toward achieving that?"

His words were a blade cutting through her inner turmoil. She drew a deep breath as she thought about what he'd said. Yes, it was time to move forward instead of standing still and burning. "That is the most useful advice I've yet received. You've implied that your life was also shattered. Did you learn wisdom by handling disaster well?"

He smiled with wry self-mockery. "No, I learned by handling it badly. I'm willing to tell you the whole disgraceful tale if you're interested."

Her eyes narrowed as she studied him, wanting to see beyond the handsome features to the man's soul. Once she'd thought herself a good judge of people, but recent years had destroyed that belief.

Now she forced herself to lower her defenses and really *look*. Perhaps she was wrong, but she felt that Lucas Mandeville was a man she could trust, at least a little. "I'd like to hear that disgraceful tale, preferably over a brandy. Will you join me for talk? *Only* talk."

"Only talk," he agreed, looking mildly amused at her wariness.

She unlocked the door and stepped inside, leaving it open for Lord Foxton to follow. Thorsay House was quiet at this hour. There were no other guests at the moment, and Mr. and Mrs. Brown, the couple who maintained the house, were in bed by now.

A candle was burning on the narrow table in the vestibule. She lifted the candlestick and led the way into a small sitting room on the left. While she lit the lamps, Foxton knelt on the hearth and roused the embers of the coal fire to warmer life. Like a Scot, he didn't stand on ceremony and wait for someone else to perform mundane tasks.

After the fire was burning easily, he stood and gazed around the sitting room. The walls were festooned with Scottish weaponry: arcs of swords and battle axes, daggers and shields, and a range of other implements of death. He moved to a wheel of dirks and traced his fingertips over the foot-and-a-half length of one.

"A Highland dirk," she said. "Very good for close fighting."

He smiled a little and turned back toward her. "Does Thorsay House expect to be invaded by the English?"

"If they come, we're prepared." The drinks cabinet was locked, but Kendra had paid to have it well stocked so she had one of the keys. It was a matter of moments to pour two glasses of good French brandy.

She handed him a glass and settled in the wing chair to the left of the fire. "I'm interested in learning about your errors in dealing with a shattered life. When we met, you were a young midshipman eager to test your mettle against the French and eventually become an admiral. How did you become tarnished?"

He took the other chair, his long, lean body shadowy in the flickering light. Under his well-tailored clothing he looked a little too thin, but whipcord strong. "I was much like an enthusiastic puppy in those days. After I discovered the realities of the Royal Navy, I lost my desire to become an admiral. But I generally liked the life and fighting the French mattered, so I stayed with it. Then my ship was sunk and I was taken captive along with the handful of other survivors. That led to my dishonor."

"Cowardice under fire?" she asked. "I can understand how anyone might succumb to terror in a lethal situation."

He shrugged. "By then I was a seasoned veteran of sea battles and wounds and had become fatalistic. My unforgivable sin was something else. Are you familiar with how prisoners of war are treated and what a parole is?"

She thought a moment. "A paroled prisoner is given freedom of movement around the town where he is imprisoned in return for giving his word of honor as an officer and a gentleman not to escape. Besides living in more comfortable conditions outside the fortress, he may be exchanged for an enemy prisoner of the same rank. A lieutenant for a lieutenant, a captain for a captain." She bit her lip as she guessed what was coming.

"Exactly. A man who breaks his parole and escapes has betrayed his honor. His reputation is tarnished past redemption. Honorable men give him the cut direct. They may spit in his face. They blackball him from their clubs and certainly do not play cards with him. I escaped and having broken my word, I stand thus dishonored." Foxton swirled his brandy in the glass "Just as well that I dislike playing cards."

Wanting to understand, she asked, "Did you crave freedom more than honor? Or was the situation more complicated than that?"

She hadn't realized that he was tense until she saw his face ease. "It was indeed complicated." He took a small sip of brandy. "Like most captured officers, I was first sent to the prisoners' depot at Verdun. Not particularly enjoyable, but bearable. Then I was transferred to a smaller depot at Bitche, which has the deserved reputation of being the most hellacious of French military prisons. There I was unfortunate enough to attract the attention of the commander, Colonel Roux, a man known for his cruelty."

When he fell silent again, she asked, "What sort of attention? Were you insolent? Disobedient?"

"No more than other young captives. But he singled me out in ever more difficult ways." Foxton rolled his glass of brandy restlessly between his hands. "He wanted me to cower from him, but I'm not good at cowering. Perhaps I would have fared better if I'd learned how to do that."

"As someone who is bad at cowering myself, I can attest that changing one's nature is difficult," she said. "I tend to throw things instead of cowering."

"That does not surprise me," he said with a brief smile. His voice became darker. "Roux first granted me parole, then he revoked it and had me thrown into the vilest dungeon in Bitche. He did this again and again over the following months. It was a cat-and-mouse game with him, and the cat held all the power."

She winced, sensing that his experiences had been far more painful than his terse words described. "Did he treat other prisoners that way?"

Foxton finished his brandy with one long swallow, then rose and began pacing the room, his unseeing gaze sliding over the weapon displays. "He was abusive in different ways to most prisoners, but he had a special hatred for me."

"Do you know why?"

Foxton paused in front of an array of axes set in a circle, the handles radiating inward like the spokes of a wheel. "Roux was the son of a laborer and rose through the ranks of the army to become a colonel. Admirable, really, but he was an angry man who despised those who were born to wealth and privilege. He also despised the British and above all he loathed filthy British aristocrats. He was short, dark, and – not well favored. I epitomized everything he hated: tall, blond, heir to a title. He wanted to break me. He was quite creative in his attempts to do that."

Kendra hadn't thought of him in those terms, but Foxton was the very image of a blond, handsome young English lord, an ideal seldom found in real life. No wonder a short, dark, ugly son of poverty had hated the very sight of such a prisoner. "I have had some experience of being the victim of a powerful man who did his best to break me," she said quietly. "Did Roux rely on torture?"

"Sometimes, but his specialty was mental cruelty. His favorite trick was to call in several prisoners at once and announce they would be exchanged very soon. Everyone but me. When I finally asked when I'd be exchanged, he said never; he'd see me dead before that would happen."

Foxton's flat voice gave Kendra chills. "Parole is linked to the possibility of a prisoner exchange, isn't it? Is a parole valid when the captor is not fulfilling his part of the bargain?"

"That is where the moral complexity comes in. It's also where I reached my breaking point." He drifted across the room to study a display of Highland claymores heavy enough to cleave the skull of an ox. "I was not in very good shape by then. I decided to hell with honor. I might as well die attempting to escape."

"But you didn't die."

"I came close. I was wounded by patrollers sent out to capture me. I kept staggering on until I collapsed near a village church. My life was saved by Frère Emmanuel, an elderly Franciscan bonesetter who is the closest thing to a saint I've met."

Surprised, she asked, "No one wanted to turn in an escaped English prisoner even though a reward was probably offered?"

"I speak French as well as I speak English, so no one realized what I was." Foxton gave a harsh laugh. "I survived, but in the end, Colonel Roux won. Once I recovered, I felt the full weight of my breach of honor. I hated myself too much to return to England, so for years I lived a wandering Franciscan life with Frère Emmanuel, trying to atone for my sins."

"You became a Franciscan friar?" she asked, startled.

"I never took vows." His mouth twisted. "I'm not made for sainthood. I let people think that I was a novice serving an older friar."

Kendra poured herself a little more brandy, thinking his story was becoming more and more interesting. "What form did atonement take?"

"I apprenticed myself to Frère Emmanuel and learned his trade while caring for him. We moved around the countryside and treated anyone with bone or joint problems. We stayed in small country churches and religious communities. Sometimes farmhouses or even barns." Foxton swallowed hard. "He was old and frail and I was honored to serve him. After Frère Emmanuel's death, I continued his work, but with… less sense of purpose."

"What persuaded you to return to England?"

"My cousin Simon. My almost-brother. We were raised together, and he never quite believed I was dead. He's a very persistent fellow, so here I am."

Before Kendra could ask more questions, Foxton swung around and poured more brandy before settling back into the other wing chair. "I've said enough. Your turn now."

"I appreciate that you're willing to share so much of your difficult past." His past and his pain. "Why have you done so when I am almost a stranger?"

He gave her a weary smile. "Sometimes it's easier to talk to a stranger than a friend. Also, because we're in similar situations, I feel some kinship. I hope that's a basis for friendship. Do you feel the same?"

She did with a sudden fierceness that shocked her. "I have a few friends who have not completely abandoned me, but none who truly understand the essence of being dishonored. Yes, we are kindred spirits." And she must match his honesty, no matter how painful. "Your words about moving past the pain resonated in me. That, and how I must decide what I want most and work toward it."

"And that is?"

"My son." She closed her eyes against tears. "*I want my son!*"

Chapter 3

"I want my son!"

Her anguished words echoed around the small room. Lucas felt a jolt of surprise, though he shouldn't have. Enough years had passed that Kendra, Lady Denshire, could have a nursery full of offspring. But it sounded as if she had only the one child, and he realized instantly what the problem was. "Under English law, the father has all rights to children. Denshire won't let you see your son?"

She nodded, her fingers tightened around her half-empty glass. "Since I'm a scandalous woman, it's positively his *duty* to keep me away from Christopher." Her voice was scathing in its bitterness.

"Where does your story begin?" he asked. "Why did you marry Denshire?"

It was Kendra's turn to get up and pace with long, tense strides. "Not long after you left to join your ship, I met Gilbert Stafford. He was intelligent and handsome and kind, and we made each other laugh. My grandfather approved of him, and his parents liked me. I had visited his estate and could see myself living there with him and raising children and being happy. We became betrothed."

She fell silent. Lucas asked gently, "He died?"

Kendra swallowed hard. "It was the most absurd thing. He cut his hand on a rusty bridle. It seemed to be nothing, but it became inflamed. Three days later, he was dead. It was a long time before I could imagine marrying anyone else.

"But I wanted a family. I wanted to be a married woman with responsibilities, so eventually I allowed the elderly cousin who presented me the first time to coax me back to London. I didn't find anyone I could fall in love with, but Denshire was attractive and seemed pleasant. We married and did well enough at first." Her mouth tightened. "I didn't realize until after our marriage that his pleasant exterior concealed a mean, selfish soul. Did you know I'm a considerable heiress?"

"No," he said, surprised. "Since I wasn't looking for a wife, I never thought about that. Was Denshire a fortune hunter?"

She nodded, her face almost hidden in the shadows as she stalked around the small drawing room. "My maternal grandfather was a very successful merchant and he gave me a large dowry. But he was a Scot and didn't believe that a husband should control a wife's property, so my money was secured in a trust that my husband couldn't access without my permission."

"Not the sort of thing a fortune hunter wants to deal with! But surely Denshire learned that when the settlements were being negotiated?"

"Yes, and he tried to negotiate full access to my money, but my grandfather and his lawyers wouldn't budge. Denshire had a substantial fortune of his own, so eventually he accepted the terms with the appearance of graciousness, but I found later that he was furious. He never got over that." She sighed. "I wish he'd withdrawn from our betrothal then. It would have been humiliating, but I would have been far better off."

"Heiresses aren't easy to come by so he didn't want to let you get away," Lucas said cynically. "I imagine he thought that when he needed more money, he could persuade or bully you into giving it to him."

"He did think that, which was poor judgment on his part," Kendra said. "But the first few years of our marriage weren't bad. I paid my own bills and contributed what I thought was a reasonable amount to the household expenses. Christopher was born and I spent a great deal of time with him in the country while Denshire was busy with a gentleman's activities in London. We got along as well as most couples do, until Denshire ran short of money."

"Gambling?"

"Mostly, though I'm sure he had a full range of expensive vices. He became very demanding." She touched her left cheek, and Lucas wondered if her husband hit her when she didn't obey him. Very likely.

"I didn't see Denshire except when he came to demand money. I was fool enough to agree the first time, but never after that." She touched her cheek again. "He became more and more furious. I eventually decided the situation was intolerable and asked for a legal separation. That triggered his retaliation."

"Which led to scandal and disgrace?"

Her mouth tightened. "Exactly. Another trigger was my grandfather's death. He left the bulk of his fortune to me. He'd come to loathe Denshire, so the trust keeping the inheritance from my husband's hands was even more stringent than before. In retaliation, Denshire decided to divorce me and do it in such a way that my name would be utterly blackened."

"The only ground for divorce in England is adultery by the wife," Lucas said in a neutral voice. "Were you having an affair?"

"Of course not!" she scoffed. "I didn't even want the man I had, much less another one!"

Lucas frowned, seeing that this discussion was getting into difficult territory. "Since the divorce was granted, there must have been some compelling evidence. What really happened?"

"Three of his good friends testified in court that there was a drunken dinner party at our house and that I begged them to lie with me," she said tautly.

He winced. "I assume they were lying?"

She began pacing again like a captured panther. "I believe they told the truth as they knew it. That night is a blur to me. Apparently Denshire hired a prostitute with a general resemblance to me, then drugged me into unconsciousness. In the dark and saturated with drink, his friends believed that I was the woman they lay with, and they testified to that."

Lucas sucked in his breath. "That is appallingly devious and cold-blooded! How could a man do such a thing to his wife? The mother of his child!"

"He was concerned only with his own pleasures and desires," she said coolly. "By this time, he despised me. I imagine he devised this plan as a way to inflict the maximum amount of public humiliation."

"Is there any chance that you were assaulted when you were too insensible to realize what was happening?" he asked gently.

She shook her head. "I've been celibate for years. If I'd been assaulted by three men, my body would have known the next morning. I'm sure I spent that night alone. For that, at least, I'm grateful."

"Was your maid able to testify in your defense?"

"She disappeared that night. I'm not sure whether Denshire paid her to leave, or whether he had her murdered." Kendra shuddered. "I fear it might have been murder."

Lucas tried to imagine what Kendra had endured. A lesser woman would have been broken. "Would no one listen to you?"

"A woman cannot testify in her own defense!" she spat out, her outrage vibrating in her voice. "I could do nothing to defend myself. *Nothing!* Denshire divorced me, told me I'd never see our son again, and he has instituted legal proceedings to allow him access to the trusts my grandfather set up because I owe him a huge fine as restitution for my wicked behavior. He is *evil!*"

"Evil or mad," Lucas agreed. "May I ask more questions? I want to try to understand what was in your husband's mind."

"Go ahead," she said wearily. "I've had plenty of time to think about what happened."

"At least Denshire wasn't ruthless enough to have you killed, which would have simplified his life in all ways." Lucas's inflection turned his words into a hesitant question.

"My death would have put my fortune forever out of his reach," she said flatly. "The money would eventually go to Christopher, half when he turns twenty-five, the rest at thirty. If my son died in some horrid 'accident,' the money would go to charity and more distant relatives. Denshire would never see a penny of it."

"Your grandfather sounds like a wise and suspicious man."

She smiled a little. "That he was. Ferocious and frightening and a darling to me."

He'd also been her protector, and now he was gone. A woman alone and disgraced was in dire straits, and Lucas guessed it was possible that under the circumstances, a court might rule that Denshire had the right to manage the money on behalf of his son. "It's fortunate that you were unmolested that night, but it did complicate matters to hire a woman to pretend to be you," Lucas said. "Do you know why he didn't choose the simple way?"

"I've thought about that," she said slowly. "I believe Denshire decided to hire a substitute because if I became with child as a result of that night, he would legally be the father and he wouldn't want responsibility for a child not his own."

Lucas shook his head. "It's a monstrous story. No wonder you're in a rage for justice."

"Do you believe me?" she asked, sounding on edge. "When I say the words out loud, my tale seems too bizarre to be true."

"Yes, I believe you," he said steadily. "Not only is it hard to imagine someone making up such a tale, but even though we've only met half a dozen times or so, the Kendra Douglas I once knew was honest to a fault. I believe you still are."

She exhaled and finally returned to her chair by the fire. Briefly she lifted the brandy decanter as if considering another drink, then set it down again. "I'm glad someone believes me. I'm trying to decide what to do next. Shooting Denshire would be very satisfying, but I don't want to end up on the gallows."

"If Denshire can be revealed for the monster he is, you might regain custody of Christopher," Lucas said. "We need to find witnesses to support your story. Your maid, for one, and the woman hired to impersonate you."

"I hope Molly is still alive, but if she is, I don't know how to find her." She cocked her head. "You said 'we.' You would help me?"

Lucas smiled, feeling a tingle of anticipation. "You need an ally and I need a good cause to fight for." He extended his hand across the space between their chairs. "Shall we make a pact to pursue justice on your behalf?"

Looking as if she wanted to weep, she caught his hand in a tight clasp. "Yes! I hope you have a better idea of where to start than I do."

After he released her hand, he said, "I have a few thoughts, and I have friends who will have more. I've been staying with my cousins Simon and Suzanne. Will you dine with us tomorrow night so we can discuss the possibilities?"

"This is the Simon who is your almost-brother?"

Lucas nodded. "He was also a colonel in the army intelligence service, so he has a number of useful skills as well as useful friends."

"Will his wife mind having a disgraced woman at her table?" Kendra asked warily.

"Suzanne is the most tolerant of women. She has also had a complicated past and may have some good insights into your situation."

"Then I thank you for the invitation." Kendra exhaled roughly. "I must rest now. Thank you for coming to my rescue at the ball, and for listening to me."

Lucas rose. "Between now and tomorrow night, think about everyone who was involved and might have information about what happened to you. Servants. Neighbors. Your husband's friends."

"Do you think that will help?" she asked.

"I don't know, but it might be a start."

"I hope so." She drew a deep breath. "Thank you, Lord Foxton. I feel steadier for having talked to you. Step by step, I will move forward as best I can."

"That's all we can ever do." He smiled. "You should call me Lucas if we're to be allies. That will balance the fact that I keep wanting to call you Kendra Douglas."

She pursed her lips thoughtfully. "I want to be Kendra Douglas again. She was stronger and more clear-sighted than I. Scottish women keep their own names, so I'll claim that right. I do not want to be Lady Denshire anymore."

As they'd talked, she'd become more like the Kendra Douglas he remembered. He was glad because she would need that strength and clarity to fight her way out of the wreckage of her life. "I'll collect you tomorrow for dinner, Kendra. I hope you sleep well."

"Perhaps I actually will," she said, sounding surprised as she escorted him to the door. "Good night, Lucas."

After he left, she climbed the stairs to her room, tired but feeling a cautious hope that there might be sunlight beyond the dark fog of despair that had been suffocating her since her life had shattered.

Though Denshire had done his best to destroy her, he had failed. Now she was going to fight back. Women had few weapons, but she was better armed than most because she had money and determination. Dear Lord, did she have determination!

She wondered how far Lucas would go to help her. This was such a sordid business and he had no particular reason to exert himself for a near stranger. He might eventually lose interest and she'd be on her own. But his kindness and belief had already meant a great deal to her.

After she lit the lamps in her room, she opened her jewelry box and removed the miniature of Christopher, which was more precious than any of her jewels. The picture had been painted the year before. He'd grown since then, but his sunny smile hadn't changed.

Or perhaps it had. She hadn't seen him in months, and his life had been disrupted almost as badly as hers had been. What lies had his father told him about the divorce? Had he told Christopher that his mother was a whore whose name must never be mentioned? Surely not, Christopher was only nine!

But Denshire was capable of great vileness, so perhaps he had poured the whole ugly set of lies into his son's ears. Would Christopher believe his father's stories? She and her son had been very close, while Denshire had been a distant father, not very interested in his son except because he needed an heir for the title.

She prayed the love between her and her son had not been destroyed.

Her fingers whitened on the gilt frame of the miniature as the horror of her recurring nightmare swept through. Time and again she dreamed of Christopher being wrenched from her arms. Always he was a helpless, crying infant and she could do nothing to save him, *nothing*.

She must get her son back, for both of their sakes.

Chapter 4

Lucas felt surprisingly invigorated as he walked back to Duval House, where he was living with Simon and Suzanne while they helped him rebuild a life in the society he'd been born to. He owed his family that after all the grief he'd brought them, and it wasn't as if there was some other place he'd rather be.

Only now, as he felt himself becoming focused, did he realize how long he'd been drifting. Ever since he was captured by the French, in fact. He'd drifted through the years as a prisoner of war when his life was about survival and a desperate hope that someday he would be free again.

Then there were the penance years of traveling the Belgian countryside as apprentice and servant to Frère Emmanuel. He had lived the simple life of a Franciscan friar and helped many people in pain, but never felt that he truly belonged where he was. Though he'd been mildly content, he'd neither seen nor wanted a future beyond the life he was living.

Then Simon had found him. Lucas's first reaction to their meeting had been a fearful withdrawal into his familiar routine. But in the days that followed, he'd recognized that it was time to return to the life he'd lost.

His first wary steps had taken him to Brussels. Though he was not a trained surgeon, his bonesetting and bandaging skills had helped save lives among the flood of wounded after Waterloo. He'd set bones and even used the strange, unreliable gift of healing that sometimes flowed through his hands.

After the battle, he'd accepted Simon's invitation to come home to England, first to Simon's Berkshire estate and now to the house on the street ahead of him. Simon owned the comfortable town house, but Lucas had grown up there after he was orphaned and taken in by his aunt and uncle. He'd been raised as Simon's brother and now occupied the same room he'd had as a boy. They'd been constant companions for years, studying and riding and cheerfully arguing the merits of the army versus the navy.

He let himself in with his key and collected the quietly burning lamp that had been left for him before he climbed the stairs. His room was at the front of the house, but he saw a crack of light showing under the door of the small sitting room that connected the bedchambers of the master and mistress of the house.

Thinking Simon might be awake, he tapped lightly on the door, then entered when Simon called permission. The scene that met Lucas's gaze was so warmly domestic that his whole body eased. Simon was relaxing on the sofa, his crossed legs stretched out toward the fire and his arm around his wife. Suzanne curled against him as she nursed their infant daughter. Mother and child were wrapped in a soft wool shawl so that only the top of the baby's small dark head was visible.

Lucas said in a quiet voice, "Suzanne, you and Madeline make the most perfect Madonna and child image I've ever seen."

"Indeed," Simon said fondly as he stroked a hand down his wife's arm. "Since Suzanne is doing the work of feeding Madeline, I thought it only fair that I keep her company. How was your first solo venture to a ball?"

"It went reasonably well." Lucas settled in a chair set at right angles to the sofa, careful not to disturb the pile of intertwined fur that was Suzanne's gray tabby cat, Leo, and Rupert, Simon's amiable dog of uncertain ancestry. "My status as a prosperous and eligible bachelor protected me from open disdain and cuts direct, and I had several pleasant dances with women I'd met here in your house. Then things became... interesting."

Suzanne looked at him with a sleepy smile. "How interesting?"

"In mid-evening, a woman in black swept into the ballroom and everyone drew back as if she were a plague carrier. Outraged whispers pronounced that she was recently divorced and a contemptible slut who was beyond redemption."

Simon's brows arched. "Was that Lady Denshire? I've heard of the scandal but don't know any of the people involved. I'm guessing you didn't shrink back in horror."

Simon knew him well. "No, since we were in similar straits, I asked her to dance and realized that I had met her years ago, just before I joined my first ship. She was Kendra Douglas then and as straightforward a young woman as I've ever met."

Looking interested, Suzanne said, "Did she tell you her side of the story?"

"Yes, and I've promised to help her." Succinctly Lucas outlined Kendra's situation, ending with, "I hope you don't mind that I invited her to dine here tomorrow night. I thought you might help develop a strategy to win her justice."

Suzanne came awake as Lucas spoke. By the time he finished, she was sitting upright, her green eyes flashing even as she continued nursing her baby. "Do you believe this woman, Lucas?"

"I do," he said. "My opinion is based more on intuition than facts, but I do think Kendra Douglas is telling the truth."

Suzanne's gaze turned to her husband. "Then we must help her. Women are too often the victims of predatory men." Her tone said that the decision had been made and was inarguable. Given her past, Lucas wasn't surprised to learn that Suzanne would fight for any woman who had been mistreated by a man.

Simon knew this as well, so he just nodded. "Tomorrow at dinner we can hear her story and discuss what is to be done."

A thought struck Lucas as he got to his feet. "Years ago, before I was captured by the French, I left a chest of personal belongings here in the house. Is it still here, or was it discarded after my supposed death?"

Simon became very still. "Of course I didn't get rid of the chest. It's in the back corner of my dressing room. You can collect it now if you like."

"Why there and not in the attic?" Lucas asked, surprised.

"I suppose it was a way of keeping you near," his cousin said softly. "I never opened it, but I liked knowing it was there."

Lucas felt a deep stab of guilt for what his years of self-exile had meant to Simon. "I'm sorry. I didn't deserve such loyalty."

"Of course you did, my almost-brother. Who else did I have to worry about?" Simon grinned with the openness he'd had as a young boy. "I've been proved right, haven't I? You didn't die."

"Not for lack of trying," Lucas said dryly.

His cousins laughed, lightening the mood. Suzanne said, "What do you hope to retrieve from your long-abandoned chest? Or shouldn't I ask?"

"You shouldn't ask," Simon said tartly.

"I don't remember everything I left in the chest. Some official papers and books, some small wood carvings, and a Royal Navy dirk, which is what I'm interested in," Lucas explained. "Thorsay House, where Kendra Douglas is living, has masses of Scottish weapons displayed on the walls, including Highland dirks. I think the design is a little different from the naval version, so I wanted to compare."

"Of *course*," Suzanne said warmly. "What man wouldn't be desperate to know which is longer?"

Lucas laughed. "I suspect you're implying that no sane woman would care. I'm sure you're right. Is it all right if I retrieve the chest now, Simon?"

His cousin waved a hand toward the master's bedroom. "You know where the dressing room is."

Lucas nodded and bid them both good night before he collected his lamp and entered Simon's bedchamber. It didn't look much occupied because Simon and Suzanne always shared the bed in the lady's chamber at the other end of the suite. Lucas envied their unfashionable fondness for each other.

The chest was where Simon had said, in the back corner of the dressing room with several folded blankets resting on top. He moved the blankets and picked up the chest by the leather handle on one end, leaving one hand free for his lamp. The chest had seemed large when he first took it off to school, but he could lift it easily with one hand now.

He left the dressing room through the back door, which opened on a corridor. Once in his own room, he set the chest on the bed and examined the scuffs and other signs of wear it had accumulated since his aunt and uncle Duval had given it to him when he first went off to Harrow. Simon had received a similar one, his covered with dark red leather because of his interest in the army, while Lucas's was navy blue. Their initials were picked out with small brass-headed nails on the lids.

He ran a fingertip over the initials. Aunt and Uncle Duval had welcomed him warmly after the death of his parents and always treated both boys with scrupulous fairness. He'd been very lucky, but he wondered why he'd thought of the chest on this particular night.

Because it was a doorway to an earlier life. He hadn't been ready to look at that life until now. Expression set, he turned the key in the lock and opened the door to his past.

Chapter 5

Lucas arrived to escort Kendra to dinner a few minutes early so she had less time to wonder whether he'd changed his mind. She headed down the stairs when the housekeeper, Mrs. Brown, said that her guest had arrived. Lucas was in the drawing room gazing at a circle of dirks mounted on the wall.

Since he hadn't noticed her entrance, she took the opportunity to study him. He was every inch the London gentleman, well dressed, reserved, difficult to read. She tried to visualize him with tonsured blond hair, wearing the loose brown robe of a Franciscan. She had trouble imagining that, yet years of living a religious life must explain the deep calm she sensed in him. Like her, he was dishonored and he felt that stain, but he accepted that this was his life now. She must emulate him.

"Good evening, Lucas," she said.

He turned and she saw that her peaceful friar was holding a long, wicked-looking dirk similar to those in the wheel of weapons mounted on the wall behind him. "Making comparisons?" she asked with amusement. "To find if your dirk is longer?"

He laughed. "My cousin Suzanne said much the same thing. Men aren't always obsessed with size, you know. I was studying the differences. The Highland dirks are more varied in style, as one would expect, and the hilts tend to be flatter."

He offered his weapon hilt first. "This is a Royal Navy dirk, which is a badge of office for naval officers. It's also a very effective weapon for close fighting, such as when you board an enemy ship or they board you."

The dirk was sleek and deadly, as long as her forearm, with a finely honed blade and an ivory hilt. "Is this the dirk you carried during your years in the navy?"

"No, that was lost when I was captured by the French. This one belonged to my father. He captained a frigate and died in action."

She handed the dirk back to him. "Was that why you entered the navy yourself?"

He nodded. "It seemed a worthy occupation. After his death this dirk was returned with the rest of his belongings. My mother gave it to me with stern warnings to keep it sheathed and be very careful because the blade was so sharp." He regarded the weapon, his gaze distant. "She died not long after and I was sent to live with my aunt and uncle. For months I carried the sheathed dirk all the time. I slept with it every night until my aunt Duval, Simon's mother, persuaded me to put it away."

"Why didn't you carry it when you became an officer yourself?"

"My father's dirk was too precious to risk. I left it in a chest of small treasures at Simon's house when I went off to war." He slid the blade into the sheath at his waist and his coat fell over it. "Time we were off. It's a cold night, but there's a bright moon and it's not far to Duval House."

"A good night for walking." As they stepped out on the street, she said, "I wasn't entirely sure you'd come. I

31

still have trouble believing that a virtual stranger is willing to help a scandalous woman."

He offered his arm. "I have to do something to keep myself busy. I don't like gambling or drinking or prize fights, and I don't know many people in London, so doing something useful is appealing."

She took his arm and they turned onto the street. A scattering of houses had outside lamps, but the full moon provided better light and cast dramatic shadows from iron railings and the occasional tree. No one else was on the street and the night was pleasantly peaceful. Kendra drew a deep breath, enjoying the night and the company. It had been a long time since she'd known simple peace. Lucas was a very relaxing man.

As they turned the next corner toward his cousins' house, he said, "Kendra is an unusual name. Scottish?"

"Possibly. It's a family name on my mother's side. The vicar once told me that there was disagreement about whether the name is Anglo-Saxon, Welsh, or Scottish," she explained. "It's actually my middle name. I was christened Mary Kendra Douglas."

"You didn't feel like a Mary?" he said with a smile in his voice.

"By the time I could walk, it was decided that I was not well behaved enough to be a Mary, so I've been Kendra ever since," she said with a laugh. How long had it been since she'd laughed?

A cloud drifted across the moon, darkening the street. "I wonder how long it will be until gas lighting is available throughout the city," Lucas remarked.

"Quite a while, I imagine. Just think of all the pipes that will have to be laid." Luckily in this neighborhood there were occasional streetlights and the pavement was kept fairly clean, but wise walkers still needed to be careful.

At the corner ahead, a pair of evergreen trees cast darker shadows across the pavement. She saw something moving in the shadows. A dog, perhaps?

An instant later, the peace was shattered as two figures, no, three, swaggered from the shadows, their figures dark and menacing. Kendra froze as the tallest man barked, "Give us whatever ya got and no one'll get hurt!"

"No," Lucas said mildly as he stepped between Kendra and the men. "We don't want trouble, so I suggest you move along."

"Can't say I didn't warn ya!" the leader said with a coarse laugh as he lunged forward with a cudgel and swung it at Lucas's head.

Except Lucas wasn't there. Kendra saw a dark object go flying – his hat? – as he swiftly dodged the cudgel. In the same smooth movement, he whipped his dirk from its sheath and slashed down his attacker's hand, wrist, and side. The man bellowed as the cudgel dropped from his damaged hand and blood sprayed blackly from his wound.

His movements almost too swift to comprehend, Lucas spun to his right and slammed the hilt of his dirk into the temple of the second man. The man gasped with pain and stumbled backward.

The third man yanked out a dagger and lunged at Lucas. There was a swift exchange of thrusts and shrieking metal as Lucas's weapon blocked his opponent's shorter blade. The violence ended when a stab from his dirk disabled the other man and the knife dropped to the street with a clatter.

Kendra barely had time to register the danger before the altercation was over and their assailants had fled into the night, leaving only dark splotches of blood on the street. Voice shaky, she said, "Are you all right?"

Lucas stared at the blood, seeming almost as startled by his successful defense against the thieves as Kendra was. "I'm fine. What about you?"

"Shaken, but well enough." She drew a deep breath, steadying her nerves. "Do all Franciscan friars fight as well as you?"

"As I said, I was never a true friar." He produced a handkerchief and wiped blood from the blade of his dirk before sheathing the weapon and retrieving his fallen hat. After donning it, he offered her his arm. "It's interesting how the old sailor skills are there when needed."

"Quick thinking being one of those skills." She took his arm since her knees were unsteady. "When those men attacked, I was as paralyzed as a rabbit. By the time my mind started working again, you'd dispatched all three of the villains."

"Reacting quickly to danger is developed by practice. Be grateful you haven't needed to attain that particular skill," he said dryly. "Fortunately, Duval House is just around the corner. I've had enough fresh air for the moment."

As they resumed walking, she said, "We escaped unscathed, so I guess this little incident qualifies as interesting rather than disastrous."

"Any fight one can walk away from is a good fight."

After a dozen silent steps, she said quietly, "You've lived several very different lives, haven't you?"

Another dozen steps before he replied, "Yes, and I need to get those different parts of my past into harmony with each other. The naval officer and the Franciscan are opposites. The prisoner of war…" He shook his head and said no more.

She thought about his words. Her ally was a most interestingly complicated man. That must be why he was so accepting of her.

And thank heaven for that! She needed as many allies as she could find.

Chapter 6

Lucas suspected that Kendra was nervous at meeting Simon and Suzanne, but she concealed it well. The only sign of her anxiety was the lift of her chin as she entered the drawing room beside him. It was the same damn-your-eyes bravado she'd showed when she strode into the middle of the ballroom the night before.

He'd admired her courage then. This time he felt a jolt of reaction so intense and unexpected that at first he didn't recognize it as desire. He and desire had been strangers for a very long time. As a prisoner of war, then a de facto celibate friar, he'd lacked opportunities. Not to mention that he refused to behave dishonorably again.

He hadn't stopped noticing what women looked like; when he'd met Suzanne, he'd immediately been struck by her beauty. But that recognition had been distant and impersonal and would have been so even if she weren't Simon's wife.

Kendra, with her courage and pain, touched something long frozen inside of him, a fact that was interesting and rather disturbing. Those thoughts raced through his mind but didn't interfere with introductions. "Simon and Suzanne, this is Lady Denshire, but she prefers her maiden name of Kendra Douglas."

Simon rose and gave her a friendly smile. "Welcome, Kendra Douglas. I'm Simon Duval and it's a pleasure to meet you."

"Thank you, Colonel Duval. The pleasure is mine," she said sincerely.

Suzanne also rose with a warm, welcoming smile. It was the same welcome she'd given Lucas when he showed up on her doorstep in Brussels, having left the Franciscan life behind him but having no idea what came next. Now that he thought of it, this was very like the warm welcome his aunt Duval gave Lucas when her orphaned nephew had arrived in this house. No wonder Simon had fallen in love with Suzanne.

"You're probably thinking they don't look much alike for first cousins, and you're right," Suzanne said in a soft voice with a hint of a French accent. "But they both listen exceptionally well for men."

Kendra smiled back, her expression easing at the acceptance she was offered. "A rare and wonderful trait, isn't it?"

Suzanne was about to say more when her gaze fixed on Lucas. "There's blood on your shirt!"

Simon became dangerously alert. "What happened?"

Lucas glanced down and saw the dark splatters on his white linen shirt. The stains were already turning brown. He made a dismissive motion. "Not my blood. We were attacked by some street robbers, but they were easily sent on their way."

"What he means," Kendra said, "is that using his Royal Navy dirk and some rather amazing fighting ability, your cousin drove them off before I had enough sense to scream or run."

37

Simon nodded approvingly. "Nice to know that you haven't lost your old skills, almost-brother."

Lucas gave an embarrassed shrug. "They were amateurs. No one died so it was no great matter."

"But surely it was unnerving!" Suzanne's gaze returned to Kendra. "Lucas told us something of your situation. I hope we can help you find some justice."

"I hope so, too," Kendra said in a low voice. "I haven't known where to start."

"We'll think of something," Suzanne said. "But first we will eat and drink because good food and conversation lead to good ideas."

Simon smiled and rested a hand on his wife's shoulder. "I think my good French cook was the reason she agreed to marry me."

"Not the only reason," Suzanne said serenely, "but it was most certainly on the list! Come now and relax and have a glass of wine before we dine. Later we will talk."

–

Kendra quickly realized that Lucas had been right that she would like his cousins, and that they were under-standing people. Dinner was simple, delicious French country food that helped create an atmosphere of warmth and easy conversation. By the time they'd finished the cheese course, they were all on a first-name basis.

At a signal from Suzanne, they adjourned to the drawing room and coffee was served. Her hostess handed Kendra a steaming cup. "Now we talk. Tell us your story."

Simon added, "I recall hearing the divorce case had some unusual legal features, but I don't know what they were."

Kendra's ease vanished and she cradled the hot cup of coffee to warm her shaking hands. But speaking to Lucas the night before made it easier to tell her story this time. After sketching out what had really happened, she said, "The legal case was unusual in several ways. Usually the injured husband charges his wife's lover with criminal conversation in a civil suit. If successful, the lover pays a large fine for alienation of affection.

"Then comes the ecclesiastical trial in which the husband charges his wife with adultery and demands legal separation. What made this suit different was there was no one lover to charge. Instead, Denshire claimed that my behavior was so heinous that I should pay a massive fine for my adulterous actions. The legal issues are still being sorted out, but so far, Denshire has been winning with his arguments because he convinced the courts that my behavior was vile beyond belief." Her voice turned bitter. "Naturally I can't testify because I'm a woman."

As she went into greater detail, Suzanne pressed her fist against her mouth, her eyes stark. Simon was very still and radiated a quiet, cold rage. Lucas looked... dangerous.

When Kendra finished her tale, Suzanne leaned forward and squeezed her hand. "I'm so sorry for what you've endured," she said compassionately. "I don't suppose it would be wise to just shoot Lord Denshire."

The words were so incongruous coming from Suzanne that everyone laughed, breaking the tension. "No, my bloodthirsty darling," Simon said affectionately. "It would not be wise. Denshire might deserve it, but the first person they'd come for would be Kendra, and she has enough troubles."

Lucas caught Kendra's gaze. "You said that most of all, you want your son. Have you seen him at all since the divorce case started?"

"Not even once! If I knew where he was, I'd steal him away and take him to one of the colonies," Kendra said fiercely. "But I just don't know. I'm sure he's not in the London house. He could be anywhere. In a school, with a friend or relative in the most distant part of Britain. Denshire was never interested in Christopher as anything but an heir, so he wouldn't want to keep him close. I've considered hiring a Bow Street Runner to look for him, but one small boy..." She shook her head. "He's a needle in a haystack."

"Now that I have a child of my own, I understand the passionate need to do anything to protect that child," Simon said quietly. "But if you take your son out of the country, you'd never be able to return to England, and you'd deprive your son of his heritage and his inheritance from his father."

"I know," Kendra said. "But apart from the title, there won't be much to inherit. Denshire will have mortgaged himself into bankruptcy. I think Christopher will be better off with a parent who loves him."

"That's certainly true," Lucas agreed, "but it would be better yet to have your name cleared so you could regain custody of your son while living in your own country."

"How is that even possible?" Kendra asked bitterly. "I was unable to testify in my own defense. The court decided that Denshire was the injured party, I receive no jointure or support since I have money of my own, I can't remarry even if I wanted to, and" – her voice broke – "they decided I'm unfit to be a mother to my own child!"

"That's monstrous!" Suzanne exclaimed. "You're even forbidden to remarry?"

Kendra shrugged. "I can't imagine ever marrying again, so it's the least of the injustices. Losing Christopher is by far the worst of them, but I would like to be able to move freely in society without people withdrawing in horror as if I'm a leper. I'd also dearly love to expose Denshire's monstrous behavior so that the scandal is shifted from me to him, where it belongs. But I can't imagine how that can be done."

"I don't know if that can be accomplished in the eyes of the law, but perhaps Denshire can be tried and condemned in the court of public opinion," Simon said with narrowed eyes. "A large amount of convincing evidence would be required. Credible witnesses to what actually happened that evil night. Ideally, recantation from one or more of the men who testified on Denshire's behalf."

Lucas said slowly, "I have an idea. Though it may be mad."

"Tell us the idea and we'll let you know if it's mad," Suzanne said helpfully.

"Kendra wants custody of her son and her reputation restored. Both were taken away by the legal system, and perhaps that is how they need to be restored."

Kendra frowned. "That sounds reasonable, but how can that be accomplished when women have so little legal standing?"

"As a peer of the realm, I can introduce a Personal Act in the House of Lords to redress a specific wrong once we have incontrovertible evidence," Lucas explained. "I would introduce the private bill charging Denshire with fraud and defamation, and pointing out that it's proof he's unfit to be the guardian of his son."

There was a collective gasp from the others. Simon said, "It's a bold and imaginative plan, but can it work? Has there ever been a private bill like this introduced into the Lords?"

"I have no idea, but a peer of the realm has a great deal of freedom as to what bills he introduces." Lucas's mouth twisted. "It's ironic that Kendra was not allowed to speak on her own behalf, but a man, even a dishonored one like me, will be listened to. Not fair, but the way of the world."

"It might not be necessary to go as far as introducing a private bill, Lucas," Suzanne said. "If we have compelling evidence, we can present it to Denshire and ask if he wants to make himself an object of disgust and loathing among his peers. We'll refrain from making his crimes public if he gives custody of Christopher to Kendra. It's not as good as utterly destroying his public reputation, but it would achieve Kendra's most important goal."

"Blackmail." Kendra's brows furrowed. "That might work. He has more than his share of pride and wouldn't want his reputation to be blackened before his friends. But it would take a great deal of evidence to convince him."

"There are many kinds of evidence," Suzanne said, her gaze probing. "Kendra, did Denshire ever seriously injure you? Seriously enough that it would be an outrage to decency?"

Kendra felt her blood drain away as the other woman's words struck her deepest shame. She hadn't wanted to reveal this, yet honesty was her best hope for freeing herself from her current hell. She dropped her gaze and whispered, "Yes, he beat me when he wanted money."

Suzanne gripped her hand, hard. When Kendra met her gaze, she realized that Suzanne had her own bitter experiences of male violence toward women.

That knowledge encouraged Kendra to reveal more. "Denshire's bullying and occasional brutality was why I spent most of my time in the country with Christopher. I reached my breaking point several months ago when Denshire came to the estate to demand money."

"What happened then?" Suzanne asked, her green eyes steady and understanding.

"When I told him I would never give him money again, he attacked me in a drunken rage. This time I fought back and he knocked me into the fireplace. My left leg slammed into the hot grate and at first I was too numbed to escape," Kendra said in a rush of painful words. "So he left me there to burn."

Chapter 7

Kendra's words produced shocked silence until Suzanne exclaimed, "Dear God, how ghastly! Your clothing caught on fire?"

"I screamed and rolled onto the carpet and used my shawl to smother the flames. Luckily my hands weren't badly burned." The iron bars of the grate had branded a pattern on her lower leg and the pain had been excruciating. "I vaguely remember Denshire babbling that he hadn't meant to hurt me before he bolted back to London."

"He didn't even wait to see how seriously you were injured?" Lucas said incredulously.

"He doesn't like unpleasantness, even when he's the one who created it," Kendra said dryly. She bent and raised her hem to her knees. The viciously red parallel scars on her left calf were visible even through her silk stockings. She supposed they'd lighten with time, but they'd always be with her.

Her companions stared at the scars, shocked. Kendra dropped the hem of her skirt and straightened up. "This isn't necessarily proof that my husband assaulted me. I could have just been clumsy and stumbled into the fireplace all on my own."

"What about the servants?" Lucas asked. "Was a doctor called?"

"My maid heard the commotion and found me collapsed on the floor, but she didn't actually see what happened. A doctor was called and he bandaged the burns and gave me strong doses of laudanum for the pain. When I recovered my wits several days later, I found that Denshire had taken Christopher with him."

There was another frozen silence before Suzanne whispered, "I'm so sorry."

The pain of losing Christopher had been even worse than the physical agony Kendra had suffered. Doing her best to keep her voice steady, she said, "I decided to seek a legal separation. Denshire and I hadn't been husband and wife for years, and since Christopher was young, it was reasonable to leave him in my care until he was old enough to go to school. So I traveled to London to speak to Denshire.

"He looked surly when I explained my intentions, but he didn't object. I thought that was because I said I would settle a sizable sum of money on him and he wanted money more than he wanted to see his son." She forced herself to tamp down her rising anger. "Instead, three days later he arranged his fraudulent scene for divorce."

Voice steely, Simon said, "I'm rethinking whether we should arrange to have Denshire shot."

"Very, very appealing," Lucas agreed, his compassionate gaze on Kendra. "But again, that could rebound on Kendra."

Simon lifted the decanter and poured more brandy for each of them. "I've always found a moderate amount of brandy aids in developing strategy. If necessary, Lucas can introduce a private bill, but what else might be done before that?"

"Find a good lawyer who understands the ins and outs of divorce law," Lucas said. "Civil and church courts are involved, but I don't know more than that."

Simon and Suzanne exchanged a glance. "Kirkland!" they said almost simultaneously.

"Is he a lawyer?" Kendra asked.

"Kirkland is an earl who knows many people and is very good at getting things done behind the scenes," Simon explained. "I might not have mentioned it at the time, Lucas, but Kirkland is the owner of the house in Brussels where we stayed before and after Waterloo."

"Oh?" Lucas said with interest. "The house with a staff who had so many interesting and varied talents. If he knows people like that here in England, he might be able to locate the witnesses that Kendra needs to build her case."

"Exactly," Suzanne said, her gaze going to Kendra. "Think of Kirkland as a handsome, charming spider in the center of a vast web of useful people. Now that Napoleon has been exiled to that island in the South Atlantic, Kirkland should have time on his hands, and I think he'd be willing to support justice for a wronged woman."

"He's some sort of spymaster?" Kendra guessed.

"One could say that," Simon said blandly. "Or one could merely say that he counts among his friends many influential men whom he can call upon if needful."

"And many of those men have wives who are kind and open-minded," Suzanne added. "I can invite some of the ones I know to tea so you can enlist them in your cause. That will lead to invitations to their entertainments and a chance to sway public opinion.

"But clearing your name publicly will not be easy. You will have to prove the truth of your situation by standing in front of others and showing your pain, knowing that some will spit on it. You will have to endure a great deal, and the result is uncertain. Are you willing to face all that?"

It was a serious question that deserved a serious answer, so Kendra thought hard about what she would be facing. Walking into the ball the night before had taken all her anger and resolution. She'd almost turned away from the front door, and she would never forget the searing humiliation of standing in the middle of the dance floor being treated as a monster, with loathing stares and whispered insults.

But daring to attend that ball had brought her an amazing ally, and Lucas had brought her here, where she had found kindness and understanding and hope. She raised her chin. "For the last months, I've been hiding like a fox gone to ground. It is time for me to come out and fight for justice. I know it will not be easy, but I am prepared for what will come."

"You'll need an escort," Lucas said thoughtfully. "I'd be happy to take on that role. I'm not welcome everywhere either, but at least we can face cuts direct together."

Suzanne smiled, but said, "People will assume you're lovers. I don't think that will help rebuild Kendra's reputation."

"But we're not lovers." Kendra looked at Lucas and their gazes caught with a force that startled her. She had no interest in remarrying, even if she were legally free to do so, but she was suddenly, sharply aware of Lucas's physicality. He had the lean masculine strength of a warrior and the compassion of a healer, and for the first time ever the idea of taking a lover was appealing.

Startled and uneasy at her reaction, she jerked her gaze away from him. "Perhaps we can be cousins. Not first cousins, but close enough that it would be believable for Lucas to wish to support me. Second cousins, perhaps. Once removed."

"We'll have to work out how we're related," Lucas said. "Who knows? We might actually be cousins of some degree. I have some Scottish ancestors who might be connected to your Scottish family, and that would be harder to disprove."

Kendra felt some of her tension unwinding. The challenges ahead would be easier to face if she had Lucas at her side. How did that come to seem so natural?

Suzanne stood. "I shall leave you three to your strategizing. It's time I fed Madeline."

Many women of rank preferred to use wet nurses, but Kendra had chosen to nurse her child, and obviously Suzanne was doing the same. She asked, "May I meet her?"

"I should be pleased to introduce you," Suzanne said with a smile. "Though I warn you, she hasn't much conversation!"

Kendra laughed and got to her feet. "I'll be down shortly, but in the meantime, here is the list of potential witnesses and all the details of that night that I can remember." She'd spent a long time developing that list and making fair copies. She handed two of the copies to Lucas and Simon, then followed Suzanne up the stairs.

The nursery was two stories above, softly lit with a single lamp. A maid was quietly knitting in a wooden rocking chair, but she rose at the entrance of the two women. "Mistress Madeline is ready for her supper, and I'm ready for my cup of tea!"

Suzanne chuckled and waved the girl out, then bent over the beautifully carved crib and lifted her tiny daughter out. Madeline smiled sleepily and gave a yawn. She had dark hair like both her parents, a pale pearlescent complexion, and she might develop green eyes like her mother. "She's beautiful," Kendra said softly.

"We like to think so," Suzanne said with a smile. "I love knowing that this crib has been in Simon's mother's family for many years. Simon, his mother and aunt, and generations before were cradled here."

Kendra brushed her fingertips over the dark polished wood, imagining all the sweet babies who had slept in its shelter. "How lovely to have such a family history for your child."

"Yes, particularly since there is nothing left of my own family heirlooms." Suzanne settled into the low rocking chair and unfastened the bodice of her gown. Her garments were cleverly designed to open so she could nurse her baby. "She's only a month old. She was born a little early, but healthy, as you see."

"What a miracle a baby is!" Kendra said as she sat in the other chair. "I can scarcely remember when Christopher was so small."

"We'll find him," Suzanne said calmly as she drew her daughter to her breast. "His father will have a care for his heir if not for him as an individual."

"I tell myself that." Kendra drew a deep, calming breath. "Suzanne, why did you accept my story so quickly? I myself might have trouble believing such an outrageous tale from a strange woman."

Suzanne leaned back in the chair and patted her daughter's back. "Lucas brought you here and he is seldom wrong about people. Also..." She hesitated before continuing. "I was on a ship captured by Barbary pirates and was then enslaved in the harem of an extremely

49

unpleasant Turkish official. I know a great deal about how men can abuse women. Women in dire straits need other women."

Kendra guessed that Suzanne's bare description of her captivity concealed an ocean of pain that her new friend had no desire to discuss. "I'm glad your experiences have made you kind, not angry, and I thank you from the bottom of my heart. You and your husband both."

"Simon was a soldier. He has seen much of the dark side of life, and he also trusts Lucas's judgment." Suzanne smiled. "I was an only child, and I'm so glad that I acquired a brother when I married Simon."

"I'm so glad I braved the Clantons' ball, because doing that brought me here." Kendra rose from her chair. "I'll leave you to your daughter. This time in a baby's life is so sweet, and they grow so quickly."

Suzanne grinned. "I know, but with luck, there will be another baby or two in our futures."

Kendra hoped that for Suzanne and wished she could see such a future for herself.

—

Lucas looked up when he heard Kendra's footsteps coming down the stairs. When she joined the men in the drawing room, he was struck by how different she appeared from the first time he'd seen her. She still wore black and she had the same queenly bearing, but she no longer looked angry and desperate. Now she looked... determined.

She gestured for them to stay in their seats as they started to rise at her entrance. "No need to get up. Has the strategy session been productive?"

Simon nodded. "I have some acquaintance with one of the three men who testified against you. Hollowell seems like a reasonable fellow. If presented with sufficient evidence, he might change his mind about what happened that night. Perhaps the other men are also reasonable."

Kendra cocked her head thoughtfully. "If the woman who masqueraded as me can be found and persuaded to tell the truth, she might be able to provide intimate details that could convince him that she was the woman he bedded, not me."

"That's a very good idea," Lucas agreed. "I hope your Kirkland can find the woman."

"His ability to learn things is legendary." Simon looked at a different list. "On the social side, I've been looking at upcoming entertainments to find ones given by friends who might be supportive. Also, as Suzanne said, she can arrange for you to meet influential women who might be sympathetic to your cause."

"I've been thinking of how to present myself," Kendra said. "I've been wearing black, in mourning for the death of truth. Would red be better since I'm considered an outrageous woman?"

Lucas had a brief, dazzling vision of Kendra in scarlet, blazing like a passionate flame. He swallowed hard. "I think black is better because it's serious and suits your situation. Also, you look good in black."

"That makes sense. Very well, I shall not wear colors. I had a mourning wardrobe made up when my grandfather died so I'm well prepared." She covered a yawn. "It's time for me to return to Thorsay House."

"I'll come with you," Lucas said as he stood.

She gave him a sweet, tired smile. "Having been attacked on the way here, I welcome your escort."

Simon also rose. "I'll come as well in case the villains who attacked earlier are still out there and annoyed."

As Lucas helped her into her cloak, Kendra said hesitantly, "We discussed my going to public places. Are you familiar with Angelo's Fencing Academy?"

"We both learned to fence there," Lucas replied. "The Angelos' teaching methods were far superior to any instruction we have had in the navy or army."

"What I learned there saved my life more than once." Simon considered. "Many times more than once."

"Are you interested in visiting there because they give fencing lessons to women?" Lucas asked.

"Yes! When I was a girl and visited Thorsay, my cousin Ramsay gave several of us girls fencing lessons when none of the adults were around to say we couldn't. I enjoyed it, and fencing is splendid exercise."

"Shall we go tomorrow?"

Kendra glowed at him. "Yes, please!"

Lucas felt that glow right to his marrow. The effect was – interesting.

"Do you mind if I join you?" Simon asked. "It's been a good many years since you and I crossed swords, Lucas."

"So it has, and I'm sure you're much more in practice than I. But I'd enjoy it," Lucas said. "Would you mind having both of us, Kendra?"

"Not at all." Her voice dropped to a near whisper. "I feel blessed to have found such friends and allies."

Lucas had felt much the same when Simon and Suzanne had opened their homes and hearts to him. He was glad that he could offer that kind of support to Kendra.

The return to Thorsay House was uneventful. Kendra walked between Lucas and Simon, but Lucas's arm was the one she held. She thanked both men graciously when they reached her destination and they set a time for the next day.

The moon had set and the streets were dark, but peaceful. They were about halfway home when Simon remarked, "You're whistling."

Lucas blinked. "I am?"

"Kendra Douglas is lovely and interesting," Simon said, amusement in his voice. "Is the friar part of you fading away?"

"If you're asking if I find her attractive, the answer is yes," Lucas admitted. "It's a pleasure to rediscover masculine appreciation of the fair sex. But if you're asking if I feel more than that, the answer is of course not. Her life is in turmoil and she's made it clear that she has no interest in men as more than friends and possible allies. If she can find her Christopher, she'll probably disappear with him, never to be seen in England again."

"True," Simon said thoughtfully. "I wouldn't blame her if she leaves the country with her son, but I hope it doesn't come to that. She's a strong woman, and if she can prove her case, it will surely benefit more women in the future."

No doubt Simon was right, but Lucas wasn't particularly concerned about women in the future.

He was concerned about Kendra *now*.

Chapter 8

How long had it been since Kendra had looked forward to a new day as she did on this day? She was ready and waiting when Lucas wielded the knocker at Thorsay House.

He smiled at her, looking as if he was anticipating the day as well. "Because of the rain, we decided to travel by carriage." His gaze moved to her divided skirt. "That's your fencing costume?"

"I had this outfit made for riding astride," she explained as he helped her into her cloak. "I grew up in Northumberland, you know, and we northerners are much less formal than southerners. I like riding astride, and I like the freedom of movement I have with divided skirts, so I had this one made in mourning black after my grandfather's death. I hope you're not offended?"

"Not at all," he said as he held the door open for her. "I respect practicality."

"I'm looking forward to learning how to use a sword properly," she said as they descended the steps to the waiting carriage. "It could be useful if Denshire comes near me!"

"Not advised except for self-defense," he said firmly. "But it's never a bad thing to know how to defend one's self."

They reached the light carriage and he helped her inside, where they sat opposite Simon. There was enough space for the three of them, but only just, which meant her leg and Lucas's were touching, a fact she tried to ignore. She was too aware of him – and she liked it.

"Good day, Kendra," Simon said with a smile. "Do you know the history of Angelo's Academy?"

When Kendra shook her head, he said, "The founder, Domenico Angelo Malevolti Tremamondo, was an Italian sword master." The names rolled melodiously from his tongue, a reminder that Simon was European as well as English. "The story goes that he fell in love with a beautiful English actress and followed her to London. Once here he looked around and decided the English were in dire need of fencing lessons to make them equal to swordsmen on the Continent."

"He wasn't wrong," Lucas said. "His academy prospered, he took Angelo as his last name because it was simpler, and the academy is now run by his son Henry. The last I heard, Domenico was teaching the boys of Eton and Henry's son, Henry the Younger, was preparing to eventually take charge of the academy."

"I hope they continue to teach women," Kendra said. "Why should men have all the fun?"

Lucas smiled wryly. "Because we have arranged the world to suit male tastes. But women like Mary Wollstonecraft Godwin are changing that."

Kendra was impressed that he knew about *Vindication of the Rights of Women*. Change would come slowly, but perhaps someday women would be able to speak in their own defense in a courtroom.

It was a short ride to Angelo's Academy on Bond Street, and the coachman left them right in front of the door so it was only a brief dash through the rain to get inside. Kendra looked around with interest as she shook the raindrops from her black cloak. The academy's main room had high ceilings, and molded arches on the walls featured paired swords of many styles, from rapiers to great two-handed Scottish claymores. There was even a pair of dirks, navy style like Lucas's.

The academy was clearly home to sporting men and easy laughter. Groups of chairs and small tables were scattered near the walls for the comfort of observers, and two pairs of fencers were engaged at opposite ends of the great hall. The low rumble of conversation slowed when Kendra and her companions entered, but it picked up again quickly. Angelo's denizens must be used to the sight of women.

A genial man approached, his expression welcoming. Kendra guessed it was Henry Angelo. "Colonel Duval, always a pleasure!" he exclaimed, shaking Simon's hand. Turning to Lucas, he said, "Mr. Mandeville, or rather, Lord Foxton now. How excellent to see you again! It's been too long, and rumor said you were dead."

"Rumor is an unreliable fellow," Lucas said as he shook Angelo's proffered hand. "But in this case, not too far off." He drew Kendra forward. "Allow me to present my cousin, Miss Kendra Douglas. She's interested in possible lessons."

Henry's gaze sharpened. No doubt rumor had also reported Kendra's divorce, but he took her hand with the same warmth he'd shown Lucas and Simon. "Then you've come to the right place, Miss Douglas. There are several ladies who practice here regularly. I will talk with you more later, but first, I want to see these two cross swords." He gestured at Simon and Lucas.

The cousins exchanged a glance and Simon said, "We're willing." They stripped off their coats and hats, which were collected by a servant, along with Kendra's cloak.

As Angelo provided them with two blunted small swords, Kendra said firmly, "Please don't damage each other! Suzanne wouldn't like it."

"Neither would we," Simon assured her. Eyes glinting, he said, "Now, cousin, let's see how much you remember!"

"Not much. It's been a long time," Lucas replied with a smile, but as he flexed the blade of the light sword to acquaint himself with the weapon's weight and balance, he had an air of experience.

Onlookers drifted into a loose circle that gave the two men room to fight. Lucas and Simon saluted with raised swords, then began sparring lightly, testing each other.

As the tempo of the bout quickened, Kendra watched, entranced. She'd never been so aware of the beauty of male bodies. Fencing was lethal poetry in action that displayed fit limbs and powerful shoulders, swift turns and agile footwork. Though Simon did seem more practiced, Lucas had a longer reach and was just as fast.

She wished Suzanne was here to appreciate this magnificent display of masculine elegance. It was… stimulating, but also charming. Even a novice like her could see how they understood and anticipated each other's movements, and how much pleasure they were taking in this friendly bout. Almost-brothers indeed!

The informal bout ended when Simon lunged forward and the blunted end of his sword touched over Lucas's heart. "Bout over! You're dead, cousin."

Laughing, Lucas made a sweeping bow of concession. "I shall survive to fight another day. We'll have to do this more often."

As both men accepted towels and wiped their sweaty faces, Kendra clapped her hands. "Well done, sirs! It's lovely to watch two skilled swordsmen who aren't actually trying to kill each other."

"Indeed it is," said Henry Angelo. "Do you wish to lift a small sword yourself, Miss Douglas? I'll show you myself to get a sense of your aptitude."

"I did a bit of fencing as a young girl," Kendra said. "But I have no real skill."

"That is for me to determine! Let us withdraw to the teaching room and find you a blade."

Kendra moved off with Angelo, feeling more alive than she had in a very long time. She was beginning to enjoy being a scandalous woman.

An officer friend of Simon's claimed his attention, leaving Lucas free to amble around the academy. It had been years since his last visit, but it hadn't changed much.

A bookshelf on one wall held volumes of the fencing instruction manuals written by various Angelos. The family had a long association with the army, where they were doing their best to raise the level of British swordsmanship to Continental standards.

Lucas was considering joining Simon when the door opened and five men with a family resemblance entered in a gust of wind and rain. Most were obviously sporting gentlemen like the others in attendance, but the group included a man in black who moved unsteadily on crutches.

One of the others, a burly fellow of military bearing, helped him inside, then asked, "Shall I take you to one of the chairs, Godfrey?"

"No, dammit, Patrick!" Godfrey snapped. A proud man, apparently, determined to make his way on his own. Lucas's bonesetter instincts stirred and he wondered what had put Godfrey on those crutches. A permanent injury, or temporary? It was hard to judge the man's age because his face was so distorted by lines of pain.

As Godfrey moved awkwardly toward a chair, he looked up and saw Lucas. His face spasmed in shock and he lost his balance, crashing to the floor.

Wincing, Lucas strode forward to help the fallen man. "Are you all right?"

Godfrey recoiled. "*You!*" he snarled. "Don't touch me, you vile coward!"

Lucas jerked to a stop, stunned by the rage and hatred in the fallen man's face. Two of Godfrey's companions hastened to his side. As they lifted him onto a nearby chair, Patrick asked, "What's wrong?"

"Him!" Godfrey brandished a crutch at Lucas. "Lieutenant Lucas Mandeville! A coward and parole breaker who is responsible for my crippled state. How *dare* he pollute the air of this place, which belongs to gentlemen!"

Patrick glared at Lucas. "So this is the coward you spoke of! What brass-balled effrontery! Get out of here, you scum. You don't belong under the same roof as my brother!"

Lucas had experienced avoidance and some cuts direct, but never such blatant hatred. He drew a deep breath. "I am Lucas Mandeville, but I don't recall meeting Mr. Godfrey, nor do I recall any harm I've done him."

"That makes it worse!" Patrick snarled. He pulled a pair of gloves from the pocket of his cloak and lashed them at Lucas's face.

59

Lucas jerked back reflexively, avoiding the blow. "Good God, man, what am I supposed to have done?"

"Broke your parole, which created greater danger and punishment for those left behind," Godfrey said savagely. He thumped one crutch on the floor. "You see the results!"

Lucas studied the other man's face, but it was unfamiliar. "I'm sorry for your pain," he said quietly. "But I don't see how I can be held responsible for what a stranger has suffered."

"And that's the worst insult of all," Patrick growled. "Name your seconds!"

"I will not fight you," Lucas said, beginning to feel anger himself. "I think you must both be mad, and I will not fight a madman over a crime I didn't commit!"

With a roar of rage, Patrick ripped off his coat and dropped it on the floor, then stepped to the nearest of the alcoves that held weapons and ripped a pair of crossed blades from the wall. He hurled one at Lucas and grasped the hilt of the other with the skill of a trained fighter. "Fight, dammit, or I'll run you through where you stand!"

Lucas swore as he reflexively grabbed at the sword Patrick threw at him, managing to catch the hilt rather than the blade. It wasn't one of the lightweight small swords usually used at the academy, but a cavalry saber, longer and heavier and more deadly, and with no cap on the tip to blunt a blow.

He had only an instant to evaluate the weapon before Patrick bore down on him. Lucas knocked the other man's thrust aside barely in time.

He didn't want to kill anyone, even this overprotective and misinformed brother. But if someone was to die here today, Lucas didn't want it to be himself.

Chapter 9

"You've a talent for this, Miss Douglas," Henry Angelo said approvingly as he blocked a thrust from Kendra's small sword.

"You flatter me, Signor Angelo," she said, smiling back. "But I do remember how much I enjoyed the lessons I had from my cousin, and how good it feels to exert myself physically."

Angelo moved in with a teasing series of thrusts. "Your divided skirt works well for this exercise. Some of my regular ladies wear pantaloons and find them very good for fencing."

"Pantaloons?" Kendra rather clumsily warded off her teacher. The idea of wearing male clothing was startling, but she could see the advantages. "I would like to meet some of your regular ladies."

"There are usually several here on Wednesday mornings and..." Angelo stopped, frowning as he listened to raised voices from the main salon. "If you'll excuse me, it sounds as if someone's enthusiasm has gotten out of hand."

Kendra followed him out of the small teaching room, then caught her breath in shock as she saw Lucas engaged in fierce, metal-shrieking combat with a burly man who had murder in his eyes. And their sabers had bare, lethal points.

The other patrons of the academy had gathered around to watch, some visibly uneasy about the fight, others ghoulishly excited. Angelo hesitated, perhaps considering the safest way to end the out-of-control duel.

Kendra gasped when the burly man slashed Lucas's shoulder and spurting blood saturated the white linen of his shirt. She instinctively darted forward, but was stopped when a hard hand clamped onto her upper arm. Simon.

"Don't distract him," Simon said in a tight voice. "That could be lethal. Lucas is a first-class fencer and he's trying to end this without anyone getting killed."

"*Someone* needs to end this!" she retorted as she tried to yank her arm free. Maybe a woman trying to intervene would cause both men to back off? Or maybe she'd be cut to ribbons, but she could not stand idly by.

Simon wouldn't release her, and in the next moments, Lucas did end it. With a movement too swift for Kendra's eyes to follow, he knocked his opponent's saber down and to one side while surging forward himself, reversing the saber and smashing the pommel of the weapon into his opponent's jaw with an audible crack. The man pitched backward, dropping his saber as he lost consciousness.

Lucas swept his gaze around the circle of men, his aquamarine eyes blazing. "By the rules of *duello*, the matter has been settled in front of witnesses. Presumably my victory over this Patrick person proves right was on my side. Does anyone else want to try to kill me without knowing the facts of the situation?"

"I want to!" The ragged voice came from a black-garbed man seated in a chair by the wall, his thin hands clutching a pair of crutches. "And I do know the facts!"

"I doubt it." Lucas's voice softened. "If you want to explain why you want me dead, I'll be happy to discuss the matter with you."

The man in black spat at him, but was too far away to hit his target. Lucas shrugged. "I can't refute charges that haven't been made, Godfrey. Feel free to summon me if you want an honest talk. If not, you can damned well *leave me alone!*"

Released by Simon, Kendra slipped through the group of onlookers. "I want to take a look at that shoulder wound, Lucas."

"It stings. Not serious."

"Nonetheless."

She'd almost reached him when one of the onlookers said under his breath, "Denshire's whore! A good match for a cowardly oath breaker."

Kendra had pretended not to hear such comments in the past, but not this time. She spun on her heel. "Mine is another case in which you don't know the facts, sir!"

"No?" he said with a leer.

Kendra's hands tensed and she realized that she was still carrying the small sword she'd been practicing with. She swung it upward and brought the point to rest in the middle of the oaf's chest.

He gasped and tried to retreat, but his escape was blocked by other men. "When a dishonorable man wants to rid himself of a wife while stealing her inheritance, what better way to do it than by slandering her good name, hmmm?" she asked sweetly. "Don't you agree?"

"I... I suppose so," he stammered, his gaze locked on the small sword resting above his heart. Though the tip had a safety button on, it would be easy for Kendra to pull it off and do serious damage.

"Think about it then." She pressed the sword just hard enough for him to feel the pressure through his shirt, then lowered the weapon and turned her back on him.

The crowd melted away, leaving Kendra and her two friends. Simon had taken off his cravat and was efficiently bandaging the wound in his cousin's shoulder.

A man helped a groaning Patrick from the floor and led him to a seat by Godfrey. Looking up, he saw Simon and stiffened. "Colonel Duval! You're a hero of Waterloo! Why are you supporting this… this oath breaker?"

"I have known Lucas Mandeville my whole life," Simon replied in a voice that could freeze a regiment in its tracks. "I have known no man more honorable. I have personal knowledge; you have only hearsay. Consider your sources, sir!"

The man flushed a deep red and didn't reply.

The conversation was broken when Henry Angelo approached. "Miss Douglas, Colonel Duval, Lord Foxton, will you join me in my office?"

They all nodded and followed Angelo into his office, which was behind the main hall. Lucas said, "I'm sorry for being the cause of trouble, Signor Angelo. I won't come here again."

"You were not the cause of the trouble," Angelo growled as he pulled a bag packed with bandages, salves, and other medical items from a large drawer at the bottom of his desk. "That slice on your shoulder needs attention."

Lucas looked uncomfortable, but relaxed when Simon said, "I'll take care of this. I've done my share of dressing wounds in the field."

Angelo poured water into a basin and set it beside the medical supplies. As Simon removed the bloody cravat and washed the wound clean, Lucas asked, "Do you have any idea why that fellow Godfrey is hell-bent on seeing me punished for crimes unknown?"

Angelo frowned. "Godfrey Rogers. He's the youngest of a pack of brothers, and they're all very protective of him. Patrick, the one who attacked you, is the oldest, a former cavalry officer. Godfrey was a midshipman in the Royal Navy, captured and imprisoned by the French. He was seriously injured in a fall while trying to escape, I believe, and returned home crippled."

"I don't remember meeting him, but he might have seen me in one of the French prisons." Lucas sucked in his breath as Simon cleaned the wound with stinging gin. "I don't know how that translates into my being responsible for his crippled state, but there must be a connection in his mind. I wish I could talk to him without being skewered by one of his brothers."

"If the Rogers brothers can't control themselves, they're not welcome here," Angelo said firmly. "I shall talk to them, and I hope to see all of you in the future."

Simon applied a fresh bandage to the wound, then helped Lucas into his coat. With the bloodstains covered, he looked normal enough.

Kendra collected her shredded nerves and said, "Wednesday morning, Signor Angelo. I look forward to meeting more of your fencing ladies."

As the three of them left the academy, Simon said, "Will you join us for lunch, Kendra? This morning I sent a message to Lord Kirkland, saying we wished to talk to him. With luck, he'll be available soon."

"Yes, thank you. I'd like that." Kendra climbed into the carriage, thinking that after months of paralysis, events were beginning to move. Almost too fast for her.

Chapter 10

When they returned to Simon's house, there was a message waiting from Lord Kirkland, inviting them to call on him that very afternoon. Lucas changed to a clean shirt and they had a light meal before traveling to Kirkland House, a spacious residence on Berkeley Square.

They were escorted to their host's study, where they were welcomed warmly. Kendra studied Kirkland. He was tall, dark, reserved, and enigmatic. Suzanne had described him as a handsome, charming spider in the midst of a vast web of connections. She'd been right about the good looks and charm, and Kendra had no trouble believing in the connections.

As his guests seated themselves in chairs set around the fire, Kirkland glanced at Lucas's shoulder. "I hope your injury this morning wasn't serious, Foxton?"

"A minor wound." Lucas's brows arched. "It appears that your legendary ability to collect information is well earned."

Kirkland smiled. "People talk. Your swordsmanship was much admired." Turning to Kendra, he said, "I'm told you prefer to be known as Kendra Douglas rather than Lady Denshire?"

She raised her chin, meeting his gaze steadily. "You are informed correctly, my lord. I'm glad to be rid of my husband, but I must reclaim my son and if possible, my reputation."

"Those two things are closely related," he said quietly. "Tell me your story in your own words."

She was becoming practiced at telling the sordid tale. She ended by saying, "Do you believe me, or do you have more questions?"

"I believe you," he said promptly. "I've kept an eye on Denshire for some time, and he's been involved in several unsavory situations. It's easy to believe he would act against you in such an appalling way. It might be possible to attack his unorthodox legal strategy, but better by far to reveal his lies and deceit."

As a maid came in with a tea trolley and began quietly serving tea, cakes, and small sandwiches, Kendra opened her reticule and removed another copy of her list. "Here are potential witnesses."

Kirkland scanned the list, nodding occasionally. "This is a good start. Another way to gather information is to place someone in the household. I know a woman who is good at that sort of work. You would need to talk to her about what to expect."

Kendra hesitated. "Any woman who goes to work there would be well advised to be skilled in self-defense."

"This woman is." He glanced up at the maid. "Hazel, you've proved how invisible you can be. Now sit down and join us for tea. Miss Douglas, meet Miss Wilson."

"Aye, my lord," the young woman said with a London accent. Her demeanor changed as she moved from overlooked servant to guest. She poured herself a cup of tea. "Like all good servants, I was listening at the door before

I came in with the tea cart, so I have some idea of what I need to learn, Miss Douglas."

Kendra studied Hazel Wilson more thoroughly. The young woman's features were pleasant and unremarkable, but her eyes were sharp with intelligence. "I'm impressed, Miss Wilson. I do hope you really are good at defending yourself. In recent years I spent little time in Denshire House, but I heard it was difficult to keep female servants because of the behavior of Denshire and his friends."

"They would regret misbehaving with me," Hazel said tartly. "I've taught self-defense courses to the females of Lord Kirkland's household. Everyone from the countess down to the youngest scullery maid."

"I don't suppose you know much about Denshire's friends who testified to your alleged depravity, so I'll set someone else to investigating them." Kirkland gave a slow, rather dangerous smile. "We shall see if some justice can be done."

A tap on the door was followed by a lovely blond woman, surely the lady of the house. "May I join you? What you said earlier made me want to meet your guests."

Kirkland stood and gave his wife a smile as intimate as a kiss. "I'm glad you've returned in time to meet them. Colonel Duval you know, and here is his cousin Lord Foxton, plus Kendra Douglas, who is here on a quest."

Lady Kirkland's smile was warm. "And Hazel is here also, I see, doing her best to seem invisible. Will you be free to give another defense course here soon? We have several new maids who are keen to learn."

"Not right away," Hazel said, "but soon."

"May I take the course also?" Kendra asked.

"Or perhaps Miss Wilson will teach the course in my household," Simon said thoughtfully. "You might end up as a full-time teacher at this rate."

Hazel shook her head. "There aren't many men as enlightened as you and Lord Kirkland, but I'm happy to oblige when asked."

Lady Kirkland's gaze moved to Lucas. "Lord Foxton, I'm involved with a charitable organization called Zion House, which provides shelter for abused women and children. We also operate a free infirmary adjacent to the shelter. I hear you're a bonesetter of considerable skill. Would you be interested in sometimes working in our infirmary in the East End?"

Lucas gave a blink of surprise. "Yes, I would. When and where?"

"A good thing you agreed, Foxton," Kirkland said amiably. "There is no escaping my lady and her dedicated friends."

"Indeed not," she said placidly. "Do you have a few minutes to discuss it now?"

"You two can go into one corner to discuss the infirmary, Hazel and Miss Douglas can go into another corner to discuss what she needs to be doing, and Simon and I can stay here by the food and drink and discuss general strategy," Kirkland suggested.

"Well played, sir!" Kendra said as she and Hazel withdrew to the right-hand corner, where Hazel began asking questions about Denshire's household, taking notes in a small notebook. When they were done, she closed the notebook and tucked it away. "This promises to be an interesting investigation, Miss Douglas. There is bound to be someone in the household who has some idea where your son was taken."

"You'll let me know as soon as you learn something?"

"Of course." Hazel's voice was gentle. "I'm sure your Christopher is being well treated because Denshire undoubtedly values having an heir, but a young boy needs his mother."

"I certainly think so!" Kendra rose to her feet. "You be careful at Denshire House. I don't want another woman to be injured."

"Oh, I can take care of myself." A short, sharp knife appeared in Hazel's hand. Just as quickly she made it disappear. "A girl learns that early in the East End."

Kendra wished she'd learned such skills, though if she had, perhaps she'd have killed Denshire, and she didn't want murder on her soul. Lucas and Lady Kirkland had finished their discussion, and he was looking very pleased.

Kendra and Lucas and Simon took their leave. Outside, Lucas said, "Simon, I know you have work to do in the City, so you can take the carriage. Kendra and I will walk home since it's turned into such a pleasant day."

"That's a good idea. Tell Suzanne I'll be home before dinner." He grinned at Lucas. "One of these days you'll have to start attending these business meetings, too."

"But you're so much better at such things," Lucas responded.

Simon responded with a roll of his eyes and climbed into the carriage. Kendra loved watching the brotherly interplay between the two cousins. She would have liked to have a brother or sister. She'd wanted to give Christopher one. The thought of her failure produced a surprising wrench of pain.

Burying it, she took Lucas's arm and they began strolling back across Mayfair. "Are you in business with Simon?" she asked.

"Yes, though I've not been very active. Our mothers were sisters and their father was a very successful businessman. He left his property to his daughters and to us, his only grandchildren. Simon is very active in the management and he's been dropping dire hints that I should be, too."

"Will you join him?"

"As I said, Simon is better at it." Lucas smiled wryly. "Being missing and presumed dead for years was a good way of avoiding work, but my conscience is prodding me to start paying more attention."

"A conscience is useful but so often annoying," she murmured.

"Very true." He glanced down at her. "How do you feel about our progress?"

"Surprisingly pleased," she said. "Kirkland is an impressive spider, and if Hazel is a good example, he finds excellent people for his investigations."

"When I was in Brussels before and after Waterloo, I met other people of Kirkland's and yes, they're all very intelligent and good at what they do."

"Hazel will surely find where Christopher is, won't she?" Kendra asked wistfully.

"I believe she will," Lucas said. "And if she fails, we'll find him in another way."

"Thank you for saying what I need to hear. I hope I'm not becoming tiresome." She swallowed hard. "Ever since Christopher was born, I've had nightmares of him being ripped from my arms," she whispered. "Even though he's a proper little boy now, I still see him as a helpless infant, and there is nothing I can do to save him."

He put his hand over hers where it gripped his arm. "You've some Scots blood, so perhaps it's a touch of the

Sight, and you saw him being taken from you some time in the future. Now that that has happened, it's time to change your nightmares to dreams of being reunited with him."

"Do you think that will help?" she asked doubtfully.

"It can't hurt. Our worst fears can take over our minds, yet often things turn out better than expected."

"Has that happened to you?"

"Oh, yes, several times I was sure I was going to die, and I didn't," he replied. "I also felt that I would be forever estranged from my earlier life and family, yet here I am. Somewhat confused, but slowly sorting myself out."

"You looked very pleased when Lady Kirkland asked if you would work as a bonesetter at her infirmary."

"I am. I'm as much a healer as a sailor, and that part of me has been neglected since Waterloo. Burned out, perhaps. So many wounded." He fell silent for a dozen paces. "It seemed as if anyone in Brussels who could carry water or wrap a bandage or help a wounded man walk was helping. It was quite extraordinary, equally rewarding and exhausting."

She'd read stories of the quiet heroism of the people of Brussels. "I imagine that Suzanne was working right next to you?"

"Yes, along with every other person residing in the house." He sighed. "I wish I could have done more."

"All we can do is our best." She smiled wryly. "Guilt at not being able to do more is optional."

"What? I thought guilt was compulsory." He glanced at her and they both laughed. She was rather amazed that despite all the problems she faced, she could laugh with Lucas.

"A bonesetter once reset my shoulder after I was thrown from my horse," she said. "The pain was excruciating, yet he was able to end it within moments. Extraordinary."

"That sort of work is very satisfying," he said. "Not all joint problems are so easily solved, but usually I can help at least a little. Frère Emmanuel trained me very well. He came from a family of bonesetters and since he had no sons, he taught me everything he knew, which included techniques he said were unique to his family."

"Have you considered teaching others how to be bonesetters?" she asked. "Surely such special knowledge should be passed along."

"I hadn't thought of that." He was silent for half a block, thinking. "But perhaps I should. Frère Emmanuel would always help anyone in need. I'm sure he would approve of sharing his knowledge." They were approaching Duval House, so he continued, "Would you like to say hello to Suzanne before we go on to Thorsay House?"

"I'd like that."

They entered and found Suzanne in the drawing room with Madeline sleeping peacefully in her lap. As Lucas removed his hat, he said, "Kirkland is already setting some impressive wheels in motion."

"I'm glad to hear that. I considered going with you, but…" She chuckled. "I feel as if I've turned into a potted plant since Maddy was born. About all I want to do is sit and hold her."

Kendra laughed. "This will pass, so enjoy it while you can."

"Would you like to hold her?" Suzanne offered. "I could use a good stretch."

"I'd love to." Gently Kendra took the baby in her arms and settled in a chair as Suzanne stood and stretched her arms wide. "So beautiful, and so clearly a little girl," she said softly. "Christopher was equally beautiful but equally clearly a little boy. How can that be when people say that babies all look alike?"

"Telling boy from girl isn't easy when they're so small," Lucas said. "But they are all their own selves from the moment they're born."

Kendra realized she'd only ever held Christopher like this, never a baby girl. As she studied the rose-petal complexion, she felt a strange, deep stirring of pain so long buried she'd forgotten it. Pain and confusion and a man's voice saying, "*A girl and sickly. I have no need of a daughter. Get rid of it!*" Kendra screaming silently as the infant was ruthlessly wrenched from her arms.

Pain. Confusion. Frantic despair.

Empty arms…

The world darkened and she was having trouble breathing as the suffocating past drowned the present. Terrified of hurting Madeline, she stood and returned the infant to her mother, then lurched away.

Cradling her daughter, Suzanne said urgently, "Kendra, what's wrong? You look like you've seen a ghost."

Kendra stumbled blindly over a chair and almost fell. "I had a daughter," she gasped. "*I had a daughter!*"

Chapter 11

Unseeing, Kendra missed her footing and would have fallen if strong male arms hadn't caught her and drawn her down to the sofa. Lucas's warm embrace enfolded her against his chest, and the steady beat of his heart helped steady her shattered nerves.

"Suzanne, order hot tea," Lucas ordered. "And brandy as well."

Kendra heard Suzanne ring for the tea, felt Lucas wrap a knee robe around her shaking shoulders. "You're safe here, Kendra," he said in his low, soothing voice as he cradled her against him. "Whatever horror has attacked you is from the past. Now you're safe with friends."

It wasn't long before a hot mug fragrant with tea and brandy was pressed between her clenched hands. "Drink," Lucas said firmly.

She took a sip, then a larger one. Warmth began curling through her and her mind began to clear. "I'm sorry," she said in a ragged voice. "That was... very strange."

"But also very real," Lucas said quietly. "What are you remembering?"

She began to shake again.

Suzanne sat on her left side and slid a comforting hand around Kendra's waist, below Lucas's arm, which encircled her from the right. "Terrible memories lose some of their power when they are spoken aloud." Wry humor entered Suzanne's voice. "Ask me how I know."

Kendra managed a crooked smile, knowing that Suzanne must have survived shattering difficulties herself. "I didn't realize what I had forgotten until I held Madeline." Her gaze sharpened and she looked around the drawing room. "Where is she? She's all right?"

"I sent her up to the nursery with her nurse," Suzanne said. "She's fine and happy. It's you I'm worried about."

Kendra closed her eyes for long moments as she pieced together jagged fragments of the past. Opening her eyes, she said, "I was nearing my time when Denshire decided that he wanted his son to be born at the family seat, Denfield Park. He was convinced the child would be a boy even though I pointed out to him that daughters happen."

"Indeed they do," Suzanne said. "It must have been a difficult journey."

Kendra shuddered at the memory. "It was winter and we were traveling a particularly rutted section of road when my labor began. After that…" Kendra shook her head. "Everything is so confused. We stopped at the next village inn we came to and a midwife was called. I don't remember her name, but she had fair hair and… kind hands."

She took a deep swallow of tea. "There was terrible pain and bleeding and I heard myself screaming but it seemed a long distance off. I felt very separate from what was happening. Later I was told that no one thought I'd survive.

"My next clear memory was the midwife putting Christopher to my breast and saying very firmly that I had a fine baby boy and I must take care of him. When I held him, I became determined to survive and the mists began to clear. But I'd lost a lot of blood and had childbed fever and was very weak for a long time after."

"You had twins and one was stillborn?" Lucas asked quietly.

"Twins, yes," Kendra said, her voice tightening. "But the other baby, a girl, wasn't stillborn. I... I remember holding her. She made a feeble little cry, like a kitten. She was so tiny and frail! I had decided that if I had a girl, I would name her Caitlin, for my mother. She had dark hair like Madeline, but she was a shadow child, not robust and healthy like your daughter, Suzanne."

The sight of Madeline in her arms had awoken the memory of her Caitlin. So fragile, so precious and fleeting. Kendra's voice turned savage. "The true horror was hearing Denshire say to get rid of it, he didn't need a sickly girl that surely wouldn't last the night. He yanked her from my arms and... she gave a terrible little cry."

As the agony of that moment seared through her mind, Kendra began sobbing uncontrollably. She turned her face into Lucas's shoulder.

"*Mon Dieu!*" Suzanne whispered in a horrified voice. Her arm tightened around Kendra at the same time as Lucas's. The warmth of their joint embrace saved Kendra from fracturing.

As she sobbed her pain and anger away, she found a clarity she hadn't known in years. At length she lifted her head and drew a deep breath. "Lucas, I'm sorry for soaking your coat."

He smiled at her. "No apology is necessary. It makes a man feel very manly when a beautiful woman cries on his shoulder."

His light tone surprised her into a crooked smile. "Best not to encourage me!"

She hoped she never wept with such grief again. She rose to her feet, giving both companions a brief grateful hand squeeze first.

Then she paced across the room as she ordered her thoughts. Now that light had been shined on the dark core of her hidden tragedy, she felt strong again after years of weakness. She turned to face Lucas and Suzanne, profoundly grateful for them. Suzanne, who had a Madonna's warmth and a survivor's steel. Lucas, who had endured a fractured life and become strong and compassionate.

Aloud, she said, "Lucas, thank you for sharing your family with me."

"The pleasure is ours," Suzanne said with a smile. "I always wanted a sister."

"I hope you're not saying that just to be polite," Kendra said wryly. "If I'm a sister, I'm an exhausting one! The last few days since we met have been educational, Lucas. At Thorsay House, there's a clever little device called a kaleidoscope that a visitor left. It's a silver tube, and inside, colored fragments of glass move as the tube is turned, creating different, unexpected patterns. That is what is happening to my life."

"Education about life makes us stronger, though generally at a steep cost," Lucas said.

"An understatement!" Kendra said fervently. "Now that I remember what happened, I see how everything changed after Christopher's birth. As I recovered, I could hardly bear to let him out of my sight because I feared something might happen to him. I was grateful that he looked more like me than his father."

Her voice hardened. "That was also the true end of my marriage. I no longer wanted Denshire to touch me.

Not that he made any real attempt to woo me back to his bed. He had his heir and his freedom to do as he wished in town while I lived in the country and tended to Christopher and the estate. I could have gone on that way indefinitely if he'd left me alone."

"What will you do now?" Suzanne asked softly.

The answer came with absolute certainty. "I must go back to that village and find out what happened to my Caitlin. I hope someone baptized her and she was buried in holy ground and not just tossed away like…" Kendra's voice broke and she couldn't finish the sentence. "I'd like to say good-bye to her now since I couldn't then."

"Of course you must go and learn what happened," Lucas said calmly. "I'll go with you. It's not a mission that should be undertaken alone."

Kendra's gaze locked with Lucas's and a shiver ran down her spine. There was intense awareness between them and a sense of connection they had only just begun to explore. She had come to trust Lucas, and there was no one she'd rather have at her side on such a difficult journey. But… "The two of us traveling together would be rather scandalous."

"As has been pointed out, we're both rather scandalous already." His voice was calm, but she saw in his blue eyes how much he wanted to take this journey with her.

Would it be wise to travel with the most attractive man she'd ever met? Was she ready for that? Perhaps it was time to find out. "Thank you, Lucas. I would appreciate your company. Not to mention that it might be a good idea for you to leave town before another Rogers brother can challenge you."

He chuckled. "I'd like to think that nonsense is over, but they seemed a pigheaded lot. If I'm out of sight, perhaps I'll fade from their minds."

"I wouldn't count on it," Suzanne said. "But this sounds like a worthy mission to undertake while you're waiting for Kirkland's investigators to come up with useful information. Kendra, where is the village where you took refuge?"

Kendra frowned. "I'll have to find a map of the area. We didn't take the usual road. Denshire insisted on a shortcut that he said would be faster. It wasn't a good decision. Denshire Park is between Cirencester and Gloucester, so not a great distance from London. The village was... Little Dauntrey, I think."

"As a former exploring officer, Simon loves maps," Suzanne said. "I'm sure he has some of that area."

"Would you object to calling on my great-aunt and uncle at Camden Keep?" Lucas asked. "It's on the way and would be a convenient place to spend the night."

Kendra hesitated. "They may not welcome a scandalous woman into their house, and I can't say that I'd blame them."

"They won't mind. They lived in India for years while my uncle was the British Resident in one of the royal courts, so they are more broad-minded than most."

"And it will give you a chance to visit the Magdalene," Suzanne answered. "Give her a kiss for me."

"The Magdalene?" Kendra asked warily. "That could refer to me."

Lucas laughed. "The Magdalene is the mule who was my mount and companion during my Franciscan years. She was already old when I acquired her, so I brought her back to England to give her a comfortable retirement.

She might have ended up in a stew pot if I'd left her in Belgium."

"Which would be a tragedy," Suzanne said firmly. "She is a noble beast of great moral character and has earned kindness, green pastures, and a full manger."

"All of which my aunt and uncle provide. They rather dote on her," Lucas agreed.

"With such references, I cannot but honor her when we meet," Kendra said with a straight face. "I'd like to leave as soon as possible, but tomorrow is the luncheon with influential ladies that you arranged for me, Suzanne. Lucas, what does your schedule look like?"

"I'm going to visit Lady Kirkland's infirmary tomorrow," he replied. "She's interested in my bonesetting skills. But after that I'm free to go."

"So day after tomorrow. That will give us time to study maps and hire a carriage and arrange the other necessities of travel." She sighed. "I suppose there is no reason to rush after all these years."

"This journey isn't so much about reason as about heart," Lucas said quietly.

He understands. Kendra needed to leave London to lay to rest the ghost of her lost child. But she also looked forward to spending time with Lucas.

Chapter 12

Lucas was buzzing with anticipation when Lady Kirkland called for him at Duval House the next morning. After greeting Suzanne and admiring Madeline, the countess led the way outside, saying with a smile, "You look like a schoolboy being taken to Astley's Circus for a birthday treat."

He grinned as he helped her into her carriage. "Is it that obvious? I am looking forward to seeing your infirmary. It's been too long since I've done anything useful."

"You sound like my brother Daniel," she said as she settled into the leather seat. "Surgery and medicine are his passions. When he inherited a barony, he went searching for a wife who could manage the estate while he continued his medical work."

Amused, Lucas asked, "Was he able to find a capable female estate manager who was willing to marry him?"

"He did, and she has become another passion for him. She's a most satisfactory sister-in-law," his companion replied with a smile. "Not only is Daniel able to continue his doctoring, but he's established cottage hospitals in towns near where he and his wife live and he hopes to start more."

Intrigued, Lucas said, "It sounds as if you're creating an empire of good works! How did you begin?"

"Daniel and I started a free infirmary in Bristol where we lived," she explained. "It wasn't long before I realized that abused women and their children needed a shelter to escape violent partners, so we established Zion House. Now there are Zion Houses in several cities, and each one has at least a small infirmary."

"Impressive! Where do you get your funding?"

The countess's eyes gleamed. "I importune wealthy people. My husband says I have a genius for cornering prospects and convincing them to open their wallets."

Lucas grinned. "No doubt you got your start by practicing on him, Lady Kirkland?"

She chuckled. "Of course. But please, call me Laurel. Since I have high hopes of enlisting you as part of our medical team, I want to be on friendly terms with you."

"Call me Lucas then." He shook his head admiringly. "You're a dangerous woman, Laurel."

"My husband says that, too," she said mischievously. With her determination and charm, it was easy to see how she'd built a large charitable institution. She continued, "Tell me about your own medical background. Suzanne and Simon speak highly of you, but I'd like to know more about your experiences."

"You know that bonesetters aren't trained like surgeons and physicians," he replied. "We serve apprenticeships."

She nodded. "My brother has wanted to be a doctor since he was in the nursery. Were you the same?"

"No, I wanted to captain a ship in the Royal Navy, like my father," he said. "But I did seem to be drawn to fixing people up. After sea battles, I often helped the ship's surgeon clean and bandage wounds when he needed help. Later when I was a prisoner of the French, that experience came in handy since prisoners received little medical treatment. I did the work since I was willing to do it. I liked helping people feel better."

"It's a very good feeling," she agreed. "I understand that after you escaped, you worked with a Franciscan friar who was a bonesetter and traveled with him through Belgium and northern France?"

"Yes. Frère Emmanuel saved my life after I was wounded in my escape from the French prison." Lucas swallowed hard as he thought of the gentle old man who had become his teacher and friend. "Since he was frail, I slipped into the role of servant and apprentice. We traveled an irregular circuit through the countryside, going where we were needed and staying in farms and villages. Bone-setters were often the only medical people available, so we did what we could no matter what the problem."

"Versatility is useful in a place like our infirmary," she said with approval. "Broken bones and dislocated joints are common. We have surgeons who do such work, but we could use a really skilled specialist." She gave him a slanting glance.

"Frère Emmanuel trained me well," he said, thinking this was no time for false modesty. "He came from a family of skilled bonesetters who over the years had developed special techniques for challenging problems, and he developed some himself. I learned those as well as the more usual methods."

"Our infirmary will give you ample scope to practice your skills, if you choose to volunteer with us."

"I'd like that," he said. "Tell me more about how it's organized."

"Zion House and the infirmary are run by a combin-ation of paid employees and volunteers," she explained. "Many of our employees were originally clients of Zion

House or patients at the infirmary. Several physicians and surgeons are paid to work half time, and there are also volunteer physicians and surgeons who work when they can. We have several training programs for our clients, including ones for nursing, cooking, and being a lady's maid. We also have guards who were soldiers or sailors and had nowhere to go after they left the military."

His brows arched. "Are guards needed often?"

"Not often, but sometimes violent husbands come seeking their wives. The thieves and drunks usually avoid us because we are valued here and our neighbors don't want us to be troubled."

For the rest of the drive to London's East End, they discussed the kinds of patients and resources the infirmary had. When the carriage halted in front of a long building on a quiet street, Laurel announced, "Welcome to our empire! We recently acquired this old warehouse which has given us more space. The infirmary is on the ground floor and the two upper levels have been turned into housing for clients of Zion House. We have several smaller buildings on this street, too."

Though the structures were old, they were in good repair and the street was well swept. They climbed from the carriage, and Laurel escorted Lucas inside. There was a reception room with people waiting in chairs around the edge and a calm older woman at the desk taking notes as she spoke with patients. A broad, capable-looking man with a wooden leg and the bearing of a soldier sat by the door, keeping a watchful eye on everyone else.

"Patients are sorted here depending on what ails them and how severe the problem is," Laurel said as she led Lucas through the reception area to the treatment rooms behind. "I'd like you to meet our apothecary. Mrs. Simmons learned the trade from her husband. After his death, their landlord put her and her children out on the street and they ended up at Zion House. She's an excellent apothecary, so we put her in charge of our medications. Now she's training her daughter in the trade."

Laurel led the way to a stairwell that took them up to the top floor. The spacious corner room had large windows for light – and bars on the windows in case opium addicts were willing to climb up two floors to break in. The room was lined with shelves holding bottles and jars as well as tables for compounding medications.

Mrs. Simmons, a plump, no-nonsense woman with silver in her hair, glanced up from the mortar and pestle she was using to grind some white substance. "Good day, Lady Kirkland!" she said in a strong Cockney accent. "Did you bring me a patient?"

"Not this time! I'm giving Lord Foxton the grand tour. He's a bonesetter who has worked in Belgium and France."

Mrs. Simmons's brows arched as she surveyed Lucas. Bonesetters were traditionally from the lower orders, not aristocrats, but she refrained from commenting on the anomaly. "I'm pleased to meet you, Lord Foxton, and even more pleased to learn that you've worked on the Continent. As her ladyship knows, I have an interest in collecting traditional remedies that work, and you might know some I've never heard of."

"We could have a long and interesting conversation about that!" he replied. "Joints and bones can be such sources of pain. I have recipes for some good soothing salves, as I'm sure you do also. Perhaps we can compare them?"

"Have you found any that are particularly effective?"

Before Lucas could answer, Laurel said with a chuckle, "I'll leave you two to discuss your remedies while I take care of some accounts. I'll come back to collect you, Lucas. If you finish your discussion sooner, feel free to explore the building."

"Her ladyship knows when to leave others to it," Mrs. Simmons said with amusement. "Would you like to look at the recipes for my salves?"

"I would. I've also just realized that I should write down recipes for compounds that Frère Emmanuel and I used before I forget them," Lucas said as the apothecary produced a large notebook with carefully written recipes on occasionally stained pages. "Of course, for fever and general pain there is nothing better than willow bark tea, but that's well known in England."

"I dispense a great deal of it," Mrs. Simmons agreed. "Now take a seat and we'll look over the ingredients in my various salves."

The two of them pulled up chairs and studied the recipes, discussing various ingredients. Lucas recognized that he and Mrs. Simmons could hardly have been more different, or enjoyed discussing their shared interests more avidly.

When they came to the end of Mrs. Simmons's salve recipes, she closed the notebook. "I do hope you choose to work here regularly. I think you'd fit in well."

"If Lady Kirkland will have me, I'll be happy to volunteer here," Lucas said, realizing how much he wanted to work with these dedicated people.

"Have you ever found anything that works well with arthritis? It's so common, especially with old folks, and it can be crippling." Mrs. Simmons flexed her right hand, where some of the joints were visibly enlarged. "There are days when I need my daughter to do the grinding and measuring, I have such trouble doing it."

Lucas hesitated. "Frère Emmanuel had a traditional remedy that often seemed to help with the pain, but if you haven't heard of it, you'll laugh."

The apothecary's brows arched. "I don't laugh at anything until I've at least tested it enough to decide it doesn't work."

"Soak raisins made from white grapes in gin for a fortnight," Lucas said. "Use good strong gin with juniper. The raisins will plump up with the gin. After a fortnight or so, eat nine raisins a day. I'm not sure the exact number matters, but that was what Frère Emmanuel recommended. The drunken raisins were surprisingly effective for a number of our patients."

Mrs. Simmons leaned back in her chair and pursed her lips thoughtfully. "That may not be as strange as you think. My husband liked studying the history of different medicines. Gin is derived from genever, which was a tonic and medication used in the Low Countries for centuries. It was said to be good for fever and digestion, among other things. The drink we call gin comes from that and the ingredients are similar."

"I didn't know that, but it makes a great deal of sense. Will you try it?"

"I most certainly will!" She flexed her fingers thoughtfully. "And I'll try it on some of my arthritic regulars. If it works, I'll be buying a good bit of gin!"

Laurel entered the room. "Lucas, a young man has just been brought in with a serious knee injury. Are you willing to take a look at him?"

"Of course." Lucas rose. "I look forward to hearing your results, Mrs. Simmons."

She grinned. "If drunken raisins work, I'll tell all of London!"

"I think you've made a friend," Laurel said after they left the apothecary's room.

"I hope so. You're very lucky to have her."

"I know. Zion House and the infirmary are blessed in our people." Laurel led the way downstairs to one of the treatment rooms behind the reception area. She opened the door, saying, "Here's the young man with the injured knee, Alfred Roberts, and his brother Martin."

The patient lay on an examination table, his face white with pain as his brother hovered worriedly over him. "Can you help Alf?" Martin asked worriedly. "Our pa owns a tavern not far from here. We were loadin' casks of beer when one slipped and fell on Alf and busted his knee."

"I'll see what I can do," Lucas said in a soothing voice.

"It bloody *hurts*!" Alf hissed through clenched teeth.

"Of course it does, but you've come to the right place to get fixed," Lucas said as he rolled Alf's loose trouser leg above the swollen knee. "I have to examine the injury and that will hurt more, I'm afraid."

He closed his eyes and offered a brief prayer for healing Alf's injury. He didn't know if the prayer helped, but he was sure it didn't hinder.

He'd found that talking helped distract a patient, so as he carefully probed the lower leg from knee to foot, he asked, "Is there numbness anywhere?"

"N… no. I wish it *was* numb!"

"In this case, pain is good. Numbness would mean worse damage." He examined the area around the kneecap to learn whether the bones were broken or merely misaligned. "What's the name of your family tavern?"

Alf gave a sharp bark of pain, then said raggedly, "The Three... Sails."

"Is the beer good?"

"The best in London!" Alf said.

"Aye, it is," Martin agreed.

"I'll have to come by for a drink." Lucas checked the pulse in Alf's foot. It was steady, if a little fast, which meant there wasn't serious damage to the blood vessels.

After he finished his examination, he said, "Your knee has been partially dislocated, which is not wonderful, but it's better than a complete dislocation. Next time, try to drop the barrel on your shoulder. Dislocations are more common there and more easily fixed. Though they still hurt like merry Hades."

Alf tried to smile. "The shoulder it is next time."

Lucas rested both hands around the knee and visualized the healing energy that sometimes blessed his treatments. Pure white light that flowed through him from some higher place, entering his hands and passing into the mangled knee.

"Your hands are warm," Alf choked out.

"All the better for fixing your knee. Martin, could you stand at the head of the table and hold both of Alf's hands? This next part will be quick but very painful."

"Worse than now?" Alf asked in a shaky voice.

"Yes, the dislocated bone needs to be moved back into place as soon as possible. It took a lot of pressure to displace that bone, and it will take a lot of pressure to return it to its proper position. But it will be over in a few moments."

Once Martin had a firm grasp on his brother's hands, Lucas applied the necessary force to reposition the bone. It took strength to be a bonesetter, and as Frère Emmanuel had become increasingly frail, Lucas eventually did all of this sort of work.

Pressure, white light…

Alf screamed in agony, his body jerking up from the table, but between them, Martin and Lucas kept him from falling off. The scream diminished into anguished panting as Lucas continued to rest his hands on the knee. "It should feel better now."

Alf exhaled roughly. "It does. A lot better. Still hurts, though!"

"That's because the ligaments that bind the leg bones together have been wrenched about. The knee will have to be splinted for a time so you can't move it. After the splint comes off, you should use a wrap around the knee to reduce the strain, and you should carefully exercise the joint to help it regain strength and stability. If you do that and all goes well, you should make a good recovery."

Laurel's soft voice said, "We have a couple of nurses who have developed exercises to help a damaged limb regain function as it heals."

Lucas hadn't realized she was still in the room, but he imagined she had wanted to see him work. She moved forward, her hands full. "I sent for opium to ease the pain and materials to splint the knee."

"Thank you." He gave Alf a dose of laudanum, then splinted the knee. By the time he was done, a male nurse had come in to further discuss Alf's follow-up treatment and recovery.

After wishing Alf well, Lucas withdrew with Laurel at his side, feeling the fatigue that always followed serious energy healing. When they were back in the reception area, he said, "Did I pass?"

"Indeed you did. Were you pleased with this day's work?"

"I haven't felt this good in…" He tried to remember and couldn't. "A very long time. A very, *very* long time."

Laurel gave him a warm smile. "Doing good for others has that effect. Do you want to become a regular volunteer?"

"Very much so. I'm leaving town tomorrow for several days, but when I return to London, I'll pay a call on you and we can decide where I'll be of most use."

"I already have ideas about that!"

So did Lucas.

Chapter 13

Kendra would rather have scrubbed floors on her knees than have lunch with half a dozen powerful wives who would know the public version of her disgrace, but she trusted Suzanne. Even so, her hands were clenched as they waited for the luncheon to begin.

"Relax," her friend said soothingly. "These are all women who know something of the world and will listen with open minds."

"I know you think that, but you seem to believe the best of people," Kendra said.

"And I'm usually right." Suzanne chuckled. "These women were all open-minded about me, and my past is even more lurid than yours."

Remembering what Suzanne had endured, Kendra smiled wryly. "You were considered a victim, I am considered a slut. I'm not sure which is worse!"

"I wouldn't have chosen either. But it's our trials that make us strong and interesting."

"I would rather be less interesting!"

Their banter was interrupted when the doorknocker sounded. As the butler responded, Suzanne peered out the drawing-room window. "Our first guests are arriving. Lady Julia Randall and Lady Masterson. They're half sisters, though you might not notice the resemblance immediately because Athena Masterson is half a head taller."

Warned in advance, Kendra observed that the first arrivals did indeed have similar dark hair and features. Lady Julia was petite and reserved in her demeanor while her sister was very tall and more outgoing, but they both regarded her with interest rather than scorn when Suzanne introduced them.

The same was true of Lady Kingston, Lady Wyndham, Lady Romayne, and the Duchess of Ashton, who had the most elevated title but turned out to be a petite and smiling golden blonde. The guests were all punctual, so soon the drawing room was filled with friendly women greeting one another and exchanging hugs.

After the initial chat and distribution of drinks, Suzanne said in a carrying voice, "I'd like to call this meeting to order, please!"

Her request was greeted with good-natured laughter and full attention. Suzanne continued, "As you know, besides the pleasure of your company, I wanted you to meet my friend Kendra Douglas, the former Lady Denshire. She has quite a story to tell, and I thought you would all find it interesting. Kendra, the floor is yours."

Kendra gulped. "I thought you'd want me to talk after we ate!"

"You'll enjoy the food more if you aren't tied in knots," Suzanne explained.

"You're probably right, but might I exchange my sherry for brandy?"

There was a ripple of laughter as Suzanne complied. Kendra took one sip of brandy before she stood, setting her glass aside. "I imagine you've heard the story of the scandalous divorce of Lady Denshire. That story is based on wicked lies. Suzanne thinks I should tell the truth to a group of powerful, open-minded women. I'm not sure it will make a difference in my life or in the grand scheme of things, but – the truth matters."

"I shall be glad to hear it," said Lady Kingston. "Even without knowing you, I thought the story sounded strange. Improbable. Since I'm a curious beast, as my husband says, I've wondered. The truth will be welcome."

Once more Kendra explained what had actually happened. There were gasps when she showed the burn scars on her leg, and frowns when she spoke of how Denshire had drugged her and thrown her out of the house and refused to let her see Christopher.

When she finished, Lady Julia said, "It's a shocking tale, and having met Denshire a few times, I have no trouble believing it."

There were murmurs of agreement from the others. Mariah, the Duchess of Ashton, said, "Denshire is not popular among intelligent women. He has social aspirations, and once he sought me out at a ball and attempted to ingratiate himself with my grand duchess self. I kept backing away and was considering tossing my champagne in his face when Ashton joined us." She grinned. "My usually mild-mannered husband gave Denshire one of his *looks*. Denshire made an undignified retreat and has avoided me ever since."

Lady Masterson, tall and incisive, said, "You have been treated outrageously, and as a woman, you've had no recourse legally. But situations change and scandals fade. What would you like to see happen?"

"I want my son back!" Kendra said without hesitation. "I'd also like my reputation back. I want people to know that I didn't behave in such a shocking way. I took my marriage vows seriously and never considered breaking them even though the marriage had died. Unlike Denshire, who broke his wedding vows regularly and in every manner available. I would like to see his reputation blackened."

After a moment's further consideration, she added, "I'd like to see him shipped off to whatever penal colony has the worst climate."

Lady Masterson laughed. "A suitable punishment for a vile man. I'd like to see all those things happen, and a good precedent set for other women in the future."

"I agree. A woman wronged needs allies," Lady Kingston said thoughtfully. "I think all of us here have had experience of how abusive some men are. I don't know if anything can be done for you through the legal system, but collectively we have a great deal of social power, and we all are lucky to have fine and reasonable husbands. We might be able to help you regain your reputation, and from that, perhaps your son."

"I would be so grateful if you could!" Kendra exclaimed, startled by what Lady Kingston was suggesting.

"If we are going to be conspirators, I think we should be on more intimate terms," Lady Wyndham, a striking redhead, said mischievously. "I'm Cassie."

"Not to be confused with me, Callie," Lady Kingston said. "I lived several years in the United States, which enhanced my rebellious streak. I'm all in favor of fighting injustice." Her smile showed teeth. "I would *love* to see justice visited on your horrid ex-husband."

"I was also once threatened legally by an appalling bully," Lady Romayne added, her face shadowed. "A greedy brute who wanted to take my daughter from me."

Her expression eased. "Sometimes justice does prevail. Please call me Jessie."

"I'm Mariah," the duchess said. "If Denshire craves acceptance in the highest levels of society, we definitely have weapons to wield against him."

"I'm Julia, of course," Lady Julia said. "My courtesy title makes it obvious." She cocked her head to one side. "The standard divorce decree does not allow remarriage. Do you think you might wish to remarry some day?"

A swift image of Lucas flashed through Kendra's mind. "I haven't been able to imagine taking another husband. But who knows what the future holds? I'd like to have the choice available."

Callie nodded approvingly. "Half the women here are on their second husbands."

"Or third," Jessie said under her breath.

Callie chuckled. "Perhaps practice improves our judgment. In my experience, a second husband is far superior to the first, so it would be good to make acquiring one possible for you."

"I have a cousin who might be able to help with that," Julia murmured, but added no details.

Athena lifted her almost empty glass. "A toast to finding justice for Kendra Douglas!"

The others all raised their glasses and chorused, "Justice for Kendra Douglas!"

Kendra bit her lip, unable to stop her eyes from tearing up. "I don't know what to say," she whispered.

"Thank you," Suzanne prompted. "And now let's eat!"

Chapter 14

Kendra was ready when Lucas arrived at Thorsay House shortly after breakfast to collect her for their journey in search of the past. The coachman loaded her modest luggage and they set off. They hadn't seen each other the day before because they'd both been busy, and she'd rather missed him.

The coach seemed an intimate space with just the two of them. Their legs were almost touching. She shouldn't find the idea so pleasant. To distract herself, she asked, "How was your visit to the infirmary? You look more relaxed than usual."

"It shows?" he said. "Yes, Lady Kirkland has fine, dedicated people working there, and I even had the opportunity to reset a dislocated knee. Very satisfying."

She chuckled. "In other words, good medical fun. Will you make a habit of volunteering at the infirmary?"

"Indeed I will." His gaze shifted to the city streets they were passing through on their way out of London. "I haven't worked since the aftermath of Waterloo. I've missed being useful."

She sobered. "I've read about the battle and the vast number of casualties, but my imagination surely can't match the reality. I've heard that thousands of people were helping in any way they could to tend the wounded. You participated?"

His gaze returned to her. "Yes, besides bonesetting, I'd had experience cleaning and dressing wounds. The streets were filled with volunteers working in emergency clinics. I set one up in front of Simon and Suzanne's house. Everyone in the household was helping. If not nursing, then by bringing water or writing down last messages."

Kendra bit her lip as she imagined the pain of recording the last words of a young soldier to his family. "It's moving to imagine you and Suzanne and the other members of the household working side by side. Humankind at its best."

He smiled fondly. "You're quite right. We all worked together until Simon was well enough to travel home."

Surprised, she said, "Simon was wounded?"

"Quite gravely, but he's made a complete recovery." Lucas glanced out the window again, his classic profile very still. "I didn't return to England until August. By then all the casualties were either recovering or dead. By the time the Magdalene and I arrived at Simon's estate, all I wanted to do was sleep."

The weeks of intense medical work had surely depleted him emotionally as well as physically. His left hand rested on the seat to her right, so she laid her hand over it. "You earned the right to rest as long as you wanted."

"Perhaps, but it's time I woke up to the world." He turned his hand under hers and gently squeezed her fingers before drawing away. "Don't be offended if I keep my distance. It's going to be awkward sharing a carriage with you for days on end when I'm increasingly attracted to you."

Feeling heat rising in her face, she matched his directness. "I believe that I'm equally attracted to you."

His face relaxed into a warm, sweet smile. "I rather hoped you might be. But there are far too many good reasons not to act on that attraction."

The air between them felt charged and full of promise. She edged away as far as the seat would let her. "Part of me says that I might as well throw off social constraints because I'm already thoroughly disgraced. A wiser part is saying that if I can find some way to challenge Denshire in court, I need to be above reproach. Yet even though I know that, I wanted your company on this journey."

He smiled ruefully. "I was equally aware that traveling together was not wise, yet here we are."

"Didn't we decide that we are cousins? You are respectfully escorting your widowed cousin on a sad journey."

"I will remind myself of that often," he said gravely. "And will find other topics of conversation. For example, how was your luncheon with the powerful women who might be supportive of your position?"

"The six women Suzanne invited were impressive. A duchess, a marchioness, daughters of dukes, and more. Several are patronesses of Zion House, which is affiliated with your infirmary." Kendra smiled dryly. "Anyone who had met Denshire was quite willing to believe that he'd behaved abominably."

"I believe that and I've never even met the man," Lucas observed.

"They all pledged to help in any way they can. It was… very moving." Kendra swallowed hard. "They have influence with their husbands, and they have social power of their own. Apparently Denshire craves acceptance in the highest social circles, and it seems likely that will be denied him."

"Good! Social censure might persuade him to let you see Christopher, which is your first and most important goal."

Kendra prayed that would be so. Wanting to lighten the conversation, she said, "As a very nice bonus, three of the women are among the Angelo's Wednesday morning Fencing Females group. I've been invited to join them whenever I wish. Thanks to Suzanne, I made friends yesterday, Lucas. It's a good feeling."

"That could prove useful if I have to introduce a parliamentary bill charging Denshire with crimes," Lucas said. "The more people who believe you, the better. Especially those women whose husbands sit in the House of Lords."

Her mouth twisted. "For now, my scandalous reputation seems a distant problem. This private pilgrimage has all my attention."

"I saw how devastated you were when you remembered your lost child," he said quietly. "You seem more composed today."

It wasn't quite a question, but she wanted to be honest with Lucas. "Remembering my Caitlin was shocking and painful, but at the same time... freeing. I hadn't realized there was a dark hole in my past until I recalled her, and that brief moment when I held her." She fell silent for the length of a city block before continuing. "Remembering her, I feel the lost possibilities. I've wondered what she would be like if she had survived. Would she be a tomboy like me? Would she look like Christopher? As twins, would they have been very close?"

"Inevitable questions," he agreed.

"Yes, but losing infants is sadly common, something many parents have endured." She drew a slow breath before adding, "My pain is not unique, and there is comfort in that knowledge."

"You're very wise."

"I'm not sure about wisdom, but I'm trying to accept what cannot be changed and move forward. The most important part of my future is getting Christopher back."

"Tell me about him," Lucas said, looking as if he really was interested.

Once again, his understanding was a balm. "Never ask a mother about her child for your ears will be bored off!" How to describe her son, who was the light of her life? "I'm completely biased, of course, but I think he's a lovely little boy. Healthy and sunny-natured and terrifyingly fearless. He loves riding and playing with the neighborhood children, but he also loves reading and learning."

"Is he kind?"

"That's an unexpected question, but it's one of the most important traits, isn't it?" she said thoughtfully. "Yes, he's kind to other children and he'd bring home injured animals and we'd nurse them together. He adores his pony, Patches." She swallowed, a catch in her throat. "Or he used to. When Denshire took him away, Patches was left behind." Christopher had been wrenched away from everything he knew and loved. She tamped down the despair she felt at the knowledge that she might never see her boy again.

"We'll find him," Lucas said with quiet firmness.

She drew an unsteady breath. "Sooner rather than later, I hope. But let's talk about you. What was your life like when you were a traveling friar?"

"It was generally quite pleasant," he said, accepting the change of topic. He gazed out the window, where the thinning edges of London were visible. "It was a quiet, rural life. We traveled on our mules and Frère Emmanuel was greeted with pleasure wherever we went. We would stay in farmhouses or villages or barns. Sometimes sleeping on straw in stables."

"How very biblical!"

He chuckled. "Surprisingly comfortable if there were good supplies of hay or straw. Our patients didn't have much, but they were eager to share. When word spread that we had arrived, people would come for treatment from miles around. Sometimes we could help with their problems. Sometimes all we could offer was our prayers. No one ever left Frère Emmanuel's presence without feeling blessed and happier."

"What about your presence? Did the local girls try to lure you into sin?"

Lucas made a face. "Occasionally. I gained a reputation for being boring and pious so they soon gave up."

Kendra suspected that would have made some girls try even harder to catch his attention, but Lucas must have learned how to be politely evasive. "I imagine it would have reflected badly on Frère Emmanuel if you succumbed to temptation."

"Yes, and worse, he would have been disappointed in me. I didn't want that."

They'd left the city behind and were now among rolling green hills. Kendra imagined the two men, one old and one young, riding side by side on their humble mounts through similar hills. "He sounds like an extraordinary man."

"Frère Emmanuel had a saint's kindness and faith, and he lived with one foot in heaven." Lucas smiled a little. "I couldn't match his saintliness, but I was good at dealing with worldly matters."

"Did he urge you to take vows?"

"No, he was too wise for that. He said I shouldn't become a friar unless I felt I had a true vocation. I never did." After a long pause, he continued, "After Frère Emmanuel died, I realized how much my devotion was to him and to the healing skills I'd learned from him. They were what gave purpose to my life."

"You've lost him, which perhaps makes it even more important that you resume your healing work," she said quietly.

His brows furrowed. "I hadn't thought of it in those terms, but you're right. Healing is essential to my spirit. But it's not enough."

She cocked her head. "What would 'enough' look like?"

His smile was rueful. "I have no idea. I think we both share the state of not knowing quite who we are."

His words struck with the force of a ringing bell. Kendra had once defined herself as a mother and an estate manager and a very detached wife. Now she'd lost her child and her estate and was permanently detached from her husband. She was glad that she was no longer Denshire's wife, but what was she? And what did she want to be?

She wanted to be a strong woman. She wanted to be a mother again. Most of all, she wanted to be in control of her life, not a helpless victim.

Her gaze slanted to Lucas. Once she would also have said that she wanted to be single and unencumbered by a husband. She was beginning to rethink that.

Chapter 15

The weather had been dry for several days, so they made good time. It was late afternoon when Lucas said, "The next turn will take us into Camden Keep."

Kendra had been drowsing, but the announcement brought her fully awake. "Do your aunt and uncle know that you're coming? And that you're bringing a guest?"

"I sent a note to let them know," he assured her.

She wondered if he'd explained that his guest was the notorious Lady Denshire. He was sanguine about their reactions to her, but men were often somewhat dense about such matters. Of course, this was Lucas, who noticed more than most men.

As they turned through an open gate, she gazed out at the well-tended fields and the masses of daffodils. "Spring is such a beautiful time to be in the country. This estate is well kept and lovely."

"When Uncle William retired from India, he decided to dedicate himself to becoming a proper gentleman farmer, and anything he does, he does well."

The road turned into a curving drive in front of a sprawling house that was a patchwork quilt of styles from different eras. Delighted, Kendra said, "I recognize bits from four or five different centuries. How much am I missing?"

He laughed. "I think there are another couple of centuries lurking in back. The oldest section is that fortified tower on the left side. That's the original keep. More bits were added on as needed, and no one felt the need to be consistent. It's a comfortable family house, not a showplace."

No wonder she liked it. She found families more interesting than showplaces. As the coach rumbled to a stop, she smoothed her hair and tucked a stray lock out of sight in an attempt to look as respectable as possible.

Lucas stepped from the coach and offered her a hand. "It will be all right, Kendra. Really."

"I hope so." Her smile was wry. "If not, I can find out what it's like to sleep in the stables with the Magdalene."

"I'm tempted to do that myself for old times' sake," he said with apparent seriousness.

He tucked her hand around his elbow and they ascended the steps. By the time they reached the top, the door was opened by a butler who was very properly dressed, other than the fact he was wearing a turban. He must be from India.

The butler bowed. "Welcome, Lord Foxton and Miss Douglas."

Obviously notice of their arrival had preceded them. By the time the butler had taken their cloaks and hats, a silver-haired couple appeared in the entry hall.

"Lucas!" The petite, elegant woman hugged him. "It's been too long!"

"Not that long, Aunt Anna," he protested as he hugged her back. "Less than a month."

"But there are years to make up for," his uncle said as he offered his hand. Tanned by years in a tropical sun, he had the same tall, lean build as Lucas.

After a firm handshake, Lucas drew Kendra forward. "Let me introduce my friend, Kendra Douglas. We have decided that we must be cousins of some sort. Kendra, meet my great-uncle and aunt, Sir William and Lady Mandeville." He gave a fond smile. "Aunt Anna and Uncle William, who sent marvelous letters and small presents all the way from India when I was a boy. And added more gifts for Simon when I was taken in by the Duvals."

His aunt chuckled. "I find it best to treat all the children in the household the same. That doesn't mean they won't quarrel, but it gives them less reason to do so."

Sir William must have been knighted for his service in India and he had an air of authority. Feeling shy, Kendra said, "Lucas insisted that you wouldn't mind having a stranger foisted off on you, but if you'd rather not, I can go to an inn."

"Nonsense! Any friend of Lucas's is welcome." Lady Mandeville's smile was welcoming but her eyes were shrewd as she assessed Kendra. She was probably trying to determine the nature of the relationship between her nephew and this strange woman, and likely wondering why Kendra wore mourning black. "I'll show you to your room so you can refresh yourself. Then we can all have a nice cup of tea."

Tea, cakes, and an inquisition. Kendra supposed it was only to be expected. "Thank you, that would be lovely."

Lady Mandeville escorted Kendra up the stairs to a well-furnished, spacious bedchamber. With a canopy bed, desk, sofa, and wardrobe, it was decorated in elegant, feminine shades of green, rose, and cream. Kendra smiled and moved across the room to the window. "What a beautiful room, and what a beautiful view."

The ancient tower was to her left, the stones glowing golden in the late afternoon sun. Her window overlooked formal gardens that were just waking from their winter sleep, while in the distance rolling hills were checked with fields and pastures. "I love the way the house reflects so many eras. Is Camden Keep an old family property, or did you and Sir William acquire it after you returned from India?"

"It's an old family property, but it belongs to Lucas, not us."

Surprised, Kendra turned back to the older woman. "I didn't realize that. He referred to it as yours."

His aunt smiled. "He's been very respectful of our feelings. You know that Lucas was missing and presumed dead for a number of years?" At Kendra's nod, the older woman continued, "After seven years, he was declared deceased, so the title and estate came to William. He grew up here as a younger son and was happy to return. Then Lucas most wonderfully returned from the dead and everything changed again."

Curious, Kendra asked, "Was it hard to give all this up?"

"Not at all. Though the lawyers made a meal of it, in practical terms nothing really changed. Lucas said we should continue to treat Camden Keep and the London town house as our own. Naturally he's welcome in both houses at all times."

"It's lovely that you all get on so well."

Lady Mandeville laughed. "It's not difficult. We have no children who might covet the title and property. Lucas is the closest thing we have to a son, and the day we learned that he was alive and coming home was one of the happiest of our lives." Her gaze became thoughtful.

"Of course, things will change when Lucas marries, but we won't cause trouble for him or his wife."

Hearing what wasn't said, Kendra said, "You needn't wonder if I might become a problem. I'm a divorcée, my reputation is ruined, and I'm forbidden by law to marry again. I hope I can build a case that will allow me to be reunited with my son, but the reputation is irredeemable. Lucas and I are friends, not lovers."

The other woman's gaze sharpened. "You were Lady Denshire? We'd heard of that affair. It was quite... lurid."

Kendra sighed, disappointed but unsurprised. "Very lurid indeed. I could tell you that the evidence against me was fabricated by Denshire, but you have no reason to take my word for it. I don't wish to cause you discomfort. I'll ask the coachman to take me to the nearest inn."

Lady Mandeville's brows arched. "There's no need for that. Quite apart from the fact that you're Lucas's guest and this is his house, I can't believe that he would befriend you without good reason. You are welcome here. I look forward to hearing more of the scandal from your point of view."

Kendra caught her breath, wishing there was a way she could be part of Lucas's generous, open-hearted family. It wasn't possible, but she was grateful for Lady Mandeville's acceptance. As Lucas had said, his aunt and uncle were very tolerant. "Thank you. I'll be happy to explain what really happened."

"You can tell us about it over tea," Lady Mandeville said. "Then Lucas will want to introduce you to the Magdalene. Has he told you about her?"

"Yes, and I'm looking forward to meeting her."

"She is a most wonderful mule." Lady Mandeville gave a mischievous smile. "Lucas can have Camden Keep, but he would have trouble taking the Magdalene away from us!"

–

Lucas was pleased but not surprised that their tea went so smoothly. He suspected that Kendra and his aunt had enjoyed a woman-to-woman talk while Lucas and his uncle had taken care of some estate business.

As his aunt and uncle listened intently, Kendra had briefly described her situation and hopes for regaining custody of Christopher. She had told her story often enough that it was polished, yet still convincing. But she didn't mention her lost daughter or the purpose of this journey. Lucas suspected that was too private and painful.

When the tea and cakes were gone, Lucas said, "It's turned into a lovely day. More summer than spring. Would you like to take a walk while it's still light, Kendra? I'd like to introduce you to the Magdalene."

She laughed as she got to her feet. "I'd love to meet this wonder mule."

"Enjoy the sunshine, dear," his aunt said. "Dinner will be at the usual time."

Lucas escorted Kendra to a side door that led toward the stables. When they stepped outside, he said, "My aunt and uncle like you."

Kendra took his arm, her touch light and relaxed. "And I like them. You were right about how tolerant they are." She gave him a slanting glance. "I didn't realize the estate belonged to you until your aunt mentioned it."

He shrugged. "It's entailed so it came to me, though it would more justly belong to Uncle William. He grew up here, and he's been managing the estate and doing it very well for years."

She gestured at the neat gardens and pleasantly weathered stone outbuildings. "Does this feel like your home?"

It was a question he hadn't considered. "Not really," he admitted. "This fits with our earlier conversation about not quite knowing where we belong. My earliest memories are here, but after Simon's family took me in, I made only occasional visits. It feels like Uncle William's home. He grew up here, he and Aunt Anna married here. I feel like a visitor."

"Is that because you haven't spent much time at Camden Keep, or because you don't feel worthy of being the owner?" she asked softly.

He felt as if she'd punched him in the midriff. What would his father, a naval hero, think of his dishonored son? Would his father think Lucas was worthy of the family title and fortune? Impossible to guess. His father had spent so much time at sea that Lucas hadn't known him well.

Frowning, he said, "You have a gift for difficult questions. Let me ask you one. Did Denshire Park feel like your home? Do you miss your life there?"

She was silent for a dozen steps as they crossed the yard to the stables. "I was comfortable there. I felt it was Christopher's home and I was his steward, doing all in my power to secure it for his future. I vaguely thought I might live there as an elderly dowager with my grandchildren around my knees as I told them stories about their father's childhood."

"It's a good dream," Lucas said quietly. "It could still happen."

She sighed. "My future is too uncertain for dreaming. Let us speak of more interesting things. Tell me about mules. Did you ride one as a matter of friarly humility?"

"That's an insult to mules," he said, smiling a little.

"They aren't as pretty as horses and they aren't as fast, but they have endless stamina and they're more intelligent. They're very admirable and every bit as good as horses. Just different."

"How did you acquire the Magdalene?"

"A Belgian farmer and his family were heading to market when their wagon slid off the road and several of them were seriously injured. Frère Emmanuel and I were nearby, so we were summoned to help. We splinted the injuries and cared for the family for the next fortnight. We told the farmer that no payment was necessary, but he wanted to do something so he offered his old mule. He said she was too worn down for heavy farmwork, but she might prove useful to us."

"He was obviously right," Kendra said with an enchanting smile. With her exquisite fair complexion, she was lovely in black.

He reminded himself to reply to her comment. "Frère Emmanuel had a mule named Caesar that had carried him faithfully for years, so this mule became mine. She had been called nothing but 'Mule.' I thought she deserved a grander name, so I christened her the Magdalene. She was in poor condition when the farmer gave her to us, but with time and care she improved considerably." Lucas had used some of his special healing ability on her and learned that it worked for animals as well as people.

Kendra laughed. "I hope she appreciated the pampering."

"She seems to." They entered the stables and Lucas headed toward the back corner. When he saw a groom, he asked, "How is the Magdalene doing, Harris?"

"Well, sir." The young man bobbed his head politely.

"She feels the cold more these days so I brought her in for the night. She's in her usual box."

As the groom headed outside, Lucas murmured, "You see how she inspires protectiveness. There she is, in the loose box in the corner."

The interior of the stables was shadowy, but the white mule in the loose box was unmistakable. Recognizing Lucas, she raised her head and trumpeted a greeting that was something between a whinny and a bray.

"Kendra Douglas, may I present the Magdalene?" Lucas said with tongue-in-cheek formality. He opened the door and stepped into the loose box. The Magdalene was floppy-eared and ungainly in the way of mules, with great liquid eyes that seemed to hold the wisdom of the ages. As she gave him an affectionate head butt, he said, "Yes, old girl, I'm glad to see you, too."

"She's large for a mule, isn't she?" Kendra observed.

"Yes, my guess is that her dam was a draft horse." Using both hands, Lucas scratched her scruffy mane fondly. If the Magdalene had been a cat, she'd have purred at the attention. "Wherever we went, children wanted to ride her. Three or four could fit on her back at once if they were small. She was always very gentle and patient with them."

Kendra entered the loose box, cooing, "Aren't you the pretty girl? Those great floppy ears are quite adorable."

"They make horse ears look rather undersized," Lucas agreed with a smile.

"She's a big mule with a big personality." Kendra curved her fingers to scratch through the coarse white hair. The Magdalene gave a happy bray and swept her head to one side so energetically that she knocked Kendra backward.

As Kendra lost her balance, Lucas stepped forward and caught her from behind. She fell against him... and for an instant the world stopped.

Kendra had held his arm when they walked and had wept in his arms, but they hadn't touched like this before. She was pressed full length against him, all warm feminine curves and subtle, provocative scent. The contact was intimate and deeply arousing.

Almost against his will, his hands skimmed down her arms to her waist. He felt the pulse of her blood through the layers of her clothing. There was a long moment of absolute silence. Then she turned in his grasp and looked up at him, her changeable eyes intense. Their gazes met and he knew that she *saw* him as he *saw* her.

He couldn't even remember the last time he'd held a woman close, and he was hungry, so hungry. Moving with infinite care, he bent into a kiss, giving her time to move away. She didn't. Instead, she leaned into him, her arms going around his neck, and in the warm depths of her mouth he found a hunger that matched his own. She tasted sweet, so sweet, as they explored each other.

Tension and desire were rising, mutual and urgent. He'd been alone so long. Now he wanted to be this close to her forever, to follow this passion to its natural conclusion. It was madness, but a madness that brought him fully alive.

Yet though he'd dishonored his word, he was still a gentleman, and he told himself he must let her go. He *must*.

His resolve was aided by the Magdalene, who brayed and bumped her head between them, knocking them both back on their heels. Lucas gave an unsteady laugh and pulled away, still supporting Kendra, but the kiss over. "I always knew the Magdalene was a wise old soul."

Kendra smiled ruefully. "Wiser than we are, obviously." She brushed hair from her face as she tried to compose herself. "I've been wondering what it would be like to kiss you, and now I know. Unfortunately, I want to do it again."

"I could become addicted to your kisses." He gently brushed the back of his hand down her cheek. Soft, so soft. "I'm reminding myself of all the reasons it's a bad idea. Rather than ride with you in the carriage, I'll borrow a horse from the stables here and ride alongside for the last leg of our journey."

"It will probably rain. Much more comfortable to be in a carriage."

When he hesitated, she continued, "We're adults. We should be capable of keeping our hands off each other."

"We're capable of it, but will we want to?"

"No, but we'll do it." Her expression sobered and he saw bleak acceptance replace the teasing warmth in her eyes. Her situation was so difficult that it would take a miracle to resolve it in a satisfactory way.

Luckily, he believed in miracles.

Chapter 16

The rest of Kendra's stay at Camden Keep was entirely respectable, with no impropriety on the part of her or Lucas. They were invited to stay again on their return trip. Perhaps by then Kendra would be able to talk about the purpose of this journey.

The next morning they set out in their carriage for Little Dauntrey, which was about half a day's travel to the west. Lucas sat facing her, his long legs carefully angled away from her. All very proper.

But she would cherish the memory of the previous day's hot, sweet kiss forever. She couldn't see an honorable future for them, so she refused to believe they would ever exchange more such kisses in the future. She didn't have enough hope in her to think it possible. Fortunately, her memory was very, very good.

At midday, they stopped for a meal in Great Dauntrey. After they ate, Lucas took the map he'd borrowed from Simon, and Kendra joined in a conference with the landlord. Lucas said, "Is there a village called Little Dauntrey near here?"

The landlord, a solid fellow with grizzled hair, replied, "No, but there's a Lower Dauntrey not far from here. Might that be the place?"

Kendra considered, thinking back to the pained confusion of that nightmare journey. "It could be. I'm reasonably sure about the Dauntrey, but it could have been Lower, not Little. Is there an inn called the Red Lion?"

The landlord nodded. "Aye. It changed hands two or three years ago but the name is the same."

After the route had been determined, Kendra accompanied Lucas out to the carriage and they set off again. She had to force herself to unclench her hands as they drove along. Now that she was so close to learning the fate of her lost child, the stress was almost unbearable.

It wasn't actually raining, but the gray sky and lowering clouds were threatening. Fitting weather for the day. Gazing out the window, she said, "Even though the inn has changed hands, perhaps there will be longtime employees who might remember what happened."

"We'll find someone who knows what happened that day," Lucas said calmly. "We'll stay as long as it takes."

Another hour of driving along a lane that was more track than road brought them to a scattering of houses, the outskirts of Lower Dauntrey. He asked, "Does this look familiar, Kendra?"

"Perhaps." She tried to imagine the village covered with blowing snow. "I was in too much pain to remember much."

"The landlord said the Red Lion is at the other end of the high street."

Kendra caught her breath as the parish church came into view. "This is the place! I remember the church tower. Round at the bottom, hexagonal at top. I've never seen another like it. I sent a few confused prayers in its direction."

"Let's stop and see if we can look at the parish register," Lucas suggested. "Births in the village should be recorded here."

117

"Would there be a record of children born here even if the mother was just passing through?" she asked uncertainly.

"Perhaps. Registers vary in the amount of detail listed depending on the person keeping the records." Lucas signaled their coachman to stop in front of the church. A weathered sign said it was called Saint Mary of the Fields. The building was small and obviously very old, but it had an air of peace, and the churchyard was well kept.

The arched oak door was iron bound and heavy, another proof of age. Lucas swung it open and Kendra walked in ahead of him. The interior was cool and the gray sky outside made it dim, but Kendra heard laughter when she entered. As her eyes adjusted to the light, she looked up the nave and saw a young woman arranging two tall vases of spring flowers and greenery, aided by a little girl of perhaps three or four.

Smiling at the sight, Kendra dropped a donation in the poor box, then headed up the aisle. The young woman glanced up as they approached. Her gown was worn and had obviously been remade more than once, but her voice was well educated. "Welcome to Saint Mary of the Fields. May I help you?"

"Thank you," Kendra said. "We'd like to see the parish register. Is the vicar available?"

The young woman smiled. "My husband, Mr. Hutton, is curate here. He's in the church study working on a sermon, but I'm sure he'll be happy to be interrupted! His study is just back here." She gestured for them to follow her through a narrow door in the right corner of the nave, next to the lady chapel.

The study was a small room lit by a pair of lanterns, and the walls were lined with full bookshelves. There was also a fireplace not currently in use. Curates were the lowest rung of the clerical ladder, and they were often paid barely enough for survival, which meant no money was wasted on unnecessary fuel. A battered desk took up most of the space, and behind it sat a bespectacled young man who was frowning at the page in front of him. When they entered, he looked up inquiringly, then stood when he saw a woman was entering.

"Good day, Mr. Hutton," Kendra said. She and Lucas had discussed how to introduce themselves and she'd decided to use her married name since that was how she'd been known when she gave birth in this village. "I'm Lady Denshire and this is my cousin, Lord Foxton."

"A pleasure to meet you," he said amiably, though he looked puzzled at having such elevated visitors.

His wife said helpfully, "They want to look at the parish register, my dear. There's no rule that says they can't, is there?"

"Not at all, they are public records." Mr. Hutton fumbled in his pocket for a small key ring, then turned to a double-locked cabinet. When he'd opened the doors, he said, "I presume you're interested in a particular year?"

"Yes, 1806." Kendra pulled off her gloves and began twisting them nervously. "Nine years ago in December, my husband and I were caught in a blizzard while heading home for the birth of our child. The baby was coming early so we took refuge at the local inn, the Red Lion. A midwife was summoned, but I was very ill and my life was despaired of."

Mr. Hutton pulled the volume marked 1806 from the middle shelf and laid it on his desk. "Yes?" he said encouragingly, understanding that there was more to the story.

"My son, Christopher, was born and is a fine, healthy boy. But since I was near death and in pain, I was dosed with a great deal of opium. There were several days of which I have no clear memory." She took a deep breath and realized that she was holding Lucas's hand as she came to the most painful part of the story.

"What I didn't remember until several days ago was that Christopher had a twin sister. I believe she was born second and was terribly frail. I remember now hearing that she wouldn't last the night." Her mouth tightened. "No one told me about her later. I presume they didn't want me to grieve over her loss.

"But now I have remembered, and I came here to find out what happened to her." She couldn't bear to repeat Denshire's cruel order to *get rid of it*. Lucas squeezed her hand comfortingly, so she continued, "My hope is that she lived long enough to be baptized, and perhaps buried in your cemetery. Do you remember any of this?"

He shook his head, his expression compassionate. "I'm sorry, I've only been at St. Mary's for three years. I've heard nothing of your story. Wasn't your husband able to tell you what happened?"

Wanting to say as little as possible, she said, "After the birth of his heir, we led largely separate lives and are now permanently estranged. There is no chance he will speak to me, and he had no interest in a girl child that didn't survive. Once I remembered her birth, I realized that Lower Dauntrey would be the best place to find answers." Her voice dropped to a whisper. "If she is buried here, I'd like to visit her grave and... and say good-bye."

"I'm so very sorry," Mrs. Hutton said as she tightly clasped the hand of her own small daughter. "No doubt those who didn't tell you of your daughter were well intentioned, but it's wrong to keep such knowledge from a mother."

"I quite agree," Kendra said, unable to keep a bitter edge from her voice.

Lucas squeezed her hand once more before releasing it. "Let's look at the parish register. That might tell us what we need to know."

The curate opened the register. "December, you said?" He flipped the pages to the end of the book. "Here is the section on births and baptisms." There were a dozen or so listings. He said indulgently, "A rather large number of births for one month, but I always think that December shows the results of celebrating the arrival of spring."

Kendra and Lucas crowded around him to study the page. The notations were written in crabbed, difficult-to-read handwriting. Three quarters of the way down she saw "*Hon. Christopher Douglas Hawthorn, son of George Hawthorn, Lord Denshire of Denshire Park, gent. & his wife, Kendra, late Douglas, Spinster, 11th Dec. 1806, baptized privately.*" But there was no listing for a little girl born that day.

Mouth dry, Kendra said, "What about the listings for deaths?"

Hutton flipped to that section of the book. She scanned the page and saw a listing for a stillborn boy late in December, but there was no mention of a girl child that month.

The curate said carefully, "Is it possible that because of your illness, you imagined a daughter?"

Kendra thought of the slight, warm weight of the baby in her arms, then said flatly, "I'm quite sure."

"Do you remember the name of the midwife who attended you?" Lucas asked. "She would surely remember. You told me that she was kind, and she must have been competent since you and Christopher survived a difficult birth."

"I don't remember her name. I'm not sure I ever knew it." Kendra frowned. "She might not have been from Lower Dauntrey. I have a vague feeling that she was summoned from some distance away. Perhaps another parish."

Hutton said to his wife, "Your midwife was from Great Dauntrey, wasn't she? I remember that you were pleased and comforted by how she cared for you and the baby when Elizabeth was born."

"Mrs. Lowell," his wife said immediately. "Yes, she had been recommended to me as the best midwife in the county and she was excellent. I can give you her directions if you want to call on her."

"Thank you," Lucas said. "Would there be any point in visiting the inn to see if anyone there might remember what happened?"

Hutton said, "I don't think so. The new landlord brought in family members to serve in the inn after he bought it. I don't believe any of the previous servants are still there."

"The name Mrs. Lowell sounds familiar," Kendra said slowly. "Can you give us her directions? I'd like to call on her this afternoon."

"I'll draw you a map," Mrs. Hutton said. "She's this side of Great Dauntrey, so not too far." She perched in the plain wooden chair by the desk and drew a clear, simple map. Handing it to Kendra, she said softly, "I hope you learn what you need to know."

Throat tight, Kendra nodded her thanks and she and Lucas took their leave. Outside, they conferred with their coachman about their new destination. He remembered the route they had taken from Great Dauntrey and said there would be no problem finding the midwife's home.

In the carriage, Kendra silently caught Lucas's hand and drew him down on the seat next to her. Though they'd agreed that they could only be friends, surely friends could innocently hold hands when touch was needed. With wordless understanding, Lucas's large, warm hand clasped hers.

Feeling her tension ease, Kendra said, "Thank you for taking this journey with me, Lucas."

He smiled at her. "I'm glad to be of use, and I enjoy your company."

"I'm not sure why," she said wryly. "I've been a tangle of problems ever since we met again at that ball."

"I like the way you face your problems," he said seriously. "I turned away from mine for years. You're a good example."

She had to laugh. "I don't think anyone has ever called me a good example! But I like the sound of it."

As they relaxed into the swaying of the coach, Kendra gazed out the window. "I do hope Mrs. Lowell was my midwife. As I said, the name sounds vaguely familiar, but I might be imagining that."

"If she was the midwife who attended you, she'll know what happened," Lucas said confidently. "If she wasn't, she'll know the other local midwives who might have been called. One way or another, you'll be able to make your peace with your child."

She hoped so. Lucas was a wonderfully comforting man.

As they turned onto the main road to Great Dauntrey, Lucas said reflectively, "As a baron, I control the livings for all the parish churches that are on my properties. The rector of Camden is old and in failing health. His wife died recently and he wants to move in with his oldest daughter and her family. Do you think Mr. Hutton would be a good replacement?"

"I think that's a splendid idea!" she replied. "He and his wife were kind, intelligent, and helpful. They both seem caring and if all those books are any indication, Mr. Hutton is a learned man as well. Any parish would be fortunate to have them." And rectors had good secured incomes, which would surely be a blessing to Mr. Hutton and his family.

"I'll talk to Uncle William about this. He'll want to meet Mr. Hutton, but I think he'll approve."

"Denshire controlled several livings. When one became vacant, he sold it to the highest bidder, which is typical of him." She gave Lucas a sidelong glance. "I'm glad you're more concerned with the welfare of your parishes and their congregations than with your income."

He grinned at her. "I have no expensive vices, so I can afford to be generous."

She laughed. He'd be embarrassed if she said that he was generous because he was a good man, but he was. The world needed all the good men it could get.

—

Mrs. Hutton's directions were clear and it wasn't difficult to find Mrs. Lowell's home, a small stone cottage set back from the road. Smoke trickled from the chimney, so there should be someone home. Lucas helped Kendra from the carriage. "You may have your answers soon," he said quietly.

She managed a smile. "I hope so. When I know what happened to my Caitlin, I'll be free to return to worrying about my other problems."

Lucas knocked on the door, and it was swiftly opened by a slim, blond girl of sixteen or seventeen. Her apron, the flour on her hands, and delicious aromas said that she'd been baking. Kendra caught her breath as the girl's round pretty face immediately evoked the kind face of an older woman who spoke comforting words as she bent over Kendra's pain-racked body. "You must be Mrs. Lowell's daughter?"

"Yes, I'm Maggie Lowell." She glanced at Kendra's waist. "Are you wishing to engage my mother's services? She usually sees patients in the morning."

"I'm not a patient now," Kendra said, "but I once was. I'm Lady Denshire and nine years ago in December, I was brought to bed prematurely when traveling and gave birth at the Red Lion in Lower Dauntrey. I was very ill and remember little, but your mother attended me and I need to speak with her about what happened."

The girl's brows furrowed and she stepped aside, gesturing them to come in. "I heard about you since it isn't often my mother treats a ladyship. She didn't come home for several days. When she did, she said she'd feared she'd lose you, but you came through and had a fine bonnie boy."

"Did she say anything about a little girl?" Kendra asked tensely. "I only just remembered that my son had a twin sister who was too weak to survive. I hate that I actually forgot my own child! I hope to find where she is buried so I can visit her grave."

The girl's expression closed. Glancing at Lucas, she said, "Is this your husband? He should know what happened because he was there."

"I'm her cousin and friend," Lucas explained. "I was on military service at the time so I don't know what happened, but I offered to escort Lady Denshire on her search."

Maggie Lowell hesitated for a long moment before coming to a decision. "It's best you speak with my mother. She's visiting her sister, my aunt Jane, who lives in a cottage at the far end of our property. Just a few minutes' walk away."

Finally Kendra would know. Lucas touched her lower back reassuringly. "Can you point us in the right direction?"

Maggie nodded and led them through the house. Several loaves of bread and savory pies were cooling on a sideboard in the kitchen. Lucas said appreciatively, "If my nose doesn't lead me astray, you're a fine baker, Miss Lowell."

The girl gave a swift smile. "I'll never make a midwife, but I'm a dab hand in the kitchen if I do say so or shouldn't. Hold a minute and I'll put some food and tea in this basket if you'd be good enough to carry it over, sir."

"Of course."

Maggie packed the basket swiftly, as if it was a customary task, including a couple of sweet cakes. After handing the basket to Lucas, she led them through the kitchen to the back of the house. She opened the door and pointed. "It's that cottage at the end of this path. You can't miss it."

The cottage was barely visible but the path was clear. Kendra was vibrating with excitement as she and Lucas walked swiftly through a vegetable garden and then along a fenced pasture where several placid cows grazed. The beasts were lean from winter and greedily enjoying the new grass.

The cottage was very small and looked as if it might have been a converted outbuilding. Kendra knocked on the door.

A woman's voice called, "A moment."

When the door swung open, Kendra's first sight of Mrs. Lowell triggered a cascade of images of kindness and concern. Soft words, a cool hand on Kendra's forehead, brisk orders to *push!* This woman had surely saved her life, and perhaps Christopher's as well.

Mrs. Lowell's expression froze. "Lady Denshire. You... you're looking well. And your son?"

"He is also well, but that is not why I'm here today. I was so ill that for years after giving birth, I recalled very little of what happened. Then a few days ago, I remembered that I also bore a little girl who was not expected to last through the night." She swallowed hard before she continued. "Was she baptized? Is she buried in the churchyard at Lower Dauntrey? I need to know."

After a long, undecided pause, Mrs. Lowell sighed. "You have the right. Best come in." She stepped back, giving Lucas a sharp glance. "You're not Lord Denshire."

"No, I'm Foxton, Lady Denshire's cousin."

Mrs. Lowell accepted his words at face value. They were in a small sitting room that included a table, several chairs, a rag rug, and a cooking corner with a fireplace. Lucas set the basket of food on the table. "Your daughter sent this. Bread and cheese, a meat pie, soup, tea, and probably a few other things."

"Maybe she'll be able to take the soup," Mrs. Lowell murmured. She lifted the lid of the crock and filled a mug with the gently steaming soup. Then she crossed the room and opened the door into a small sleeping chamber.

Dim light came through an oil paper-covered window to reveal a haggard woman with fair hair lying limply on a narrow bed. She was asleep, her breathing strained and her cheeks flushed with fever. A little girl perched on the side of the bed petting a cat, but at the sight of the newcomers, she stood.

Kendra felt as if her heart had stopped. The little girl had dark auburn hair and changeable eyes. She looked like Christopher.

She looked like Kendra.

My daughter!

Chapter 17

Kendra whispered, "Caitlin," her face so pale that Lucas feared she would faint. He took her hand and she gripped his fingers fiercely.

Ignoring Kendra's shock, Mrs. Lowell entered the room and gave the mug of soup to the little girl. "See if your mother will take some of this nice soup, Katie."

"Thank you, Aunt Mary." After an incurious glance at the visitors, the little girl accepted the mug, balancing it carefully as she sat on the edge of the narrow bed. She dipped the spoon in the mug and said coaxingly, "Have some nice chicken soup, Mama. It smells very good."

Mrs. Lowell left the bedroom, closing the door behind her. "That's my daughter!" Kendra said in a low, fierce voice. "*I'm* her mother!"

"Yes, you gave birth to her." Mrs. Lowell folded wearily into one of the plain wooden chairs and gestured for her guests to sit. "Do you remember how weak she was?"

"I now have a very clear mental image of holding her," Kendra said unsteadily. "She was so fragile I feared she would never draw another breath. Then she was gone. Taken from my arms."

The midwife nodded. "Do you remember your husband saying to *get rid of it*?"

Kendra hissed through her teeth. "Yes, and I can't believe that I was ever fool enough to marry that man!"

129

"I wondered that myself," Mrs. Lowell said dryly. "I didn't think your little girl would last through the night, and I was so busy trying to save your life and keep your little boy breathing that I had no time to spare for the poor wee mite. My younger sister Jane Potter lived in Lower Dauntrey then, so I sent for her. I wanted to give the babe into loving arms for as long as she survived.

"Jane was grief stricken because she'd just lost her own baby. When she arrived at the inn, I asked if she'd look out for your little one till the angels came for her. That you wanted her named Caitlin and since it was an emergency situation with the blizzard and the infant's life so precarious, Jane could perform a lay baptism. Jane cradled the baby in her arms and swore she would take care of her. She was covered in snow from the walk to the inn, and she used melted snow from her cloak to perform the baptism immediately."

"I hoped Caitlin had been baptized," Kendra said tremulously.

"She returned to her home and dedicated herself to nursing the babe into life." Mrs. Lowell smiled reminiscently. "Jane is deeply loving and she was determined to save your little girl. Your child is as tenacious as you are, Lady Denshire. I didn't think either of you would survive, but you did. A pair of miracles and no mistake."

"So you let Jane just keep my child?" Kendra said, aghast.

Mrs. Lowell nodded. "I didn't know that Katie had survived until weeks later. When your life was no longer threatened and you were on your way to recovery, I went home so exhausted that I slept for days. The weather was foul and it was after Christmas before I saw Jane and found the baby was alive and doing well. Jane called her Katie and later had a church baptism here in Great Dauntrey, naming the baby Catherine Potter and listing herself as the mother."

Kendra bit her lip. "You made no attempt to find me?"

Mrs. Lowell's eyes narrowed. "You and your husband were long gone, and I didn't know how to find you. Nor did I want to! You had your sweet little boy to love, and your husband was never going to value a daughter. He didn't deserve her! Jane did."

Kendra's eyes closed and she whispered, "My head understands that, but my heart cries for my lost child."

"Your coming is timely. Perhaps divine intervention," Mrs. Lowell said, her expression stark. "Jane is dying, so Katie may need another mother."

"Consumption?" Lucas asked.

Mrs. Lowell stared at him. "How did you know?"

"I recognized the symptoms. It looks as if your sister's case is very advanced."

The midwife sighed. "You're right. Jane's husband died of consumption. I thought Jane might not be affected, but then she began to develop the symptoms."

"What about Caitlin? Katie?" Kendra asked.

"I think she has also been affected," Mrs. Lowell said with deep regret. "After Jane's husband died, she was left penniless, and I fixed up this little cottage for her. I wanted Katie to live with me so she'd be less likely to contract the disease, but she refused to leave her mother." She glanced at Kendra and changed her words to, "To leave Jane."

Kendra turned an intense gaze on Lucas. "Suzanne said that sometimes you perform miracles, and that you saved Simon's life. Can you do anything for Jane?"

Mrs. Lowell's brows furrowed. "Miracles? I've seen some recoveries that seemed miraculous, but never from consumption."

Lucas said reluctantly, "I've spent years working as a bonesetter. Sometimes, not often, I've also been able to heal with prayer and the laying on of hands. But it's a very uncertain ability." He'd tried to save Frère Emmanuel and failed, and that failure haunted him. He'd failed other times, also. Too often. "There are no guarantees."

"I have had some similar experiences," Mrs. Lowell said, her brow furrowed. "When I'm worried about a mother or infant, I'll hold them and pray and whisper words of hope and comfort. I believe that sometimes that healing touch has made the difference. If you have that gift, surely it's worth trying with Jane! It doesn't hurt to make the attempt."

"That's... not entirely true. Whether I succeed or fail, there is always a price." Lucas drew a deep breath, knowing he could not refuse to help. "But if you wish it and give me permission, I will try."

"And look at Katie as well," Kendra said, her voice tight.

He looked at her compassionately, seeing on her face the shock and pain of finding her lost daughter only to risk losing her again. "Of course I will look at Katie."

"Is there anything we can do to help?" Mrs. Lowell asked.

"I'll be resting my hands on Jane's shoulders. If you two can each lay one hand on me and the other on Jane while praying for her health, that might help." In a previous critical case, two others had joined him and he believed they'd helped, though it was impossible to be sure. But he was sure that Kendra and Mrs. Lowell would feel better for aiding his efforts.

Mrs. Lowell opened the door to the bedroom and led the way in. Jane was sleeping, her breathing labored, and she clutched a bloodstained handkerchief in one hand. Katie had crawled under the covers and was holding her foster mother as if trying to protect her from eternal night. Silent tears ran down her cheeks from changeable eyes. Gray now, and exactly like Kendra's.

She tilted her head up and looked at Lucas. "Who are you?" she asked in a thin voice.

"My name is Lucas Mandeville, and we're going to try to help your mother feel better," he said gently.

She nodded and closed her eyes, burrowing deeper under the blankets.

Lucas went to the head of the bed and rested his hands on Jane's thin shoulders. He sensed her spirit fading. If they failed today, she would have very little time left.

Mrs. Lowell moved into the space between Lucas and the wall so she could lay one hand on his shoulder and the other on her sister. Kendra stepped to his other side, her left hand on his arm and the other placed so it rested on both Jane and Katie.

Lucas wasn't sure if there would be a miracle, but there was no shortage of love here. He closed his eyes and quietly said the Lord's Prayer aloud. Kendra and Mrs. Lowell joined in as he spoke the familiar words.

Then he sank into that healing space where sometimes he could channel divine energy to help someone who was ill. *With your will, oh, Lord.* He sensed white light and love flowing through him into Jane, who was fiercely loving and loved. Joining him were the prayers of his two companions. His palms warmed, almost burning as he poured all his concentration and hope into the woman under his hands.

He continued until he felt the divine light fading, along with his strength. He whispered, "Amen," removing his hands from Jane's shoulders.

And almost fell over. Kendra grabbed his arm to steady him. "Are you all right?" she asked, worried.

He smiled crookedly. "As I said, there's always a price, and part of that is my strength. The more serious the illness, the more exhausted I become. Even so, I don't know if I helped her."

As Kendra steered him out of the bedroom, Mrs. Lowell straightened the covers over Jane and Katie, then brushed a light kiss on each sleeping head before following the others into the main room. Closing the door behind her, she said in a hushed voice, "That was extraordinary. I could feel the heat from your hands."

Lucas sank into a chair by the table, shaking with cold and fatigue. "I don't know if it was enough," he said wearily, feeling hollowed out, devoid of all strength.

"Jane is breathing easily now and her color is better. You may have given us that miracle." The midwife sighed. "Even if you didn't, thank you for giving so much of yourself. I'll go sit with Jane and Katie."

After she left the room, something warm settled over his back and shoulders. A knitted knee rug. It was followed by Kendra wrapping her arms around him. Since she was standing and he was sitting, his head ended up resting on her soft breasts. As her hand slid soothingly down his neck and back, his hollow fatigue faded away. He wanted to melt into her and never let her go.

But let her go he must. He pulled back, saying, "Thank you for reviving me."

She smiled. "Food and drink should help, too. Would you like some tea?"

"Yes, please."

The tea was in a thick pottery crock that had kept it warm. Kendra poured a mug for him and set it between his hands. The liquid soothed his parched throat, helped clear his mind, and gave him some energy.

Tea was followed by a chunk of fresh buttered bread, and he realized that he was hungry. Ravenous, in fact. He murmured a thank-you to Kendra and ate the bread greedily. The bread was followed by a slice of the meat pie.

Feeling halfway human, he straightened in his chair. "When I'm doing simpler work like setting a bone, I'll sometimes use lesser amounts of healing to try to reduce the pain. But when a life is in the balance and I'm trying so hard…" His voice trailed off before he spoke again. "As I said, there is always a price, and the healing is not always successful."

Kendra sat in the chair next to him and took his hand. "But it is better to try and fail than not to try at all," she said firmly.

"It was generous of you to want Jane to be healed when your deepest desire must be to sweep Katie up and carry her off with you," he said quietly.

Her smile was rueful. "Yes, but how can I wish for the death of the woman who saved Caitlin's life and has raised her ever since? A woman whom Katie loves as her mother. What kind of woman would that make me?"

"It would make you a woman who is much less than you are."

Embarrassed, she looked away. "Even if I wanted to take her away, where would I take her? I don't have a real home now, and I'm in the midst of a major scandal that may warp my life forever. Katie is best off here, with people who love her."

"Surely you will want to be part of her life?"

"Oh, yes!" She looked wistful. "I do so want her to meet her brother. And for Christopher to meet his sister."

"That will likely happen eventually, but not as soon as you'd like," he predicted.

The door to the bedroom opened and Katie emerged. She looked like a different child, her eyes bright and her movements confident. She bobbed a curtsy to Lucas. "Mr. Mandeville." Her gaze moved to Kendra and she said hesitantly, "Lady Denshire?"

"I was once Lady Denshire," Kendra replied, "but now I'm Kendra Douglas, the name I was born with."

Katie bobbed her a curtsy as well. "It's a pleasure to meet you, sir, ma'am."

Lucas smiled at her earnest formality. Before he could reply, the cat he'd briefly glimpsed earlier wound itself around Katie's ankles, then looked up with matching earnestness.

It was the oddest-looking cat he'd ever seen, with wild splotches of black, orange, and white. One front leg was solid black, the other striped orange, the neck was white, and its face was diagonally divided into black and orange. Knowing better than to insult the child's pet, he said, "That may be the most unusual-looking cat in Britain."

"Yes, isn't she pretty?" Katie scooped the cat up in her arms. "My mama says God used all the colors left over from other cats to make her special. I named her Patches."

"A good name," Kendra said, wondering if it was mere coincidence that Christopher's beloved pony had the same name. She offered her fingers to sniff and received a raspy tongue lick in return. "Is she hungry?"

"Yes, and so am I." Katie spoke clearly, sounding older than her years. She looked at the food on the table. "Maggie usually sends over a sweet cake for me. Did she do that today?"

"Yes, but I think you need some proper food first," Kendra said, sounding very maternal. "Perhaps a bowl of soup along with some bread and cheese?"

"Oh, yes, please!"

Kendra sliced several pieces of cheese. Katie placed Patches on the floor, then set a sizable piece of the cheese in front of the cat. Patches dived into it enthusiastically while Katie sat in the third chair by the table and began eating soup with equal enthusiasm but better manners.

"You look as if you're feeling well," Lucas observed.

"I haven't felt so well in *ages*." She beamed over the soup bowl. "Mama feels better, too. *Much* better!" She tilted her head to one side. "What did you do to her?"

How could he explain the unexplainable to a child? Trying to be as clear as possible, he said, "Some people have a divine gift of healing. It's very mysterious and doesn't always work, but we decided to try with you and your mother, and it appears we may have succeeded."

"Thank you," Katie said gravely. She peered into the food basket and found the sweet cakes her cousin Maggie had included for her. Spice cakes by the look of them. She took a happy bite and washed it down with a mouthful of tea.

Her interested gaze moved to Kendra. "Your hair is the same color as mine."

"Yes, it is." Kendra pulled a long lock free so Katie could see it clearly. "A dark brown that shines dark red in the light. It's usually called chestnut."

Katie pulled a lock of her own hair out and laid it by Kendra's for comparison. "Almost the same!" she said with pleasure. "But your hair is darker."

"That's because I'm older. Yours will darken with age also." Kendra tucked her hair away again.

"Your eyes are like mine, too," Katie said, intrigued. "Not one color. Changing from blue to gray to a kind of green."

"There's a reason for that." Lucas could hear the tension in Kendra's voice.

"Oh?" Katie said, interested in knowing more.

Kendra drew a deep breath. "Did you know that it's possible to have two mothers?"

"You mean to be born twice?" Katie shook her head. "I don't believe you."

"Not to be born twice, but to have two different kinds of mother. One who gives birth, and one who raises you." Kendra lightly rested her hand on her daughter's. "You have two mothers, Katie. I am your birth mother. That's why we look alike. And Jane Potter is the mother who loved and raised you."

Shocked, Katie pulled her hand free and scooped up Patches, holding the cat against her chest as protection. "No! If you were my mother, why didn't you keep me? Didn't you want me?"

A tremor in her voice, Kendra said, "I was very, very ill. I almost died and didn't even remember that you'd been born. You were so tiny and frail that no one thought you would survive. Your aunt Mary gave you to her sister, who saved your life and has been your mother ever since. You and I were both very lucky."

Katie scowled. "How could you forget you had a baby?"

"Because I had *two* babies. You have a twin brother." Kendra showed a ghost of a smile. "He looks like both of us. The same hair, the same eyes. Because I had him to love and care for, when I recovered from nearly dying, I'd forgotten that I'd borne a daughter, too. Then a few days ago I held a baby girl who looks a bit like you, and I suddenly remembered what I had lost. So I came looking for you."

Picking out what interested her most, Katie said, "I have a brother?"

"Yes, his name is Christopher. He'll love to learn that he has a sister."

Mrs. Lowell emerged from the bedroom. "Katie, your mother wants to see you."

Grateful for a reason to escape from all this new information, Katie scrambled from her chair and disappeared into the bedroom with Patches draped over her shoulder. The cat's black and orange face studied Kendra quizzically before the door closed, separating them.

Frowning, Mrs. Lowell said, "You shouldn't have told her you were her mother."

"She had to know sooner or later. She started the discussion by commenting on the fact that we have the same color hair and eyes." Kendra caught the other woman's gaze. "I'm not going to carry her away from everything she knows. This is her home and you are her family. But so am I. I want to be part of her life. I want her to meet her brother. I want her to have the life she deserves."

"We're not good enough for her?" Mrs. Lowell's gaze was challenging.

"You and your family are the best thing that could have happened to an abandoned child," Kendra said quietly. "But your sister's circumstances were difficult even before she became ill. I want to settle an income on Katie, enough to provide her and your sister a good home. I pray they are both healthy now. Do you think they are?"

The midwife's tension eased. "I believe so. Jane is tired but I see no signs of illness." She brushed her hand over her face, briefly covering her eyes. "I don't mean to be difficult. Today has been too much for me."

"It's been too much for all of us," Lucas said as he rose to his feet. "Kendra, we need to find an inn for the night. We can return in the morning and have all the discussions that are too overwhelming for tonight."

She turned to him gratefully. "You're right. Would you mind going to the Red Lion? It's not far, and I'm curious to find out if it will seem familiar."

"You could stay here," Mrs. Lowell said uncertainly.

"That's kind of you," Lucas said, "but you don't need the extra burden of guests who are virtual strangers."

"Strangers who are also family," Mrs. Lowell said wryly. "But it will be easier if you stay elsewhere. I look forward to seeing you in the morning after we've had time to sort ourselves out."

Kendra couldn't agree more.

Chapter 18

It was a relief to get into the carriage for the return to Lower Dauntrey. When Lucas climbed in after Kendra, he moved to take the opposing seat, but she caught his hand and pulled him down beside her. "I think we can both use some mutual handholding," she said with a weary smile. "How are you feeling?"

He exhaled roughly. "Drained. I'll be fine tomorrow, but attempting a major healing as we did today leaves me feeling as if a regiment of cavalry has galloped over me. What about you? Today has been shocking even though the news is miraculously good."

"I never once considered that my daughter might have survived." Fighting tears, Kendra pressed her free hand to her lower face as she whispered disjointedly, "Even now I have trouble believing it's true."

He released her hand and wrapped his arm around her shoulders. "But there's no doubt. She's the very image of you."

"And the image of Christopher." She bit her lip at the thought of her son, then continued, "The most I hoped for was obtaining some kind of certainty about the past, and the chance to say good-bye to my Caitlin. But reality turns out to be so much more complicated. She's my miracle child – yet I can't take her home with me."

"You were right to say that you can't take Katie away from the woman who has been a mother to her," Lucas said quietly. "It will take time to build a relationship with Katie and Jane. You might end up more like a favorite aunt than a mother. But you will be part of your daughter's life, and you've acquired other worthy relatives as well. That Maggie knows how to cook!"

She smiled as he'd intended. "We'll sort things out in time. My next task is to return to London to hear whether Kirkland has discovered any weapons to use against Denshire."

"*Our* next task," he said firmly.

She raised their joined hands and brushed a kiss on his knuckles, then closed her eyes and relaxed back into the seat. That looked like such a good idea that he did the same, and they both dozed for the rest of the journey to the Red Lion. Holding hands all the way.

"Kendra?" Lucas's tap on the door was light because he didn't want to wake her if she was sleeping.

But she called, "Just a moment."

Taking that as permission, he swung the door open, balancing his silver brandy flask plus two empty tumblers.

"Oh!" Kendra blinked in surprise. Like him, she'd changed into nightwear, which in her case meant a floor-length burgundy velvet robe to ward off the chilly spring night. Her hair was down, falling halfway to her waist in rich mahogany waves that echoed the richly colored robe. "I didn't realize that door opened to another bedroom."

Trying not to stare at that glorious hair, Lucas said, "I told the landlord we were married, so he offered us this pair of rooms. The connecting door can be locked so the rooms are separate, but unlocked, the arrangement is good for families or couples who sleep apart because the husband snores. I told him that I was that husband and we'd like these two rooms."

She smiled a little. "Do you snore?"

"I don't know. If I do, I'm asleep when it happens." He set the tumblers on the table, which still held the plates and silverware from the supper Kendra had taken in her room, along with a pitcher of water. He splashed water into the tumblers. "I gather that you're also having trouble falling asleep. Care for some gently watered brandy? It might help us both to relax."

"That sounds like an excellent idea." She wrapped her arms around herself with a shiver despite the warmth of her velvet robe, then sat on the edge of the bed opposite the fireplace, where coals were quietly burning. In the soft firelight, she looked like a lovely, exhausted Madonna.

When she accepted the glass of watered brandy he offered her, she said, "I'm haunted by this room. It's where I gave birth to my children and almost died."

He sat on the bed beside her and wrapped an arm around her shoulders for warmth and comfort. "You recognize this room even though you were in such a bad state?"

She gestured upward with her brandy glass before taking a sip. "The cracks on the ceiling are unmistakable. They were about all I could see in my brief periods of clarity."

He tilted his head back to examine the faint cracks. "That looks rather like a map of Britain."

"I thought of it as a lunging wolf, which says something about my state of mind at the time." She looked upward again. "But it could be Britain. I like that better." She took a deeper swallow of brandy. "So much happened at this inn. My children were born, I almost died, and my marriage ended."

He tightened his arm around her shoulders. She tucked under it so nicely. "Ended?"

"Until I became with child, we had a reasonably civil marriage. Denshire lost interest in me when I became pregnant. Then Christopher was born and he had his heir." She finished her brandy in one long swallow. "After the birth, I no longer wanted Denshire to touch me. Though I didn't consciously remember Caitlin's birth or what he'd said about her, deep down I must have realized that my husband was contemptible. After that, our marriage was in name only and his mistresses were welcome to him. The arrangement worked fairly well for a number of years."

"I know it has been difficult for you, but at least you're free of him now. And we *will* get Christopher back to you," he said with quiet vehemence.

She set her empty glass on the bedside table, then looked up at him, her gaze intent. "Why are you doing so much for me? Because you like helping people?"

He watched the firelight playing over her lovely, determined face. "Generally, I do like helping people. But in particular, I like you."

"You seem to like having a friend or partner," she said thoughtfully. "Simon when you were children. Frère Emmanuel during your years in Belgium. Friends when you were in the Royal Navy?"

Surprised by her words, he thought back before replying. "I can certainly manage on my own, but you're right, I prefer to have a companion I enjoy and trust."

With a swift smile, he said, "But there weren't any prior companions I wanted to do this to." He leaned down into a kiss.

It should have been a light, friendly kiss but wasn't because she leaned in, too. Her lips opened under his and she raised a hand to his cheek. Her mouth was sweet and tentative as she whispered, "It's been a very long time since I've kissed a man."

"And even longer since I kissed a woman," he murmured back. "I had forgotten how wondrous a kiss can be. Though I think it's you who makes it wondrous."

"I think it's the two of us together who create wonder." Breath quickening, she slipped her arms around his neck and pressed herself against him.

She was so marvelously soft and female. His hands slid down her back and waist over enticing womanly curves. Her full breasts were intoxicating under the velvet robe. His palm flattened over her nipple and he gently rotated his hand. She caught her breath and pulsed against him, her hands equally active as she explored him with touch.

His exhaustion vanished in a flood of desire, a desire that she matched as she parted the panels of his blue velvet banyan and spread her hands on the bare skin beneath. He sucked in his breath as fire raced through his veins.

Kisses and hands and scent and breath, and how had they come to be lying back on the bed with their clothing half off? Her robe was open, revealing the translucent shift underneath. "You are so beautiful." Her nipples were visible so he bent to kiss one through the thin muslin. It stiffened under the heat of his mouth and she gasped as she arched against him.

After giving due attention to one magnificent breast, he shifted his mouth to the other, delighting in her eager

145

response. Her warm hand was sliding down the front of his body, reaching…

She touched him and he turned rigid, wanting nothing more than to complete this lovemaking in the most profoundly intimate way. And yet… huskily he said, "I'm trying to remind myself of all the reasons we shouldn't be doing this, but my memory and good judgment are dissolving."

"Perhaps tonight we should forget memory and good judgment," she breathed as her hand circled his straining erection.

Desire burned ever hotter and he could barely manage to speak. "We shouldn't… be fools for pleasure!"

"Why not?" she said with sudden fierceness. "I have been battered and betrayed for years. With you, I feel young and cared for and full of life. No one knows us here, we are traveling without servants, so why not share passion, even if it's only for one night?"

In a dim corner of his mind, he knew they shouldn't take this irrevocable step, but he couldn't resist her. He needed to be skin to skin with her, breath to breath. He stroked down her body with his palm, savoring the feel of smooth skin and underlying muscle and bone. When he reached her knee, he slowly reversed course, sliding his hand upward between her thighs, pushing aside the delicate fabric of her shift.

She was hotly ready when he touched her most intimate flesh. Moaning, she separated her legs in welcome and tugged at his body to bring him closer. He was equally ready, wanting desperately for them to join together. He shifted to between her legs, preparing her for his entry.

146

She gasped and gripped his hips as he slowly pressed into her, ravished by the pleasure that saturated every fiber of his body. Her heated hands were under his open robe, skin to skin. Her tightness was proof of her many years of celibacy, just as it had been many years since he'd known the joys of a woman's flesh. But those occasions had been the playful learning of youth, without the deep caring he felt for Kendra.

"Lucas," she moaned. "*Lucas!*"

She began convulsing around him, her arms crushing around his waist. He was falling, falling…

No! With his last shred of control, he withdrew and his seed spilled over her leg as they locked themselves together in shattering rapture. Skin to skin, breath to breath…

He never wanted to let her go, but he didn't want to crush her. He slid onto his side, holding her against him. "I wish you hadn't had to do that," she said in a raw whisper.

"So do I," he said fervently. "We have this one stolen night, but getting you with child would be a disastrous complication on top of a mountain of complications."

"I know." She gently brushed back damp hair that had fallen over his forehead, her expression wistful in the firelight. "But I would love to have another child and have it with you."

Imagining them creating a child together was bitter-sweet pleasure. He wanted that with a yearning that equaled hers. But as he drew the covers over them to keep out the chill night, he bleakly recognized what a mistake it had been for them to become lovers.

Chapter 19

Kendra drowsed in Lucas's arms, her head on his shoulder and his breath stirring her hair. She'd never known such intimacy with a man before. Not just the passion, amazing and eye-opening as that had been, but the tenderness. "You were right that this was a bad idea, Lucas," she whispered. "Because I can't bear to think we may never lie together again."

She'd thought he was asleep, but he replied in a voice as low as hers. "I feel the same way. Contented. Happy. Not wanting to move. Though eventually I should return to my room, having claimed we needed it because I snore."

She smiled into the darkness, which was lit only by the glow of the coal fire. "You haven't snored yet, but more research is needed to be sure." Then she wished she hadn't said that because there would be no more opportunities for research. Not in the foreseeable future.

He brushed his fingers through her hair. "We've already had one miracle in discovering your daughter. Maybe more miracles lie in the future."

"I like that idea. I think you're my good angel, Lucas. When we met at the Clantons' ball, I was paralyzed with anger and uncertainty. Now I have friends and allies and hope." And a daughter and a lover, even if she would see neither of them as much as she'd like.

He laughed. "I don't think I've ever been anyone's good angel." His hand slid down her body, bringing a different kind of warmth. "My thoughts now are distinctly unangelic."

She caught her breath and began her own explorations of his body. "If we only have a few more hours, let us not waste them."

They didn't.

—

Kendra tried to hide her nerves when they returned to Mrs. Lowell's the next morning. Lucas noticed, of course. "Steady on," he murmured. "Today will be easier than yesterday."

She hoped so. As it turned out, he was right. Mrs. Lowell welcomed them warmly and escorted them to the back of the house. "I hope you don't mind the kitchen. In this house, it's where most of the living is done."

Guessing this was a test of sorts, Kendra said, "I love a warm, friendly kitchen."

"I hope this one includes some of your daughter's baking," Lucas added.

The midwife laughed. "Indeed it does."

Kendra had barely noticed the kitchen the day before, but now she saw that it was spacious and full of sunshine and the enticing odors of baking. Maggie, Jane, and Katie were sitting at the large oak table, sipping tea and waiting for their visitors. Patches, the absurdly colorful cat, sat contentedly on Katie's lap, one eye on the newcomers and the other on the platter of assorted cakes.

The females stood politely and Patches flowed to the floor. Jane Potter looked very like her older sister, with fair hair and a pleasant face. She was too thin, but otherwise looked healthy and competent, if a little wary. Katie held Jane's hand, but she studied Kendra intently.

Jane said, "Lord Foxton, I believe I'm indebted to you for saving my life, and also that of my daughter."

Another test, Kendra thought. Jane was staking her claim to Katie and needed reassurance that Kendra wouldn't demand to take custody of the girl. Kendra thought of her own willingness to flee to America with Christopher if necessary. She couldn't force another woman to face such a terrible choice. Nor could she wrench another child away from all she knew as her son had been.

Lucas said, "I think thanks should be directed to the Divine. I'm very glad the healing seems to have been effective. Do you feel entirely well?"

"Better than I have in years." She considered. "I'd forgotten what it felt like to be healthy. Are you always so successful with your healings?"

He shook his head. "No, it's a chancy gift. I'm very glad it worked this time."

Katie had been staring at Kendra, and now she spoke. "What should I call you?"

Kendra remembered what Lucas had said. "How about Aunt Kendra? That's easier than trying to explain that you have two mothers."

"Aunt Kendra." Katie spoke the words experimentally, then gave a little nod. "I like having another aunt."

"Does that mean you're my aunt also?" Maggie asked.

"If you want me to be," Kendra said obligingly, wanting to enlist the good will of as many members of this family as she could.

Maggie smiled. "Then please sit, Aunt Kendra and Lord Foxton, and have tea and some of my ginger cakes while they're still warm."

Kendra took a seat with Lucas on her left and Katie on her right while Jane sat on Katie's other side. The girl continued to study Kendra, her changeable eyes more green than gray today. "Will I be able to meet my brother? Will he like me?"

"Yes, you'll meet him someday, and of course he'll like you," Kendra said reassuringly. "He's always wanted a brother or sister."

As tea was poured and the cake platter was passed, Jane asked bluntly, "Where do we go from here?"

Kendra met the other woman's gaze. "As I told your sister yesterday, I won't take my daughter away from the people who love her and the only home she's ever known. But I do intend to be part of Katie's life."

Jane's gaze was still wary, but she gave a reluctant nod. "'Tis only fair."

"I am going to settle an income on Katie that you will be able to spend for your joint benefit," Kendra continued, glad she had the money to do this for her daughter. "It will be sufficient for the two of you to live comfortably."

"Can I get a pony?" Katie asked wistfully. "I've always wanted a pony."

"That's up to your mother," Kendra said, glad she could call Jane the girl's mother in a steady voice. "If she agrees, you can have a pony, though she might want to wait until you're older. Your brother likes horses, too."

Mrs. Lowell said, "Jane, you and Katie are welcome to move into this house. I was concerned about contagion before, which was why I fixed up a separate cottage, but now that you're well, there's plenty of room here. Two widows and our daughters. I'd like that."

"I would, too," Jane said. "And your stables have enough room for a pony if we decide to get one." She glanced at Katie. "That's *if*, little miss. Not definite!"

From Katie's beaming smile, she seemed confident that her mother meant not "if" but "when."

Kendra bit into a delicious apple tart with a wonderfully crumbly crust. Continuing the conversation, she said, "My life in London is complicated now, but when I have things sorted out" – if it was possible to sort them out – "I'd like to have you and Katie visit me there." Her gaze moved to Mrs. Lowell and Maggie. "And both of you also. It could be a family visit."

Maggie drew her breath in, her eyes shining. "We could go to the theater?"

"Indeed we could. And shopping on Bond Street as well."

Maggie beamed. Kendra said softly, "I want us all to be friends, you know. Surely that's possible?"

For the first time, Jane smiled. "I don't see why not."

Kendra swallowed the last bite of her tart. "I suppose we should be on our way. We have a long journey ahead of us."

Lucas nodded and rose from the table. "Miss Maggie, you have a true talent for baking."

Looking pleased, Maggie said, "Let me wrap up some of the cakes and tarts for you to enjoy on the road."

"We'd like that." He gave the girl a smile that would melt the heart of any female.

As Maggie wrapped a dozen pastries in a piece of cloth and tied the bundle with a length of string, Kendra asked, "Katie, may I hug you?"

Katie stood and embraced Kendra. "I am so glad to have met you, Aunt Kendra! When will we be able to meet again?"

Kendra hugged her warm little girl body, mourning all the years they'd missed while reminding herself of the miracle of Jane's saving a sickly infant and raising her into a lovely young girl. "I'm not sure, but I know it will seem too long. I'll write you."

"I'd like that, Aunt Kendra," Katie said, glowing. "I'll write you back."

Kendra reluctantly released her daughter and stood. "I've written down my address and the address of my lawyer on this paper. You will be hearing from him."

After farewells all around, she and Lucas went outside to where their patient coachman was waiting. Lucas undid the bundle of pastries and offered three to the coachman, who accepted them with enthusiasm.

As soon as the carriage started moving, Kendra relaxed into the seat with a sigh and took Lucas's hand. "That went well, don't you think?"

"I do. You and Jane both want the best for Katie, and everyone will benefit." He gave Kendra a sidelong glance. "Even if she and Jane were willing, you couldn't take Katie to London now and risk Denshire finding out he has a daughter. From what I've heard of him, he'd probably grab her as he did Christopher just to make you miserable."

Kendra felt as if icy water had been poured on her head. "I hadn't thought of that! Denshire and his malice seem so far away. But you're right, he would demand custody and send her off to some horrible school just as he did with Christopher."

"That won't happen," Lucas said reassuringly. "Katie is safe and very lucky to be with people who love her."

"I won't tell anyone about her except Simon and Suzanne so she'll stay safe." Wanting to change the direction of her thoughts, she said, "I'm looking forward to returning to Angelo's for more fencing lessons and sparring with some of the women Suzanne introduced me to. It's splendid exercise. Athena Masterson promised to send me some garments that are suitable for fencing."

"I'll go with you, if you don't mind," Lucas said. "I enjoyed my previous visit, apart from being challenged to a duel, of course."

"Of course I don't mind." She studied the lean, elegant length of him and couldn't help but think of the strong body that lay under his well-tailored garments. They'd seen each other's scars the night before: the ugly parallel burn marks on her leg from when she was knocked onto the burning hot grate. The jagged, alarming scar on his left shoulder and back from the near lethal wound he'd suffered in the navy. Seeing their pasts written on their flesh, which was another kind of intimacy.

Aloud, she said, "How long until you visit the infirmary again?"

He chuckled. "Not long. I plan to work there regularly."

"I need to be doing something useful," Kendra said thoughtfully. "I wonder if Zion House could use an inexperienced volunteer. I could work with children, perhaps."

"Mention your interest in volunteering to Lady Kirkland and you'll be there the next morning teaching little children their letters," Lucas assured her.

"That sounds very satisfying." And being busy would keep her from brooding on her situation. She'd done too much of that before she met Lucas. Now that she'd decided to move on with her life, helping those less fortunate seemed a good way to help herself as well.

Her life really was getting better. It was a novel and very welcome thought.

—

As their coach rolled up the drive to Camden Keep, Kendra sat up and stretched her limbs in various directions. Lucas loved watching her and looked forward to seeing her fence at Angelo's. She had grace and strength like a great cat, and like a lioness, she protected her children and others whom she loved.

As she straightened her skirts, she said, "When we came through before, it was too difficult to speak of my search to learn the truth about Caitlin, but now that I know she's alive and well, I want to share the good news. I also feel that I owe your aunt and uncle an explanation for taking advantage of their hospitality. I presume they can be trusted to keep the story to themselves?"

Lucas nodded. "Being a British Resident at an Indian royal court is like being an ambassador. Discretion is second nature. Just ask them to keep it private and they will."

The coach halted at the Keep and Lucas and Kendra climbed out and were admitted to the house. They found their hosts in the family drawing room. "What good timing," Aunt Anna said warmly as she rose. "We'll be having tea soon."

"After I've visited the Magdalene," Uncle William added. "I was about to go out. Would you like to join me, Lucas? She's always particularly happy to see you."

When he hesitated, Kendra said, "Go along with your uncle and give the Magdalene my regards. I'll call on her later." Turning to his aunt, she said, "I'd like to tell you of our successful journey."

Guessing she wanted to speak with his aunt alone, Lucas said, "Uncle William, I trust you have carrots so I can bribe my lady mule to remember me?"

His uncle laughed. "Even better, I have apples. But no need to bribe her. You're still her favorite."

"She and I traveled many long miles together." Happy to stretch his legs, Lucas accompanied his uncle outside to the stable area behind the house. Since the weather was mild, his white mule was grazing in a small paddock. She looked up at the sound of approaching footsteps and gave a happy little bray as she joined them at the fence.

As the Magdalene had her neck scratched from two directions and daintily accepted half an apple, Lucas's uncle said, "Your lovely lady friend looked more cheerful than she did two days ago."

"Her journey turned out much better than expected," Lucas replied. "I imagine she's telling Aunt Anna about it now. I'll leave it to Kendra to explain to you."

Uncle William looked curious, but didn't pursue the point. "Now that the weather is really spring, we'll be coming up to London in a fortnight or so to get our annual dose of social frivolity. Do you want to join us at Foxton House?"

"Thank you, but I'm settled with Simon and Suzanne." Lucas smiled. "And they have a most excellent French cook."

His uncle chuckled. "Hard to argue with that." He fed another half apple to the mule. "Are you in love with Kendra?"

Lucas froze. "As a divorced woman, she is legally forbidden to marry."

"That wasn't my question." His uncle looked up from the mule to catch Lucas's gaze. "She's a fine young woman who is handling a difficult situation with grace and determination. The two of you seem very close."

Lucas wondered if his uncle suspected that he and Kendra had become lovers. He'd always been uncannily perceptive. "The fact that we're both dishonored has proved a surprisingly strong bond."

"I can see that would make a good foundation, but there seems to be more between you than that. We'd like to see you settled down with the right woman, and we both like your Kendra." William grinned. "So does the Magdalene."

Lucas's face tightened. "Unless something changes, marriage will be impossible."

"Things often do change," his uncle observed.

Deciding it was time for a change of subject, Lucas said, "In Lower Dauntrey, we met a very impressive young curate, a Mr. Hutton, at the parish church of St. Mary of the Fields. He was especially helpful to us, and he and his wife both seemed very caring. I think he'd be a good choice when the next Camden Keep living becomes available."

"Which will be quite soon," his uncle said with interest. "When the time comes, we can go to Lower Dauntry to meet him. But now it's time to go in for tea."

Tea was always good for a change of subject.

Chapter 20

Kendra rolled over and stretched. She liked being back in her familiar bed in Thorsay House, but why did it feel rather empty even though she'd spent only a single night with Lucas?

At least she'd see him soon when he came to collect her for the visit to Angelo's Academy. Speaking of which, she needed to get moving to be ready in time.

After washing up, she brushed out her hair and tied it back with a simple black ribbon. Now it was time to try on the garments that Athena had sent. It was strange to draw on the pantaloons. Made of black stockinette, they had a strap under the foot and the knit fabric stretched with movement. Perfect for fencing.

They were also quite scandalous. Kendra wasn't sure how she felt about that. She pulled on her own pair of well-broken-in black riding boots. Then, per Athena's instructions, she donned a set of short stays that provided support for her breasts but were loose enough for movement. A full-sleeved shirt went over the stays.

All black, of course. She'd explained to Athena and the others that she wore black as a symbol of mourning for the death of justice. They had agreed that it made a good statement as well as commenting that she looked good in black.

Over the shirt, she added a garment that was something between a buttoned vest and a tunic. Again black, it fell almost to her knees and made the outfit a little less scandalous. None of the garments were formfitting, but neither were they baggy. Athena had done a good job of estimating Kendra's size.

She looked dangerous. Good. Turning away from the mirror, she lifted her riding crop and lunged forward as if it was a small sword. Heavens, the freedom of movement! She twisted through several other fencing exercises and wasn't once constrained by her garments. A woman could get used to this!

Much as she liked the pantaloons, Kendra wasn't ready to be seen wearing them on a public street. She tossed her cloak over her arm and went down to find breakfast.

Thorsay House was primarily run by Mr. and Mrs. Brown. Donald was Thorsayian and his wife, Emma, was a London girl whom he'd met when he was stationed at an army barracks in the city. They ran the household with an easy competence and a Thorsayian informality. Kendra felt very lucky that she was able to live here.

Emma Brown looked up at Kendra's entrance. "Good morning. Your usual?"

"Yes, please."

Emma put an egg into simmering water and poured Kendra a cup of steaming tea. "That's quite the outfit you're wearing, but isn't it early in the day for a masquerade?"

Kendra laughed and cut a slice of bread, then stuck it on a long toasting fork and held it over the fire. "I'm going to Angelo's Fencing Academy this morning. One of the other women who fences there sent me this outfit. It's so easy to move around wearing this!"

"A good thing you'll have a sword to fight off the men who like the look of your legs," Emma said dryly.

"Lord Foxton will escort me over and back, and he's a dab hand with a dirk," Kendra explained.

"Really? He looks too pretty to be a fighter."

"He was an officer in the Royal Navy and is more dangerous than he appears." Her bread toasted, Kendra buttered the slice, then cut it into the narrow strips called toast soldiers.

Emma served the soft-boiled egg in an egg cup. Kendra neatly decapitated her egg and dipped the first toast soldier into the warm yolk. Delicious, and each bite was followed by a mouthful of tea. She loved the informality of Thorsay House, and the way she was accepted without judgment. She paid a generous fee for the use of the house, and in return received a comfortable lodging and easy company.

"The house has been quiet for the last fortnight," she remarked. "Are any other Thorsayians expected?"

Emma shrugged. "Hard to say. Most just show up at the door as you did. You're the only long-term guest we've had recently." She topped up the tea for them both. "But I did hear that the young laird may soon be coming through on his way back home."

"My cousin Ramsay? It's been years since I've seen him. Where has he been living lately?" Kendra asked with surprise.

"Constantinople, they say. 'Tis a long voyage from there to here."

"A couple of months, I'd guess," Kendra agreed. If Ramsay was coming home, it probably meant the old laird was failing in health. She'd like to see Ramsay again. He'd been like a big brother to her when she was a little girl summering in Thorsay. But he'd had restless feet and headed out to distant lands when he finished university.

She was finishing her breakfast when Donald Brown entered the kitchen, saying laconically, "Your friend is here, Miss Kendra."

"Thank you." She swallowed the last of her tea and stood, giving Donald his first look at her pantaloons.

"You're going out in your drawers?" he asked, scandalized.

"Pantaloons, not drawers," she explained. "I'm looking forward to fencing in them."

"What's the world comin' to?" he muttered, but his gaze was amused and appreciative.

"Greater freedom for women, I hope!" With a departing smile, she collected her cloak and headed toward the drawing room. When she entered, Lucas was studying a battle-scarred round shield, but he turned at her arrival, then stood stock-still, staring. He swallowed hard before saying, "Good morning."

"I think this is the first time I've seen you really surprised," she said cheerfully. "Athena Masterson sent the clothes over while we were traveling. I hope to see her at Angelo's this morning."

Collecting himself, Lucas said, "Your outfit will offer great flexibility for fencing." He grinned. "Or possibly for becoming a jewel thief."

She glanced down at herself. "I hadn't thought of that, but I'll bear it in mind if I need to take up a new occupation."

"You may cause a riot as we walk over," he said, seeming unable to wrench his gaze from her legs. "And if you cross swords with any men at the academy, you'll win because they'll be too stunned by the sight of you to put up a defense."

"I'm divided between feeling dashing and alarmed," she admitted as she donned her cloak to conceal her appearance from men on the street. "But I do love the freedom of movement that I have."

They stepped out on the street and the bright spring breeze blew her loose cloak around her legs. Her pantaloons made the effect interestingly different from her usual skirts. She also found that her strides were longer and freer. Lucas didn't have to alter his pace for them to walk side by side down the street. Yes, she liked this.

Angelo's was rather quiet when they arrived, but four women had claimed the left end of the main room and were chatting in a friendly way as two of them sparred with their blunted small swords. All wore pantaloons, though only Kendra was dressed in all black.

Kendra smiled at the sight, feeling as if she was joining a very special club. Athena Masterson was part of the group and wore black boots and pantaloons along with a white shirt and dark red tunic. She made a very convincing warrior woman. She turned to greet the new arrival. "Kendra, welcome to the Fencing Females Fighting Society! I'm glad you braved the pantaloons. It's much harder to fence in a skirt."

Kendra grinned at her, immediately feeling at home. "You did a good job guessing my size. Thank you!"

"My sister-in-law, Lady Kiri Mackenzie, is a wizard with clothing and fashion and she developed the pantaloons," Athena explained. "She often fences here but couldn't come this morning. I'll tell her how pleased you are with your new ensemble."

"I think pantaloons are a splendid idea," Lucas said. "Why should women always wear clothing that is so confining?"

"I like your point of view." Athena extended her hand. "I'm Athena Masterson and you must be Foxton?"

"Indeed I am," he said as they shook hands.

"Do you know if Henry Angelo is available?" Kendra asked. "I'd like to have another lesson with him if I could."

Another woman, this one with red-gold hair, shook her head. "He's out until this afternoon. For lessons, it's best to book the time in advance."

"I'll do that next time, Callie," Kendra said. "For today, is anyone up for a little gentle sparring with a novice?"

"It would be my pleasure since I'm no expert myself." She turned to Lucas and offered her hand. "I'm Callie Kingston. I heard about your sparring session with your cousin. I gather that the two of you put on a dazzling show. I'm sorry I missed it."

"I'll see if I can persuade Simon to join me here next Wednesday. He's my favorite sparring partner," he said as they shook hands. "I'll leave you to your mayhem and see if I can find a sparring partner of my own."

Kendra set aside her cloak, then lifted a practice sword, testing the balance in her hand. "Now show me how bad I am, Callie!"

—

Lucas took off his coat and hat, enjoying the prospect of some demanding exercise. After collecting one of the practice swords racked along the opposite wall, he looked around for a prospective partner.

A sparring match was going on at the opposite end of the room from the women, and several other men were watching, so he approached one of the onlookers who also held a practice sword and looked ready to use it. "Hello," he said pleasantly. "I'm Foxton. Would you like to do some sparring?"

"Foxton?" Looking revolted, the man scowled and made an elaborate show of turning his back.

Lucas felt as if he'd been punched in the belly. In the last few days of travel with Kendra, he'd not thought about his pariah status. Now it was brought back to him with sharp malice.

Then Athena Masterson was at his shoulder. "Would you be willing to spar with a mere female?" she asked. "Like Callie, I'm more accomplished with a gun than a sword, but the way to improve is by sparring with someone who is better, which you are."

Lucas's tension eased away. "I'd be delighted to cross swords with you. I have a suspicion that you're better than you admit."

"I'm not really," she said as they moved to a clear space in the center of the room. "But I have had some unwelcome experiences of war when I lived on the Peninsula. That produces a certain ruthlessness."

"War does that," Lucas agreed. They saluted each other with their blades, then began easily testing each other's ability. Almost as tall as Lucas and with a long reach and quick reflexes, Athena was a worthy opponent. Their speed increased to a swift, athletic bout that ended when he touched the practice sword to the center of her chest. "Touché, my lady!" he said, panting. "I'm very glad I didn't have to fight you seriously!"

"The feeling is mutual!" she said with a breathy laugh.

Kendra and Callie had also finished their bout and were laughing together. Kendra turned and came to Lucas, breathing hard, her face flushed. She looked beautiful and enticing and he was tempted to kiss her. Just as well they were in public.

"I wish I'd discovered fencing years ago!" she said.

"It's even better exercise than galloping a horse cross-country."

"I prefer fencing as a sport to fighting for one's life, which tends to interfere with the entertainment value of swordplay," he replied.

"Indeed it would!" she said fervently. From her expression, she was remembering the time they were attacked on the street when walking to Duval House.

The door to the academy opened and two men entered. The one in the lead was gaunt and scowling, with a red sore on his neck that was almost hidden by his hair. The man in his wake was shorter and milder looking.

Lucas would have barely noticed the new arrivals, except that the gaunt man stopped in his tracks as he caught sight of Kendra. "You!" he said incredulously. "You *bitch*! What are you doing here, dressed like a slut?"

Kendra's face whitened. For a moment Lucas wondered if she was about to faint. But she collected herself and said with icy calm, "Given the women you consort with, Denshire, surely you know better what a slut looks like."

"The way you're dressed is scandalous! You're a disgrace to your sex!" he spat out.

"Really?" Callie drawled. She and the other women drew closer to Kendra, pantaloons obvious, swords in hand, and expressions dangerous. "If anyone here is a disgrace to his sex, surely it's you, Denshire. A fornicating fraud and a bully to boot."

He sputtered incoherently, looking ready to strike someone, but he was outnumbered and out-armed. His friend put a hand on his arm and murmured something, perhaps a suggestion to leave, but Denshire shook the other man off. "I'm not leaving until I find out what that bitch has done with my son!"

Chapter 21

Kendra gasped at her former husband's words. "What have I done with Christopher? Nothing! I haven't seen him since you threw me out of your house and said my son was your property and I'd never see him again!"

"He's vanished from the school I placed him in!" Denshire snarled. "If he didn't drown himself in the river there, you must have taken him so you can turn him into a molly boy!"

"*You lost my son!*" Kendra said in a low, furious voice. Her sword ready in her right hand, she stalked toward her former husband, her expression murderous. "You treated him badly and put him in a school so vile that he must have run away. Dear God, what has happened to him?" With her left hand, she snapped off the protective button on the end of the blade.

Swearing, Denshire backpedaled. "Get away from me, you crazy bitch!"

Lucas took two swift steps to Kendra and caught her arm, immobilizing her. "He probably deserves killing, but not by you," he said in a low voice. "Christopher will need you when we find him. You can't be there for him if you're imprisoned and hanged."

She looked up at him, wildness in her eyes. "Kendra!" he snapped. "For everyone's sake, don't do this!"

The wildness faded. As she mastered herself, Denshire bolted from the academy, his friend at his heels. In the lacerating silence that followed, Athena said thoughtfully, "He really does deserve to be skewered. Perhaps the Fencing Females should have a drawing for the privilege?"

Her words produced a ripple of strained laughter. Kendra's gaze moved around the circle of women. "Thank you for your support, my friends," she said unsteadily. "I'll take my leave now, but I hope to see you all next week."

She donned her cloak, the length swirling around her scandalously beautiful legs. Lucas also grabbed his coat, pulling it on as she left the academy. When they were outside, he took her arm. "Slow down and breathe."

"But Christopher might be dead! Denshire said that he might have drowned himself from misery," she cried, on the verge of breaking down entirely. "Denshire doesn't care about him beyond the fact that he's the heir."

A narrow alley ran between the buildings they were passing, so Lucas drew her into it, where they'd have the privacy for him to wrap her shaking body in his arms. "Christopher is your son," he said quietly, feeling her anguish. "Can you imagine the boy you love taking his own life because school is so dreadful?"

She drew a slow breath and he felt some of her frantic tension ease. "No. No, he wouldn't do that. He would run away and find a safe place to hide. Then he'd try to write me."

"That sounds like what a clever boy would do," Lucas agreed, stroking her back as he would soothe a nervous pet. "There might not even be a river. Denshire could have made that up just to upset you more."

"That sounds like something he'd do," she said, more of her tension fading. "He might even have lied when he said that Christopher had disappeared from his school, though his degree of anger at me implies that Christopher really is missing. If so, running away is by far the most likely explanation. I think Christopher would try to communicate with me, but I'm not sure he knows I'm at Thorsay House."

"Communication will be difficult for him," Lucas agreed. "But Christopher is surely out there somewhere, safe and trying to find his way home to you."

"Dear God, I hope so!" she breathed.

"We will find him," Lucas promised as he had before. "But brace yourself for some new information."

When Kendra glanced up at him, he said, "Denshire has the French pox. Syphilis. That explains a great deal about why he's become increasingly unstable in recent years."

She stepped back, her expression appalled. "The French pox!" she exclaimed. "Why do you think that?"

"Did you see that red sore below his ear, almost covered by his hair? It looks like a gumma, a kind of soft tumor that's a sign of the advanced disease," he explained. "When I saw that, I looked more closely and saw some subtler signs as well."

Kendra bit her lip. "Do I have it?"

"You don't have any of the symptoms," Lucas said reassuringly. "You told me that you haven't lain with him for years, so it's likely he contracted the illness after you separated."

"I hope you're right! For your sake as well as mine." She closed her eyes, shuddering. "I'm so sorry. I… I would never have allowed any intimacy with you if I'd known I might carry the disease."

"I know you wouldn't have." He raised a hand and tenderly brushed a loose tendril of hair behind her ear. "Because you have honor and Denshire does not."

She gave a crooked smile. "He certainly doesn't, but any honor I have is debatable."

"You have honor," he repeated. "And also amazing strength. You have been struck by one blow after another, yet you're still standing."

"More like leaning on you." She took his arm and guided him from the alley. As they resumed their walk back to Thorsay House, she asked, "Aren't you getting tired of the maelstrom that is my life?"

He remembered the colorless drifting that had been his life before meeting Kendra. "If not for your troubles, we wouldn't have met again, and that would have been a great loss for me, though probably not for you."

She gave him a swift, shy glance. "Not meeting you again would have been a *very* great loss for me."

For a moment their gazes held, saying more than they wanted to admit aloud. The emotional moment was buried when she continued, "Without knowing where Christopher's school is, it's impossible to know where to start looking for him."

"From what you know, the school had a particular reputation for discipline?" When she nodded, he continued, "That might narrow the search down some. We need an expert on British public schools. Simon and I both attended Harrow. There might be someone there who could give us some suggestions."

"I hope so. I have no better ideas." Her voice became tight. "Since Denshire does know the school's location, he'll know where to search."

"If that's the case and Denshire has men who locate Christopher, the worst that is likely to happen is that he'll be sent back to the school, or possibly to Denshire Park," Lucas said. "As heir to Denshire, he has value. He won't be injured."

She smiled ruefully. "I know you're right, but it's a mother's job to worry about her children."

"And it's a job you do very well," he said solemnly.

She chuckled slightly. "Sadly true. I'm glad Caitlin is safe with her foster family."

He could see her visibly girding herself to deal with this new worry. It was a trait he admired, given that he'd spent years in Belgium hiding from his problems.

When they reached Thorsay House, Kendra said, "Would you like to come in for tea? The Browns are out for the day, but Mrs. Brown left some of her excellent shortbread."

Guessing that she wanted company, he said, "I'd like that," and followed her into the house. The small entry hall had a table on one side with a basket for mail. There was only one letter, and Kendra frowned as she picked it up. "This is from Kirkland."

"Let us hope for interesting news, and that we won't need the tea to revive ourselves. Or worse, brandy!"

She smiled a little before she settled on the sofa and broke the seal of the letter. "Kirkland wants us to meet with him tomorrow for a strategy session. What do you think that means?"

Lucas considered. "My guess is that he's uncovered some information and wants to discuss how to use it."

"That makes sense. We have information for him as well." Her brow furrowed. "I don't see any reason to tell him about Caitlin. The more invisible she is, the better, don't you think?"

"I'm sure Kirkland can be trusted to keep secrets, but as you say, there's no reason to tell him about her."

"I do need to tell him about Christopher's disappearance. He might have more ideas about how to look for him. Did Kirkland attend Harrow or Eton? Those are the two elite gentlemen's schools."

"Neither. He went to the Westerfield Academy. It's a very small and very good school for boys of good birth and bad behavior."

"Kirkland studied there?" She glanced up with surprise. "I wonder what kind of bad behavior he indulged in. I'm having trouble imagining it."

"He was probably planning to take over the Houses of Parliament or some such," Lucas replied with a smile. "It wouldn't have been anything trivial like gambling in the stables with the grooms."

She laughed. "I wonder if I dare ask him?"

"Better you than I!"

The tea tray arrived and Kendra poured for both of them. The shortbread lived up to its reputation. Lucas was reaching for his third piece when a small knock sounded on the front door.

The Browns were still out, so Lucas rose and crossed into the hall to answer it. A small and very scruffy boy stood on the front step. A boy with chestnut hair and changeable eyes.

The boy said politely, "Is Lady Denshire here?"

At the sound of the boy's voice, Kendra bolted in from the drawing room. "*Christopher!*"

"*Mama!*" The boy hurled himself into her arms and hugged her as if she was saving him from drowning.

Tears were rolling down Kendra's cheeks as she whispered, "Oh, Kit, my darling boy! I was afraid I might never see you again."

He was clinging to her like a limpet. "Papa said you were wicked and I should have nothing to do with you!"

"Your father was wrong," Lucas said as he ushered them both toward the drawing room so he could close the front door.

Having been a small boy once himself, he asked, "Would you like tea and shortbread, Christopher?"

"Oh, yes, sir, please!" the boy said. "I'm *starving*!"

Kendra laughed and pulled him down on the sofa beside her, keeping one arm around him. "I'm happy to see that your appetite hasn't changed! How did you get here?"

"The school was in Yorkshire and it was *horrid*." Christopher took a piece of shortbread from the plate. Since Kendra had finished her tea, Lucas used her cup, guessing that the boy would prefer to have his tea quickly rather than to wait for a new cup to be delivered.

Christopher accepted the teacup, but his brows furrowed as he stared at Lucas. "Who are you, sir?"

"My name is Lucas Mandeville and I'm a friend of your mother's," he replied. "We met many years ago before I left for my first posting in the Royal Navy."

"And a very good friend he has been." Kendra's arm tightened around her son's shoulders. "I've needed friends since your father divorced me."

Christopher took two more pieces of shortbread. "Divorce means never having to see him?"

"That's one of the results of divorce." She frowned. "I hadn't seen your father in months, but I had a chance encounter with him earlier today. He was furious and accused me of having abducted you from your school."

"I wish you had!"

"I would have if I'd known where you were," she said fiercely. "But your father wouldn't tell me what school you attended. You said it was horrid?"

The boy's expression darkened. "The Scranton School. Bad food, bad boys, bad masters. It was always freezing cold. Beatings from bigger boys, canings by the masters."

"It sounds dreadful!" Kendra said, appalled. "I've heard that boys' schools are difficult, but I didn't think they were that bad!"

"Few are that bad," Lucas said grimly. "I'm not familiar with Scranton, but I gather Denshire wanted to put Christopher in an unusually harsh school on the theory that such places build strong men."

"More likely they turn out brutes!" Kendra exclaimed. "Yet you escaped, Kit. How did you do it?"

Christopher grinned, looking very pleased with himself. "Instead of sleeping in a dormitory, I was locked into a separate little room every night. The only window was small, but so am I. I managed to steal a rope from the stables by wrapping it around me under my shirt. Then I took the money of the biggest bully in the school. I escaped out the window that night before he found it was gone."

"Generally stealing isn't a good idea," Kendra said, bemused, "but it sounds as if it was necessary this time. What did you do after you escaped from your room?"

"I hiked to the nearest town. I had to sleep in the woods one night but at least it didn't rain. From there I caught a coach to Leeds. In Leeds, I got the coach to London."

"No one questioned why such a young boy was traveling alone?" Kendra said with surprise.

Her son looked impish. "I looked sad and said that my mother was very ill and I'd been ordered to come home. There was no one to come get me so I had to travel alone. I had enough money to pay for my tickets, so the coachies believed me. It was a long ride, but at each stage, nice women looked after me. One gave me a piece of the best currant cake."

"Your mother said you were clever," Lucas said admiringly, understanding why motherly women had been inspired to care for him. "She was right."

"How did you know to come to Thorsay House?" Kendra asked.

"You brought me here once, remember? You introduced me to Mr. and Mrs. Brown and said this is kind of a family house. I thought you might be staying here and if you weren't, they might know where you were." He used his hand to cover an enormous yawn. "Mama, why are you dressed like a man?"

"I was fencing with some other ladies." Kendra stood and made a pretend lunge. "Wearing pantaloons makes it possible to be a better fencer."

Christopher accepted that explanation with a nod and covered another yawn.

"It's time you went to bed, my lad. I'll take you up to my room so you can get some sleep," Kendra said.

The boy was tired enough that he didn't protest. Kendra took his hand and led him away but said over her shoulder, "Can you stay, Lucas? I have some matters to discuss with you."

He didn't doubt it. And the top of the list would be deciding where Christopher could be kept safe.

Chapter 22

Christopher had grown in the months since she'd last seen him, and he seemed more mature as well. That wasn't surprising given his experience at his horrid school and the challenges he'd overcome to find her in London. Should she tell him that he had a twin sister? No, it was too soon for that; her son had too many other changes to deal with. She'd wait until life calmed down.

When they reached her room, she hugged Christopher again. "You were so brave, Kit! Brave and clever both."

His new maturity vanished as he burrowed against her and began sobbing. "Papa said the most awful things about you, Mama! He... he said you were a whore and wanted to turn me into a molly boy. I asked a boy at the school what 'whore' and 'molly boy' meant and he laughed in a mean way and told all the other boys and they started calling me a whoreson!"

Kendra thought savagely that if Denshire were here and she had a sword, she'd run him through. "That is absolutely not true, Christopher! For all the years of my marriage, I was a faithful and honorable wife." That night with Lucas didn't count because she was no longer married when they came together.

Kit's voice dropped to a shaky whisper. "He... he said you didn't want me anymore, but I didn't believe him.

Didn't *want* to believe him! That's why I had to find you again."

Forget having a sword – if Denshire were here Kendra would kill him with her own hands. "That was a horrible lie! I was frantic when he took you away and told me I'd never see you again. More than anything on earth, I wanted to find you." She drew a deep breath, thinking she should be calm and strong for her son. "Instead you found me. What a blessed day this is!"

"Why did he tell such lies?"

How to explain the end of a marriage to a child? Choosing her words carefully, she said, "He decided he didn't want to be married to me anymore, Kit. The only way a man can divorce a wife is to say bad things about her. That's what he was doing."

Kit lifted his head. "How could anyone say bad things about you?"

As much as she loathed Denshire, she shouldn't descend to his level. Remembering what Lucas had said about the French pox, she said, "I believe he has a disease that can affect a person's mind and make him act differently than he used to."

"Like the king?"

Mad King George was a good example. "Something like that. I don't think they have the same disease, but in both cases, their minds are affected." She swallowed hard, then forced herself to say, "Your father is to be pitied, but that doesn't make his actions right."

"I don't ever want to leave you again, Mama," Kit whispered.

"Oh, my darling." She hugged him close, wondering how long it would be until he would consider himself too old to be hugged by his mother. "I want to keep you close too, but that won't be possible. If your father found out that you were with me, he'd take you away from me again, and he might lock you up in an even worse place than the Scranton School. The law says he'd have the right to do that."

Christopher jerked his head up. "Why does the law say that?"

Kendra wanted to spit out that the law had been created by bullying males, but she didn't think that would help her son understand. "English law has been developed over centuries and it says that a man's wife and children belong to him, like a horse or a pair of boots. He can do anything he wants with us."

Christopher's eyes narrowed to slits. "That's stupid!"

"I agree. Someday the laws might change, but for now, your father has the legal right to take you away from me." Wanting to emphasize the danger, she continued, "He might even charge me with kidnapping you and try to put me in prison."

Christopher looked horrified. "He could do that?"

"He could try." She shivered. "I don't want to know if he would succeed. But don't worry about that now. Rest. You're safe here for now. While you're sleeping, I'll go downstairs to talk to Lucas about the best way to hide you from Denshire."

Kit covered another yawn. "You like him?"

"Yes, I like him a great deal. He's trying to help me change my situation so that you can stay with me again."

"Is that possible?" Christopher asked hopefully.

"I don't know," she said honestly. "We'll certainly do our best. Now get some sleep."

"Couldn't sleep much on the coaches," he muttered, his fingers so tired they were fumbling as he tried to undress. "Too much lurching around."

"Then you have every right to be tired," she said lightly as she helped him take off his outer clothes. When she tucked him into her bed, he was asleep almost before she pulled the covers over him.

She leaned over and lightly kissed his forehead. Her beautiful boy was here, her greatest wish fulfilled. Now for the complicated question of how they could remain together.

Kendra descended and entered the drawing room. Lucas stood when she entered and she walked straight into his arms, craving the warmth and safety of his embrace. In fact, she thought wryly, she was behaving like Christopher when he burrowed into her embrace. "What a day it has been," she said with a sigh.

"Indeed." He scooped her up in his arms, then sat on the sofa with her in his lap.

After a startled moment, she relaxed into him and rested her head on his shoulder. "Retrieving Christopher was my most important goal, and now I have him. The question is how do I keep him?"

"I've been thinking about that, too," Lucas said. "Obviously it would be a disaster for Denshire to learn that Christopher has run away to you. Even though the boy doesn't want to be separated from you again, I don't think it's safe for him to stay in London."

She sighed and absently stroked Lucas's arm. "I know you're right. But we need to find a good place for him, and it has to be close enough for me to visit."

"What about Camden Keep?" Lucas suggested. "I think my aunt and uncle would love to have him, and he'd have the Magdalene, who is a very soothing mule."

She smiled. "That might work. More thought is required. There may be a better solution."

"We might not have much time. Does Denshire know about Thorsay House? Is there a chance he might come here and accuse you again of abducting Christopher? Maybe even demand to search the house?"

She caught her breath. "I don't think so, but I'm not sure! If he came with some men to back him up and demanded to search the house, they'd find Kit and it would cause trouble for Mr. and Mrs. Brown as well."

"If the Browns don't know that Christopher was ever here, it would be safer for them," Lucas said. "Might they return soon?"

Kendra shook her head. "No, they're visiting their older daughter today to see their new grandson. They didn't expect to get home much before dark."

"So we can take Christopher out before anyone notices there's a child here."

"That might be best, but where would we take him?"

"Duval House," he said immediately. "Simon told me to treat the house as my own, and I intend to take full advantage of the invitation. Not that I think Simon or Suzanne would object to sheltering a child in need. It would only be for a few days."

"And there are a cat and a dog to keep him company. He'd like that. Does Duval House have a guest room Christopher and I can share? He needs to have me near him for now. And I need it, too."

"There's a good-sized room in the attic that would work. Shall we take him over? I can get a small closed carriage and take it to the mews behind the house."

Kendra nodded decisively. "Yes, please do. I have some of his clothing. It was a wishful hope that I'd find him before he completely outgrew his current clothes."

He slid his arms under her and neatly transferred her to the sofa beside him so he could stand. "I'll go to Duval House to make sure that Simon and Suzanne don't object to having guests. Simon has the right kind of carriage as well. I'll borrow it and return here. I should be back in one to two hours."

She rose also. "I'll pack a few things for Christopher and myself and be ready when you return."

Lucas put a finger under her chin and gave her a swift kiss. "Now that we have him back, we won't lose him again."

As soon as he left Thorsay House, Kendra began making preparations for a few days away. When she entered her room, Christopher was still sleeping like a hibernating bear. Like a boy who had been frightened and exhausted and who knew that he was now safe and loved.

She changed from her fencing costume to one of her usual black gowns, then swiftly packed a small canvas bag for both of them. When she was done, she took the bag downstairs and cleared the tea things from the drawing room. Then she left a note for the Browns, saying that she was visiting friends for a few days and would be back soon.

Finally, she waited, and tried not to think of all the things that could go wrong with a crazed ex-husband nearby.

Lucas returned in just under an hour. When he entered the drawing room, he said, "I acquired a driver. Simon is waiting in the mews behind the house. Time to collect Christopher and be off before the Browns return."

She nodded and led the way up to her room. Christopher was still deeply asleep. Lucas said, "I'll carry him out to the carriage."

Kendra wanted to say that was her job, but her son was getting too heavy for her to carry easily, especially down a staircase. "Wrap him in the blanket so he doesn't get cold outside."

Lucas peeled off the upper covers, then lifted Christopher with tender care. Kendra thought how natural he looked with a child in his arms. He would be a far better father than Denshire had ever been.

They descended, Lucas careful not to bump any part of Christopher on the walls of the narrow staircase. In the drawing room, Kendra collected the bag of their belongings and they headed out the back of the house.

Simon was waiting by the carriage. "Thank you for being our coachman," Kendra said.

"It's my pleasure. That brave little boy of yours deserves protection," Simon said seriously. He took Christopher while Kendra and Lucas climbed into the carriage, then passed her son up to Lucas again. "Suzanne will be glad to have him. She has a history of taking care of people when they're in need."

Simon swung onto the driver's seat and drove the short distance to Duval House. They entered from the mews. Kendra didn't think anyone had seen them. Perhaps they were taking more precautions than strictly necessary, but she wasn't going to lose her son again.

Suzanne met them inside and peered at Christopher's peacefully sleeping face. "What a beautiful little boy! He's the picture of you, Kendra. They sleep so soundly when they're young, don't they? I imagine you'll want to stay with him for now. You can join us for dinner, or food can be sent up if you prefer."

Kendra felt tears stinging her eyes. "I can't thank you all enough for what you're doing. I don't know what I would have done without you."

"You would have managed," Suzanne said seriously. "But I'm glad we can make it easier for you. Rest now."

Kendra nodded, thinking she was almost as tired as her son. Then she followed Lucas up the stairs as he carried Christopher to the attic room. It was pleasant, with a bed large enough for them both and a view of the back garden through the small window.

She turned back the covers and Lucas gently laid Christopher onto the bed. He straightened and said, "Tomorrow we'll figure out what comes next, but tonight, sleep in peace with Christopher."

"Thank you for all you've done," she whispered as she gave him a light kiss on the cheek. But they both shifted and their lips met and the kiss turned serious. His mouth was warm and welcoming and she wanted to fall into him forever. Her arms went around him, his around her, and they were pressed together with swift, unexpected heat.

After an endless interval that was over too soon, Lucas released her and stepped back, his breathing unsteady. "Wrong time, wrong place," he said. "Until later."

She kissed her fingertips, then brushed them down his cheek. "Until later," she whispered.

Later couldn't come soon enough.

Chapter 23

Christopher awoke the next morning hungry and full of energy. Before he'd finished his breakfast, he'd fallen in love with Suzanne, which Kendra thought was entirely reasonable. By the time she and Lucas left to go to Kirkland's house, Christopher was playing with the dog, Rupert, under Suzanne's indulgent eye.

When they entered Kirkland's study, they found that he was not alone. He got to his feet behind his desk and greeted them affably. "Thank you for coming. Please take a seat. As you see, I've brought in two associates who can be trusted to honor your need for confidentiality. Hazel, you've met, of course."

Kendra smiled at Kirkland's agent. "Is this your half day, or have you left Denshire's employment already?"

Hazel returned her smile. "I left day before yesterday, after I had to damage one of Denshire's friends who wanted something I objected to giving."

"How seriously injured is the fellow?" Lucas asked.

"He should be walking again in a week," Hazel said. "During my brief time at Denshire House, I did learn that your maid, Molly, ran away that night of infamy. Apparently she objected to what was being done to you and was threatened with violence if she interfered. She was afraid for her life, so she escaped while she could. No one in the household had any idea where she'd gone.

The servants survive by shutting out the coarseness and unpredictability of their master."

"I'm so glad Molly wasn't harmed!" Kendra said. "Thank you."

Hazel glanced at Kirkland. "You don't need me for anything else, do you?"

"Not at the moment. Thank you for joining us," Kirkland replied.

After Hazel left, Kirkland gestured to the other woman present. "You've both met my wife."

"It's lovely to see you again, Lady Kirkland," Kendra said warmly.

Lady Kirkland, a gentle blonde with an expression of quiet but indomitable determination, offered her hand. "Please call me Laurel. I wanted to join the group of subversive ladies that Suzanne Duval gathered to support you, but I was busy that day introducing Foxton to our infirmary."

Kendra took the other woman's hand. "I'm Kendra. Lucas told me about Zion House and the infirmary. You do such valuable work. Do you need volunteers to help with the children?"

"I'd love to have you as a volunteer!" Laurel said. "We must set a time when you can visit Zion House and become acquainted."

"Another victim falls to my lady wife's charming wiles," Kirkland said with a chuckle. "But that's not why I asked you here. I have some new information that might prove useful, and it's time to determine what strategy has the best chance of success."

Kendra sank onto a sofa beside Lucas. "The situation has just changed dramatically – in a good way. At Angelo's Academy yesterday, Denshire saw me when he came in and began shouting accusations that I'd kidnapped our son from his school. Which I might have done if I'd known what school it was, but I didn't."

The Kirklands looked appalled. "He lost your son?" Laurel exclaimed.

"Yes, but the story has a happy ending. Lucas and I returned to Thorsay House and were having tea when there was a little knock on the door. It was Christopher." Kendra couldn't prevent herself from beaming. "He'd made his way to me at Thorsay House all the way from the Scranton School in Yorkshire. I don't know if you've heard of it?"

Kirkland frowned. "I have, and it was nothing good, particularly not for a boy as young as Christopher. He's a brave and clever lad to have escaped and found his way home to you. Will he be safe staying with you?"

"We weren't sure, so we moved him to Duval House," Lucas replied. "But he'll be safer out of London. We've discussed taking him to Camden Keep to stay with my great-aunt and uncle."

Kirkland leaned back in his chair and looked thoughtful. "You might consider my old school, the Westerfield Academy. It's small, with excellent teachers, and most importantly, bullying is not allowed. It's a remarkably civilized place for a boys' school."

"'For boys of good birth and bad behavior?'" Kendra inquired.

Kirkland grinned and looked much younger than his usual reserved self. "So it is said. In truth, Lady Agnes Westerfield, the founder and as fine a woman as there is in Britain, prefers students who don't quite fit the aristocratic mold so she can teach them how to survive in their world without being driven mad."

"That sounds an excellent goal." Kendra couldn't resist asking, "Why were you sent there?"

Amusement sparked in his eyes. "Nothing interestingly lurid. My arrogant English father hated that I preferred my mother's relatives, who were mere merchants as well as being appallingly Scottish. My father assumed that Lady Agnes, being a duke's daughter, would be as snobbish as he was. Instead, she encouraged me to look for every person's true value. My Scottish relatives are better than my father was in all ways."

"It might be a good place for Christopher," Kendra said thoughtfully. "Where is the school? I'd like to talk to your Lady Agnes. How difficult is it to gain admittance?"

"The school is in Kent, not far from the Dover Road. She likes taking on boys in difficult situations, so I think she'd be willing to accept Christopher. As it happens, she's in London now for a nephew's wedding. She's joining us for luncheon here tomorrow. I can bring her to Duval House after so you can meet her and she can meet Christopher."

"That would be ideal. Much as I like having Christopher with me, he needs to be safe and with other boys. Your old school sounds good if there really is no bullying."

"Boys will be boys and occasionally one loses control," Kirkland allowed. "But bad behavior is stopped immediately, if not by a master, then by one of the older boys because the 'no bullying' philosophy is part of the fabric of the school."

"I like the sound of that," she said. "I look forward to meeting your Lady Agnes tomorrow. Now what about new information and strategizing?"

"The identities of the three men who claimed they'd had relations with you are known because they testified in the trial." Kirkland frowned. "I wish now that I'd attended the trial, but I was very busy and it seemed too sordid a matter to waste time on."

"Even more sordid than you thought," Lucas said. "Though in a very different way. Do you know if those men are completely convinced that they bedded Lady Denshire, or might they admit that they were deceived?"

"I haven't probed them too deeply, but at least one of them is apparently uncomfortable with the whole business and how it played out," Kirkland replied. "I'm not sure about the others."

"Have you located the woman who impersonated me?" Kendra asked.

"Yes, and there's a definite resemblance to you in her height and figure and coloring," Kirkland said. "She calls herself Aphrodite and she's a rather exclusive courtesan who specializes in performing male fantasies. She didn't realize when Denshire hired her that he wanted to create a fraudulent basis for a divorce case, and she was not happy when she found out how she'd been used."

"If so, why didn't she speak out when the divorce became public knowledge?" Kendra asked.

"She didn't want to become involved with any legal proceedings and she wasn't sure her evidence would be of any use to you," Kirkland explained. "But she might be willing to cooperate under the right circumstances."

"What kind of circumstances?" Lucas asked.

"This gets into the area of strategy, and my wife has some thoughts about that." Kirkland nodded toward Laurel.

"From what you said, you want to have legal custody of your son," Laurel said. "For that, your reputation needs to be rehabilitated in the eyes of the world and the law. I doubt the divorce could be reversed even with proof that it was based on fraudulent evidence, and I assume you wouldn't want it to be."

Kendra shuddered. "I don't even want to be in the same room with that man, much less married to him!"

Laurel nodded acknowledgment. "You told the women's group that your first priority was to get your son back. Now that you have him, the new priority must be keeping him legally. That means restoring your reputation, which can only be done by publicly proving that Denshire not only lied, but orchestrated an elaborate fraud designed to vilify you."

"That's a good summary," Kendra said. "Do you have any thoughts about how it might be done?"

"You said that Denshire is socially ambitious," Laurel said. "Your female allies have a great deal of social power, and they've started what could be called a whispering campaign saying that he has behaved despicably and is not a desirable guest. He is getting fewer invitations, especially to more prestigious events, and he's said to be outraged by this."

"I approve of anything that annoys him," Kendra said, "but can this be used to help me to my goals?"

"Perhaps. The strategy I have in mind is unpredictable, but it might help your reputation and your chances of getting custody of your son. We can arrange a very exclusive event, perhaps a ball or soiree hosted by two duchesses, and send invitations to Denshire and the three friends who testified to your alleged wanton behavior," Laurel explained.

"I'm sure he'd love that," Kendra agreed. "Then what?"

"Once he's there, we confront him with his sins. Perhaps the woman who took your place will testify and confront the men who lay with her, making it clear that it was she, not you. If we can find your missing maid, she can attest that you were drugged that night and she herself was threatened." Laurel smiled wickedly. "And among the other guests will be a high-ranking cleric or two. Perhaps even the Archbishop of Canterbury."

Kendra gasped. "You can arrange all that?"

"It will be a joint effort, but yes, I believe it could be done," Laurel assured her. "Mariah, the Duchess of Ashton, would host the event at Ashton House, which is a very fine venue for entertaining. Co-hostess would be the dowager Duchess of Charente, one of the most highly respected women in society and Lady Julia's grandmother. Lady Julia's brother is the young and rather reclusive Duke of Castleton, and she might be able to lure him to attend."

"What about the Archbishop of Canterbury?" Kendra asked faintly.

Laurel chuckled. "He's some kind of cousin to Lady Julia and very fond of her. If he's unavailable, I'm sure we can find another leading cleric or two. The clerics would be useful in clearing your reputation, because if influential members of the Church believe you were unjustly accused, most of the rest of society will agree. This would help you retain custody of Christopher."

"I surely hope so!" Kendra considered. "Much of Denshire's rage is because he wants the money left to me in trust by my grandfather. He's made several unsuccessful legal attempts to claim the funds and my lawyers could attest to that. Would having one of my lawyers attend be useful? It would prove how low Denshire's motives are."

"That would surely be helpful," Kirkland agreed.

Kendra looked over to Lucas. "What do you think?"

"It would certainly be an interesting evening for anyone whose life doesn't weigh in the balance!" His brows furrowed. "People are unpredictable, and Denshire more than most. I don't think I mentioned that he seems to have advanced syphilis?"

Kirkland gave a low whistle. "That goes a long way to explaining his unreasonable behavior."

"It doesn't make him any less dangerous. Rather the opposite." Lucas returned Kendra's glance. "Such an event might help your cause and is unlikely to make your situation worse. Given the elaborate fraud Denshire created to destroy you and your marriage, perhaps it's appropriate to create an equally elaborate trap to expose his crimes."

"How long do you think it will take to arrange the event?" Kendra asked.

Laurel considered. "Two to three weeks? That would fall at the height of the season so our exclusive gathering will be much talked about."

"The doors of the ballroom should have capable gentlemen standing guard to prevent any of the guilty from leaving early," Lucas said. "I'll volunteer for that duty."

Kirkland gave a dangerous smile. "So will I."

Once again, Kendra was amazed at how lucky she was to have such friends and allies, and she owed it all to Lucas. "With luck, Christopher will be safely out of Denshire's grasp by then. I look forward to meeting your Lady Agnes, Lord Kirkland."

"I'm sure you'll like her. You're both very direct females." He stood and offered a farewell smile. "Until tomorrow afternoon then."

Kendra rose also. Now to persuade her son to go away to another school.

Chapter 24

Kendra waited until after lunchtime the next day to tell her son that the headmistress of a school was coming to meet him that afternoon. His small face screwed up at the news. "Why can't I stay here with you? I like it here!"

"This is a lovely place to stay," Kendra agreed. "But it's not our home. You need to be somewhere outside of London, where it's safe."

"Don't want to go to another school! I liked when you taught me," he said stubbornly.

"I don't know everything you need to learn," she explained. "Don't you think you might like to be with other boys? Ones who are nice, not bullies like at your old school."

Unconvinced, Christopher turned his attention to Rupert, Simon's friendly young dog, and the two romped to the other end of the drawing room. Lucas had joined them for their lunch, and now he said quietly, "Would Christopher be more willing to go to a school if he had his pony Patches with him? From what Kirkland said, boys at the Westerfield Academy often have pets, and many have ponies or horses."

"That's a wonderful idea!" Kendra said. "I imagine Patches is still in Denshire's stables, eating his head off and missing Kit. I doubt Denshire knows Patches exists since he was seldom at Denshire Park and he never paid attention to his son. We can send someone to go there and offer for the pony. I'll send a letter and some money. The head groom is a nice fellow who taught Christopher to ride, and I'm sure he'll cooperate."

"If that could be done, it would help reconcile Christopher to the idea of school. Assuming Lady Agnes is willing to take him."

Kendra nodded and mentally crossed her fingers. It was a relief when the knocker sounded. After the butler admitted the guests, Kirkland entered the drawing room with Suzanne, escorting a tall woman with silver at her temples and an air of good-natured authority.

After Suzanne made the introductions, Kendra rose and offered her hand. "It's a pleasure to meet you, Lady Agnes. I've heard very good things about your school." She beckoned to Christopher, who abandoned Rupert and came to her side to see what was going on.

"This is my son, Christopher. I wanted the two of you to meet. Kit, this is Lady Agnes Westerfield, the headmistress of the school I discussed with you."

Wary but polite, Christopher said, "I'm pleased to meet you, ma'am."

"Come, let's sit down and become better acquainted," Lady Agnes said. "I'm told that you were at the Scranton School? A dreadful place. Very brave of you to escape, and very clever to find your mother."

Christopher perched on the edge of a chair and said emphatically, "I don't want to go to another school! I want to stay with Mama."

"That's a great compliment to your mother," Lady Agnes said seriously, "but it's also important to learn new things and make friends. At my school, each new student is assigned an older student to look out for him like a big brother. They have to like each other – that's very important. If you don't, another student is chosen."

"I'd like to have a big brother," Christopher said, unable to conceal his interest. "I'd like to be with other boys and not be bullied. But do your students just sit in classrooms all the time?"

"Not at all! We encourage sports, and that includes a form of Hindu fighting that was taught by one of my very first students. Everyone learned from him, and the tradition continues," Lady Agnes said. "But there's also time for reading or walking or arguing philosophy. These are all good ways of making friends."

"With your permission, Lady Agnes?" Kirkland asked. At her nod, Kirkland caught Christopher's gaze. "I was one of the first students at the Westerfield Academy, and it was the first place where I'd ever been happy. My years there laid the foundation for the rest of my life, and the friends I made there are closer than brothers. Every student has a different experience, of course, but I don't know a single one who regrets having attended Lady Agnes's academy."

Looking thoughtful, Christopher asked, "Could I have a pony there?"

"Yes, all the boys ride. The stables have both school horses and horses owned by students," Lady Agnes said. "Some boys also have smaller pets."

Christopher's gaze went to Rupert, who was lying across his feet. Suzanne said firmly, "Rupert is a wonderful dog, but he belongs to Simon. There are many other wonderful dogs in the world if you decide you want one."

Christopher actually chuckled as he leaned over and scratched the dog's ears. Straightening, he asked, "Would I be able to see your school first?"

"Your mother can bring you down if she likes, but before we get to that stage, I always ask prospective students two questions," the headmistress said. "The first is what you hate and don't want anything to do with."

Christopher's expression hardened. "Don't ever want to see my father again!"

"I can't guarantee that wouldn't happen sometime later in your life, but while you're at the school, we would do our best to make sure you don't have to see him," Lady Agnes promised. "My second question is what do you love? What do you want to do? For example, do you like learning new things?"

"I do like lessons," Christopher said slowly. "But most of all, I want to have friends. Friends like brothers, like Lord Kirkland made."

"To make friends, one must be a friend." Lady Agnes studied Christopher's small face, her gaze assessing. "I think you would be a good friend. Would you like to visit the Westerfield Academy?"

Christopher glanced at Kendra. "Yes?" he said tentatively.

"Then we'll visit the school," Kendra said with a smile as she gave a private sigh of relief. She had a very good feeling about sending her son to the Westerfield Academy.

Suzanne said, "After listening to all this, I'm ready to sign up our son if Simon and I ever have one!"

Lady Agnes chuckled as she stood. "If you have that son, let me know."

The guests left and Christopher was restless. Kendra said, "Lucas, after I find Kit something to read, will you be available to talk about the school?"

"Of course. I'll be here in the sitting room looking over some papers."

She nodded and escorted her son up to their attic room. Once there, she said, "I think the Westerfield Academy sounds perfect for you, and we'll travel down to see it within the next week. I want you to like it and I think you will."

"It sounded like a good place," Christopher said as he settled in a comfortable armchair and opened a favorite book that she'd found in the library. "But I'd rather be with you!"

Kendra sighed and pulled another chair up beside him. Deciding on directness, she said, "I'm afraid that isn't possible, Kit. I don't think it's safe for you in London because the law says you can't stay with me. I will leave you at the school when I take you there."

"Are you sure I can't stay with you?" he pleaded.

She shook her head. "If you did, you wouldn't be able to go outside in case you were seen and the news got back to your father. You'd hate being inside all the time, wouldn't you?"

He nodded glumly.

"At the academy you'll be out and able to ride and play games," she said coaxingly. "If after two months or so you really hate the place, well, we'll talk about it then and find a better solution. But please accept that the Westerfield Academy will be your future home for a while."

Christopher nodded, looking resigned and older than his years. "Yes, Mama. I'll do my best to like it." He looked down at the book again.

"Thank you." She leaned forward and kissed his cheek. He was turning the pages with interest by the time she reached the door.

Now to talk to Lucas about a potential pony-napping.

-

Lucas was frowning over a page of numbers when Kendra entered the drawing room. He looked up with a smile. "Were you able to find something to engage Christopher's interest?"

She nodded. "I told him that he has no choice about attending the Westerfield Academy because it isn't safe for him in London. I think the idea of having a pony persuaded him. I need to see about retrieving Patches from Denshire Park."

"Kirkland will have a suitable agent, or if Simon can spare him, his man Jackson might want to go. Like Simon, Jackson is a former soldier and he enjoys getting out and about occasionally."

"I'll ask Simon about Jackson then." She glanced at the windows. "Would you like to go for a walk to Thorsay House? The weather is pleasant and there are a few things I'd like to collect for Christopher."

Lucas rose. "I'd love to. I've been studying financial reports and they're putting me to sleep."

"Financial reports?" she asked as they headed outside into a brisk but bright spring day. "Are you sure you wouldn't find a nice novel or travel account more amusing?"

"*Anything* would be more amusing," he said with a laugh. "Simon and I both inherited substantial ownership in several businesses from our mutual grandfather. Since retiring from the army, Simon has become interested in running them and he seems to have inherited our grandfather's business brain. Personally, I'd much rather spend a pleasant afternoon setting broken bones."

It was Kendra's turn to laugh. "Isn't it fortunate that there are so many different talents in the world!"

"Indeed," he said as she took his arm. "I'm content to let Simon run the businesses, but he asked me to spend some time familiarizing myself with how they're run and how money is made and spent. He's right, I need to have a general idea of their operations, but it's too much to ask me to enjoy it."

"I must admit that I find business and the management of money rather interesting," she admitted. "I speak with my lawyers regularly about the investments made in my grandfather's trusts. The lawyers are entirely honest and capable, but I feel it would be irresponsible of me not to pay attention."

"You're sounding like Simon," Lucas said. "I am surrounded by intimidating financial competence!"

"But I would be hopeless at splinting broken bones," she pointed out. "I know whom I'll call if Kit falls down the stairs and needs mending!"

"Different skills, as you say."

They continued bantering the last blocks until they turned a corner and saw Thorsay House. Several people were clustered around the open door and raised voices could be heard. Lucas swore under his breath and accelerated. Kendra kept pace, her expression tight.

Denshire was accompanied by two men, one a burly ruffian and the other a thin gentleman who looked pained by Denshire's shouting. Of *course* it would be Denshire. "I know my son is here," he bellowed. "Give him to me!"

Mr. Brown stood in the doorway, his wife a step behind. He was looking very stubborn and very military. "You're talking nonsense," he said, his northern accent strong. "There's no child here."

"I'd have noticed when I was cleaning," Mrs. Brown said acidly. "Now get you gone and leave us alone!"

"You're lying!" Denshire growled. "Stand aside. I'm going to find him."

"Denshire, don't be an idiot!" Kendra snapped with an authority that sliced through the angry voices. "Christopher is not at Thorsay House. You're the one who sent him to a school so dreadful that apparently he was forced to run away. And whose fault is that? God only knows what may have happened to him, but you won't find him here!"

Lucas gave silent thanks that they'd moved Christopher to a safer place. The sooner they got him out of London, the better.

Denshire spun around at the sound of Kendra's voice. "*You!*" he snarled as he grabbed at her.

Lucas chopped the side of his hand across Denshire's reaching wrist. He knew a great deal about bones and nerves and where best to strike. Denshire howled and lurched back, holding his injured wrist with his other hand.

"Who the hell are you?" he barked as he glared at Lucas.

"I'm Foxton and I'm Miss Douglas's bodyguard," Lucas said calmly.

"You don't look like a bodyguard," Denshire said suspiciously. "I've seen you sniffing around my wife before."

"She's not your wife anymore," Lucas pointed out. "You're the one who falsely accused her of immoral behavior, then divorced and threatened her. Which is why she needs a bodyguard."

"Divorce is an ugly process," Kendra put in helpfully. "But it does mean I'm free of you. Go away and stop bothering the inhabitants of Thorsay House!"

"I'm not leaving!" he growled. "You have my son in there and you have no right to keep him. The law says he's mine, and by God, I'm going to go in there and get him!"

Lucas frowned. Denshire was crazy enough to come back some night and set fire to the house if thwarted now. "Mr. and Mrs. Brown, would you be willing to allow Denshire to search the house, accompanied by you and me so that he can see that his son isn't here?"

"I won't have that man in my house!" Mrs. Brown snapped.

A sentiment Lucas understood. Kendra was looking homicidal, so it was up to him to calm things down. "It's understandable that a father would be concerned with the whereabouts of his son," he said in a mild, unthreatening voice. "It's equally understandable that you wish to protect your home from intrusion, Mr. and Mrs. Brown. But for everyone's sake, it might be best if the house is searched in order to prove that Christopher isn't here."

He scanned the people around him. Ah, the thin gentleman with the unhappy expression. "Mrs. Brown, what if you and Miss Douglas accompany this gentleman, Lord Denshire's friend, as he searches? You because it's your house, Miss Douglas because if her son is hiding under a carpet or in a closet, she'd like to know about it, and Denshire's friend to ensure that the search is thorough?"

Denshire frowned, looking as if he wanted to tear the house up himself, but said grudgingly, "I guess I can trust Hollowell to do the job properly."

Mrs. Brown didn't look pleased, but she probably had the same concerns about Denshire's behavior that Lucas did. "Very well," she said reluctantly.

Kendra gave Lucas a grateful glance. "That seems a fair solution."

"Good," Lucas said. "Mr. Brown and I will wait outside. You can do the same if you wish, Lord Denshire, but there's a tavern around the corner that might be a more pleasant place to wait."

Resigned to his fate, Hollowell said, "That's reasonable, Denshire. I'll come find you when the search is finished. I'll bring Christopher if we find him in the house." He sounded as if he didn't expect that to happen.

Denshire nodded and signaled for his ruffian to follow him down the street and around the corner. When they were gone and the women had gone into the house with Hollowell, Brown said in a low voice, "They won't find the boy in there, will they?"

The Browns might have guessed that Christopher had been there once. "No," Lucas said. "I'm hoping Denshire trusts his friend enough to believe the truth. Without the search, he might keep threatening you."

"He seems the sort," Brown agreed. He settled down on the steps of the house, then pulled out a pipe and lit it.

Lucas did the same, minus the pipe and sitting upwind of the smoke. "If Denshire tried breaking in some night, you have all those weapons decorating the drawing room."

Brown gave a baritone chuckle. "Tempting that would be, but killing a lord would cause trouble, no matter how much he deserved it."

They sat in companionable silence for an hour or so until Mr. Hollowell came out of the house. "We searched every nook, cranny, wardrobe, and under the beds as well. No hidden children."

"Told you." Brown got to his feet. "My bet is the women are making tea and complaining about the nuisance." He extinguished his pipe and went inside.

Lucas stood and quietly said to Hollowell, "You know that Denshire has advanced syphilis?"

Hollowell sighed. "Yes, but he refuses to admit it. He's been getting more and more erratic. I try to divert his more difficult behavior."

Curious, Lucas said, "You're old friends?"

Hollowell nodded. "We went to school together. He appointed himself my protector and drove off the bullies. I owe him a great deal."

"He's lucky you haven't said good riddance and left," Lucas noted.

"That could happen someday," Hollowell said wearily. "But we're not at that point yet. Good day, Foxton. Thank you for staving off potential violence." He inclined his head, then headed down the street toward the tavern.

Thinking how much luckier he was in his friends than Hollowell was, Lucas turned into the house. Tea and sane conversation sounded good.

Chapter 25

Kendra stood and moved into Lucas's arms when he entered the kitchen, not caring if the Browns deduced that she and Lucas were more than just friends. As his protective arms came around her, she gave a sigh of relief. "Thank you for coming up with a sensible compromise, Lucas. If you hadn't, blood might have been shed."

"Blessed are the peacemakers. It's a role I've always liked." He hugged her thoroughly, then released her. "I heard there might be tea on offer?"

"Tea and ginger biscuits," Mrs. Brown said as she rose to get another mug. "My thanks also. That former husband of yours is a nasty piece of work, Miss Kendra."

Kendra sighed and returned to her chair to collect another ginger biscuit. "He wasn't always so dreadful, but these days, I don't even want to be in the same room with him. And I certainly wouldn't hand a child over to him!"

"I wonder where that poor lad is?" Mrs. Brown said and she poured more tea for everyone.

"From what Kendra has told me about Christopher," Lucas said, "he's a clever lad and would have a plan to find a safe place for himself."

Kendra nodded agreement. "I'm sure he's safe and well somewhere. I just wish I had legal custody of him!"

Her comment triggered a discussion about stupidities of the law, which lasted until Kendra rose and said, "Time to get back to Suzanne. She's Lucas's almost sister-in-law. She hasn't been feeling well so I volunteered to come help out with her baby until she's feeling stronger." She smiled. "I adore babies and will use any excuse to hold one. Perhaps when she's older, your new grandson can visit here?"

"I'm sure he shall, and a more adorable baby you've never seen!"

"A very right and proper sentiment for a grandmother," Kendra said with a smile. "I'll be back here in a few days."

"I think Denshire has been convinced that Christopher isn't here," Lucas said as he pushed his chair back and stood. "But he's unpredictable and could be dangerous. Which is why I've decided Kendra needs a bodyguard."

Kendra rolled her eyes at the Browns dramatically as she left, but once they were outside on the street, she took hold of Lucas's arm. "Really, a bodyguard?"

"It seemed a good description," he replied, amusement in his eyes. "It gives me a reason to watch your very fine body, but I also think you need one, with Denshire running mad about town."

She shivered. "I'm so glad we moved Kit to Duval House! Mr. Hollowell was polite but very thorough."

"Do you know Hollowell? Apparently he and Denshire have been friends since their school days."

"I believe I met him a time or two in the early years of my marriage." Her voice turned dry. "He was one of the three men who testified that I'd lain with him."

Lucas looked startled. "I didn't realize that. I wonder if he was the one Kirkland said was uneasy with the whole business? We talked briefly. He seems to be loyal to Denshire because of their long years of friendship. He said he tries to keep Denshire in line."

"Not doing a very good job of it, is he?" She sighed. "I'll be so glad when Christopher is safely in school. I wonder how successful we'll be when we confront Denshire at this very exclusive entertainment that the ladies are planning?"

"I can't even begin to guess," Lucas said. "But I hope it will be the turning point for clearing your reputation."

"I hope so, too." She gave him a sideways glance. "How about your reputation? Are you still being scorned?"

"Sometimes," he admitted. "Another Rogers brother challenged me to a duel when we met by chance at Tattersalls. Those fellows are as stubborn as they are loyal to their little brother."

"You didn't accept the challenge, did you?" she asked with alarm.

"No. I refused on the grounds that I still didn't know what my deadly sin was and how could there be a duel with no stated cause?" After a pensive silence, he added, "I got the impression that the injured brother, Godfrey, has never told his brothers the details of my dishonorable behavior."

"That's interesting," Kendra said thoughtfully. "I wonder if his reasons for accusing you contain an element of shame at his own behavior."

Lucas's brows furrowed. "Very interesting indeed. But we'll never know unless young Godfrey is willing to speak up."

"Frustrating. A real grievance could be addressed but not dire accusations that aren't explained. At least my alleged shameful behavior is clear, if fraudulent."

"You're also facing up to the situation, not wailing and accusing." He glanced down at her, his eyes warm. "I have much more respect for your approach."

She felt absurdly pleased. "Thank you. I spent several months in an angry fog, but I've been coming out of that ever since I attended the Clantons' ball and met you."

"We're good for each other," Lucas said. "I admired how carefully you worded what you said to Denshire to avoid actually lying."

She smiled. "It's a modest gift, but sometimes useful. More useful yet will be getting Christopher out of London."

"We can leave three days from now. That will give Lady Agnes time to finish her business in London and return to her school. With luck, it will also give Jackson time to find Christopher's pony and bring him to the school."

Kendra hoped fervently that the pony could be acquired. But in the meantime, she must tell Kit that his father had appeared at Thorsay House, and he must stay inside until they took him to the Westerfield Academy.

–

Lady Agnes's school was as appealing as her description of it had been. Lucas, who was driving, said, "Kirkland told me that Lady Agnes inherited this house from her mother's family. After she spent some years in world travel, she returned to England. Being restless, she decided to start a school for boys. It's been a success since the beginning."

"I imagine that traveling in faraway dangerous lands would be good preparation for dealing with young boys," Kendra said, amused. "Kit, what do you think?"

"It looks nice," he said. "Nicer than Denshire Park. Where are the stables?"

"Behind the house, I believe," Lucas said. "There are also playing fields, and Kirkland said they recently built a new residential hall for the students. Classes are held in the main building. Lady Agnes's private quarters and office are in the right wing."

Lucas was driving because hiring a driver would mean one more person knowing of Christopher's location. He turned the carriage neatly into the circular driveway in front of the great sprawling house.

When a footman appeared from the private wing, Lucas said, "I'm Foxton. Lady Agnes is expecting us today. Could you tend to my horses?"

"Of course, sir."

After the footman took the reins, Lucas climbed from the carriage, then helped Christopher and Kendra down. At the door, a butler appeared to escort them to Lady Agnes's office at the back of the ground floor. She looked up from her paper-covered desk when they were announced, then rose to her feet. "You made good time, I see. Christopher, we've talked about the school. Would you like to tour the place and see the classrooms and the residents' hall?"

"And the stables?"

She smiled. "Definitely the stables. Also, there's someone I'd like you to meet. Benjamin, please join us."

A brown-haired youth of fifteen or sixteen had been reading in a corner of the office, but he put his book aside and stood. He wore a navy blue coat paired with buff-colored trousers for a uniform that was neat, comfortable, and practical. Kendra squinted at the embroidered circular patch on one pocket. Was that the image of a zebra? She smiled inwardly. It was a suitable symbol for a school of students who were a little different.

"Is this the new lad?" Benjamin asked with an easy smile.

"Yes," the headmistress replied. "Benjamin Thomas, meet the Honorable Christopher Hawthorn. Christopher, I'm proposing that Benjamin be your big brother if the two of you get on."

"Hello, Christopher." Benjamin offered a friendly hand. "I'm Benjamin and sometimes Ben. I hope we're going to be friends."

Christopher took the older boy's hand firmly. "I hope so too, Benjamin. I'm Christopher and sometimes Kit." He gestured at Kendra and Lucas. "This is my mother, Miss Douglas and her friend, Lord Foxton."

Kendra smiled at the older boy. "It's my pleasure to meet you, Benjamin. We'd like to see the school, too, so may we follow around after you? I'll try not to get in the way."

Benjamin gave her a sunny smile. "Of course you can, ma'am. Shall we look at the classrooms first?"

"That's the best place to start," Lady Agnes said. "I'll follow along, too. Pretend we aren't there."

"Impossible!" he said with a laugh. "Come along, Kit. There's a lot to see."

He led the way out of the office, with Christopher beside him. Kendra glanced at Lucas, who gave an approving nod. Since the classrooms were in the same building, there was a connecting door, though it had a lock on it so Lady Agnes wouldn't be disturbed unnecessarily.

The classrooms were well equipped and impressively tidy given that the students were growing boys. Several classes were in session, so the visitors just glanced in. The teachers seemed capable and kept the classes in good order.

The adults trailed far enough behind that they didn't disturb the ongoing conversation between Christopher and Benjamin. Lady Agnes made a few comments about the courses, adding, "Before Christopher would start, he'd be tested to see how much he knows so we can put him in the right classes."

"I don't know how much he learned in the Scranton School," Kendra said. "Not much, I suspect. Before that, I taught him. His reading is very good and so are his numbers. We studied geography and the globes together. No Latin or Greek because I don't know either. Kit has always enjoyed lessons and I hope that continues."

"He sounds like he has a good foundation," Lady Agnes said with approval. "I teach geography classes myself. I enjoy it and it keeps me in touch with the students."

At the back of the ground floor, they looked into a large corner room with several windows, padded floor mats, and little furniture. "This is where we learn Hindu Kalarippayattu fighting," Benjamin explained. "It's great fun!"

Lady Agnes murmured, "The padding reduces the bruises. There's always at least one older boy who is very skilled at Kalarippayattu here during teaching and sparring sessions, so if someone loses his temper and risks becoming dangerous, he's stopped until he cools down. We want the boys to learn how to defend themselves, not end up with broken bones."

"This sounds really interesting," Lucas said. "Hand-to-hand fighting is a useful skill for those who go into the army or the navy."

"I've had several old boys tell me that the skills learned here have saved their lives, for which I'm deeply grateful," Lady Agnes said as Benjamin led them all outside. A group of younger boys in the school uniform were happily kicking a ball around a playing field.

Christopher looked as if he wanted to join in, but today was for learning, not playing. As Benjamin headed to the residential hall, Lady Agnes said, "There are outside game sessions every day so the boys can work off their energy."

"I'm beginning to wish I'd studied here!" Lucas said.

"Where did you go?"

"Harrow."

"A good school, if rather too conventional," Lady Agnes said, her eyes twinkling. "Not as good as mine."

Benjamin led them to the residential hall and up a flight of stairs. At the far end of a corridor, he opened the door into a cozy parlor with a fireplace, sofa, a couple of tables, and several upholstered chairs. "This is where I live and where you'll live if you become a student. We call it the Hawks' Nest. There are four rooms off this common room, two singles and two doubles. Older boys get the single rooms. We're of different ages, some older, some younger. You'll like the other Hawks. They're a good lot."

"This would be your room." Benjamin swung open a door revealing a pleasant chamber with paired beds, wardrobes, desks, chairs, and bookcases. A framed print of a horse jumping a fence hung over the bed that was in use. "Your roommate would be Robby Bolton. He's just a little older than you and he's been hoping to get a roommate so the two of you can stay up talking half the night."

Kendra smiled, thinking it was inevitable the boys would talk long after lights out. Girls certainly would!

Christopher surveyed the room. "I was locked in a small private room at Scranton, but most of the boys slept twenty to a room. I like this better."

"Twenty boys in one room!" Benjamin gave a mock shudder. "How does anyone get any sleep?"

"Boys who wanted to sleep pulled pillows over their heads," Christopher said tersely.

"Very sensible," Benjamin said. "Now for the stables!"

Everyone followed him downstairs and outside like a string of goslings following their mother. The stables were only a short walk away. The building was large and old, like the house, and filled with stalls and loose boxes holding contented-looking equines. Several boys were there grooming their mounts or cleaning stalls, and they exchanged casual greetings with Benjamin and Lady Agnes.

Benjamin stopped by a loose box containing a handsome chestnut. "This is my Rowdy," he said proudly as the horse came whickering to him. "A gift from my stepparents. He's a very good-natured fellow. Would you like to give him some sugar?"

"Oh, yes, please!" Christopher said.

Benjamin pulled a sugar lump from his pocket and gave it to Christopher, who then held it out on his palm to Rowdy. He glowed as the horse delicately lapped the sugar from his palm.

Benjamin said, "Ponies are at the far end of the aisle. The school owns some of the horses and ponies so everyone can ride."

As he led them along the length of the stables, Christopher said wistfully, "I had a pony. I miss him."

Benjamin said mischievously, "Was his name Patches?"

He stopped by a loose box where a splotchy pony stuck his curious head over the door and whinnied excitedly.

"Patches!" Christopher said. Almost beside himself with excitement, he opened the door and popped into the box before anyone could stop him. Not that stopping him was necessary. Boy and pony were equally delighted to find each other again, and Kendra felt tears stinging her eyes. She would give Jackson a bonus for finding Patches and bringing him here so quickly.

Lucas murmured in her ear, "I think by this time Christopher is happy with the idea of coming to school here."

"Where Patches goes, Kit will go," she agreed.

A deep gong sounded three times. Benjamin looked at Lady Agnes. "It's dinnertime. Should I take Kit along to eat and meet the other Hawks?"

Kendra said, "Kit, are you happy with the idea of becoming a student here?"

"Oh, *yes*, Mama!" He reluctantly stepped away from his pony and walked out of the box, carefully latching it behind him. "Can I go riding tomorrow?"

"That's up to your teachers," Kendra said.

Lady Agnes said, "I think that can be arranged. I'll have your belongings sent up to your room. Now, you go along with Benjamin to your dinner and meet some of your fellow students."

Christopher dived for Kendra and wrapped his arms around her for a moment. "Will you visit me, Mama?"

"Yes, but I'll have to talk to Lady Agnes about when. She may prefer that parents not visit for a while."

The headmistress nodded. "That's true, Christopher. You need to settle into the school first. But the term ends soon and I'm sure your mother will write."

Christopher's gaze shifted to Lucas. "Will you write, too?"

Lucas smiled. "Unless your mother disapproves, yes."

Kendra smoothed a hand over her son's shining hair. "Of course Lord Foxton can write, and you should write him back."

"I will." Christopher stepped away from her, his lip quivering. "Is this good-bye?"

Lady Agnes said, "I'm going to invite your mother and Lord Foxton to dine with me and spend the night, so you can say your good-byes in the morning if that's agreeable to you all."

Kendra glanced at Lucas, who nodded. "We'd love to. We can say our farewells after we've all breakfasted."

Christopher gave her a big smile. "I'll see you in the morning then!" He turned to Benjamin Thomas. "Where is the dining room?"

"On the ground floor of the residence hall. Come along now, Kit." He flashed a mischievous glance at Lady Agnes. "The food is really pretty decent."

"Considering the amount you young barbarians eat, it's hard to get enough food on the table to feed you all," she said fondly. "Now off with you, lads."

The two boys headed off at a brisk pace while the adults followed more slowly. Kendra found her own mouth trembling. Lucas took her hand quietly. "I know it's hard to watch him go, but children must learn to use their wings so they can fly."

"And then they fly away," Kendra said with a sigh.

"Yes, but that one will return to you regularly," Lady Agnes predicted. "You've given him the love and confidence he needs to test those wings."

Kendra prayed that the headmistress was correct. "Do you always spend so much time introducing new students to the school?"

"It varies," Lady Agnes said. "Because Christopher is young and has gone through a difficult time with his father and his former school, I thought he needed the extra attention. Bringing his pony here was very wise."

"I'm glad Patches arrived so quickly," Kendra said. "Credit goes to Lord Foxton for knowing someone who could make it happen."

"Making things happen is a gift you share with Lord Kirkland," Lady Agnes said to Lucas. "He's always looking for talented men and sometimes women to solve problems if you're looking for work."

Lucas smiled but shook his head. "I prefer to set bones."

"In that case, you can work for me!" Lady Agnes said with a laugh. "I'm sure you can imagine the number of things a school full of adventurous young fools can break."

"Indeed I can!" Lucas said feelingly. "If you have a boy with a problem that is difficult to fix, let me know. I'd be happy to come down to see what I can do."

"I might take you up on that," Lady Agnes said.

The three of them continued to chat amiably as they crossed back to the private wing of the school. Kendra felt light enough to fly. Her children were safe. Now she could concentrate on fixing her own life.

Chapter 26

Dinner with Lady Agnes proved very enjoyable. Besides Lucas and Kendra, the company included Miss Emily Cantwell, who seemed to be universally known as Miss Emily, and retired Army General Rawlings. The two were Lady Agnes's partners in running the school. The general was in charge of sports and other manly pursuits and provided a male confidant for the boys when that was needed. Miss Emily handled most of the office and financial work, as well as giving warm hugs.

Lucas suspected that what made the three of them a good team was that they all genuinely liked their students, and they liked guiding those boys who needed extra help in learning how to find their place in society. They were also very enjoyable dinner companions.

The meal was winding up when Lady Agnes said to Kendra, "I think by morning you'll find that your son is settling in well."

"I'm sure you're right. Having Patches again has won his heart." Kendra made a face. "We took his limited possessions over to his room when the boys were dining, but because of the circumstances, he has almost nothing. Is there a nearby tailor that does uniforms and other boys' clothing?"

"Yes, there's a very competent fellow in the nearest village who spends most of his time making clothing for my students, including the school uniform. He's good with sturdy garments that are not easily destroyed by rough and tumble boys. There's also a very good shoemaker who does a fine job with shoes and boots of all sorts."

"Just what Christopher needs! Can you see that he's properly equipped and add the costs to his school fees?"

Miss Emily smiled. "We shall. It's a common arrangement here. They grow so quickly!"

Giving in to his curiosity, Lucas asked, "Is that really a zebra on your school uniform badge? It looked like one, but I wasn't close enough to be sure."

Lady Agnes laughed. "It is indeed a zebra. Partly because I've traveled widely and seen zebras and lions and elephants in the wild and the boys love hearing about such things. But also because so many of my students feel as if they're zebras in a herd of horses. The odd ones out who will never belong."

"Our job is to teach them to canter seamlessly along with the horses while not losing their stripes," Miss Emily explained.

Lucas lifted his wineglass in a salute. "It's a perfect metaphor."

Kendra raised her glass also. "Would that all schools were so wise!" She looked wistful at the knowledge that her son would be cantering out of her sight, but she didn't say that. Instead, she smothered a yawn. "Please excuse my rudeness, but it's been a long day. I'm ready to retire."

"By all means." Lady Agnes rose. "I'll leave the gentlemen to their port and see you at breakfast. Christopher will be brought over here for his skill testing, and you can say good-bye properly then."

Kendra nodded and withdrew, as did Lady Agnes and Miss Emily. When the women were gone, General

Rawlings cocked an eye at Lucas. "Do you like port, or would you prefer brandy?"

Lucas grinned. "Brandy, please."

He enjoyed talking with the general, who had thoughtful and far-reaching views. If he knew of Lucas's disgrace, and he probably did, he didn't mention it. As a man of wide experience, he apparently recognized the many shades of gray in life.

They each enjoyed a leisurely glass of brandy before Lucas excused himself for the night. The worldly and tolerant Lady Agnes hadn't asked about the relationship between Lucas and Kendra, but she'd assigned them adjacent guest rooms so they could sort it out as they wished.

When he reached his room, Lucas stripped off his coat and cravat and tossed them over a chair, trying not to think that Kendra was a mere wall away, presumably sleeping the sleep of the relieved. All soft womanly warmth... and memories of a night they both agreed shouldn't have happened.

-

Though Kendra was tired when she reached her room, she was too restless to go to bed right away. After changing from her black day wear, she donned her nightgown and robe and slippers, which were a soft ivory. She hoped the day would come when she would feel that she didn't need to wear black as a statement of injustice.

Then she settled at the desk and made a list of things Christopher might need. She suspected that the academy wasn't the sort of place where flaunting wealth was approved of, but she could buy new copies of some of her son's favorite books, like *Robinson Crusoe*. A Bible, of course. Perhaps a small bedside rug so his feet wouldn't land on a cold floor first thing in the morning.

When she finished her list, she had a modest selection of items that might be useful to a new boy at this particular school. She'd show it to Kit and Lady Agnes in the morning to see what they thought.

Then she stretched and took the pins from her hair so she could brush it out. She'd always found the ritual relaxing both physically and mentally.

She'd worked out all the tangles and was almost done when the full emotional force of what had happened this day really struck her. Christopher was *safe!* In the months since Denshire had thrown her out of his house and told her she'd never see her son again, her greatest fears and despair had concerned Christopher. Not knowing where he was had driven her half mad. She had also feared that Denshire would turn her son against her.

But now she had the result she'd wanted above all things. A few weeks before, finding Christopher had seemed impossible. Instead, her brave boy had traveled half the length of England to reach her, and now he was in a safe, supportive school where he could learn and make friends for life.

And on top of that, she had discovered her beautiful young daughter. Though she regretted not raising Caitlin herself, her girl had been loved and cherished, and in the future Kendra would be part of her life.

Joy bubbled through Kendra, so intense and wonderful that it must be shared. And who better to share it with than the man who had been with her every step of the way? Lucas and his friends had made this all possible, and she wanted him to know how much she appreciated that.

She also wanted *him.*

Not bothering to tie back her hair, she silently stepped into the corridor. Light showed around Lucas's door, so she tapped on it, hoping he was still awake.

Before she could have second thoughts, the door opened and there was Lucas, his powerful frame silhouetted against the lamp light and his hair glowing gold. He'd removed his coat and cravat and boots, and he'd unfastened the buttons at the throat of the shirt. There was intimacy in his dishabille and from the flare in his eyes, her nightwear had a similar impact on him even though every inch of her body was covered.

A little uncertainly, she said, "Since you're still awake, may I come in? As I was brushing out my hair, it really sank in that the worst of my problems are over. I feel like Atlas after the weight of the world was removed from his shoulders. Christopher is no longer lost but here in a safe place! A few weeks ago, this was a result almost beyond hoping for, and so much of this I owe to you. I feel like dancing for joy!"

For a moment she feared that Lucas would smile, offer congratulations on a job well done, then politely send her back to her own room. Instead, expression a little rueful, he stepped back so she could come inside. "Alas, we have no musicians, but you do have much to celebrate."

"Everything has become so much better since we met, Lucas." She cocked her head to one side as a thought struck her. "I just realized how much of our early relationship revolved around dancing."

He considered. "You're right. That year when you were presented to society to find a husband and I was in London to gather a bit of polish before going off to sea. We met what, perhaps a half dozen times?"

"Yes, and danced each time. Not all formal balls, several were more informal romps for young people. But I was always glad to see you, and glad when you asked for a dance."

He smiled reminiscently. "I was always glad to get one. As a beautiful young heiress, you were much in demand."

She made a face. "Too often that was because of being an heiress. One of the things I liked about you was that you seemed to have no interest in any inheritance I might have."

"There were other reasons?" he asked with interest.

She laughed. "Oh, yes! You were so handsome and dashing and enjoyable to talk with. There was no waltzing then, though. It was considered such a scandalous dance. Let's waltz now!" She held up her arms and began humming waltz music.

Unable to resist her bubbling spirits, he took her in his arms and spun her across the room, which was large enough to take a couple of turns as long as he kept an eye out for furniture.

"We were so young and life seemed to be overflowing with possibilities, didn't it?" he said nostalgically. "You were a favorite partner when we were at the same event, but there were other young ladies I liked. In the months before I joined my ship, I created a mental gallery of part-ners I particularly enjoyed. I'd contemplate their images in the middle of North Sea gales."

She laughed, easily imagining that and not insulted by the notion that there were other young ladies he'd thought about. "I was looking for a husband and you weren't on the list because you were about to leave for the navy. But you danced well then, as you do now." She tilted her head back, her hair sliding over her shoulders as she resumed humming. "And dancing at a ball brought us together again."

"My dancing was rather rusty when we met at the Clantons' ball," he reminded her.

She shivered as she remembered that night, her exuberance briefly shadowed. "I don't remember rusty dancing, only that you rescued me when everyone else was drawing back as if I were a plague carrier."

"I've wondered. What did you hope to accomplish by storming into the center of that ballroom?" he asked curiously.

She sighed, scarcely able to remember why she'd done such a mad thing. "I suppose I was looking for a friendly face. Someone who might speak for me. Or even *to* me. It wasn't until I was shaking and alone in the middle of the room that I realized how foolish I was."

"Not foolish," he said seriously as he steered them clear of the desk. "Perhaps your instincts were pushing you to break out of your fog of despair."

"Pushing me toward you, perhaps." She realized their dancing was becoming slower, more sensual. "When we first met all those years ago, I never dreamed how important you would become to me."

"Nor did I imagine this, either," he said, his gaze intent.

She loved dancing with him, being in his arms with that strong, masculine body so close to hers. She became very aware of how light and loose her night garments were. They were designed for sleep and perhaps seduction, not protection, and she wanted nothing more than to dance them both to the bed.

He would surely have his doubts about the wisdom of lying together again, but she didn't think he could resist their mutual attraction any more than she could. She had spent so many celibate years with her desire tamped down so far it seemed dead. So had he, from what he'd said. Now that they'd let desire blaze free once, how could they *not* join together again when they had the opportunity?

She murmured, "This could be another night that takes place out of sight and sound of the world. Where becoming lovers doesn't count because no one will know."

"We will, and that is more dangerous than if the world does," he said softly. "But how can I say no when you are in my arms and the most alluring woman in the world?"

"Then don't say no." She ended their dance by moving forward to press her full length against him. She wanted his weight on her, crushing her into the mattress as their bodies moved together in the fiercest and most primal dance of all.

She felt a shudder run through him and he released her hands so he could caress the rest of her body. His palms sliding down her back until he could grip her derriere. His mouth closing over hers, equally giving and demanding, igniting the latent fire between them into a bonfire.

As his kneading hands brought her yearning flesh to sizzling life, she concentrated on his clothing. He was wearing too much. *Pull his shirt from his trousers, caress the heated bare skin of his lower back. Move a hand between them so she could unfasten the fall of his trousers and find the passionate response behind it. Oh, yes…!*

He gasped, his eyes darkening. "It will be… more efficient if you give me a moment to remove my clothing."

"More efficient, perhaps," she said with mock innocence, "but less fun."

He laughed, his eyes warm. "You're a mischievous wench with wickedly roving hands." He moved a step back so she could more easily pull his linen shirt off over his head, then plant butterfly kisses on his bare throat. His trousers were already loosened, so she eased them and his drawers off, caressing his warm skin hungrily.

Then she surveyed her handiwork with satisfaction, loving the sight of his strength and male beauty. They were made for each other, she knew it in every fiber of her being.

While she admired his nakedness, he untied her robe and undid the buttons of her nightdress. Then he drew her garments over her head with one swift movement, leaving her bare except for her slippers.

She was suddenly shy of him seeing her fully naked. She was no flawless young maiden. She'd borne two children and carried scars from her marriage.

But his eyes showed only desire. "You are so intoxicatingly womanly," he said in a low, raw voice. "Made to be worshipped in every way a man can show devotion."

His words gave her a visceral understanding of the wedding service: *With my body I thee worship.* Before tonight, they'd been only words, but now they resonated through her. They weren't married; perhaps they never would be. But even without vows, they could come together as lovers, and she wanted that most desperately.

She took his right hand and held it over her heart. "Let us worship each other together on this night out of time."

His warm hand clasping hers, he bent into a deep, passionate kiss as their bare bodies pressed together. Their arms encircled each other and she found her hips rolling against him, wanting what was so close and needing to be closer yet.

"I want to make love with you slowly, savoring every touch, every kiss," he gasped. "And yet..."

With one long arm he turned back the covers on the bed, then twisted her onto the smooth sheets and came down with her, his body crushing into hers as she'd desired, his kisses ravishing her sense and her senses. Her hands clawed with need, wanting to meld them together, and her legs separated in a silent plea that they join.

A plea he answered without words, only a long, desperate groan as he entered her welcoming body. She bit his shoulder to express the fierceness of their coupling, then shattered under the touch of his clever fingers, all sensation and a fire so intense she was barely aware when he withdrew. They culminated together but not joined, and she had just enough awareness to feel a distant thread of regret.

They had shared almost everything she desired.

For now, *almost* would have to be enough.

Chapter 27

As Lucas lay with Kendra in his arms, he wondered if his heart might actually explode in his chest. But no, it was slowing down to a more normal pace, along with his breathing. He murmured into her tangled hair, "Slow savoring wasn't a very reasonable plan, was it?"

She laughed and the rich fullness of her magnificent breasts pulsed against him. "Not when there was so much pent-up desire on both sides. But the night is young. Who knows what might happen before I must slip back to my room so we can be found alone in our own beds?"

"I think the night still holds interesting possibilities, but in the morning, we must return to decorum," he said gravely. "If we are to publicly confront Denshire with his sins, you must do so as a virtuous woman. If you are known to have a lover, your quest for justice will turn into a public pillorying of you. It would be ugly, perhaps even uglier than the initial divorce."

After a long silence, she said, "I know you're right. I want to have the high ground so I can condemn Denshire to the gutter. But even if I stand unsullied on that high ground with my sword of justice upraised – what if it makes no difference? What if Denshire merely resumes his assaults on my fortune and his claims that he owns Christopher and I have no rights in my own family? What if the Archbishop of Canterbury can't or won't lift a hand to help me? What then?"

He sighed and skimmed his hand along the smooth arc of her back. "I don't think you'll be any worse off in terms of your status, though you will almost certainly feel emotionally shattered at first. I can bring a bill accusing Denshire of criminal fraud in the House of Lords as I suggested before. I don't know if there is any legal recourse beyond that."

She slid her fingers into his hair, petting him like a cat. "Have you ever thought about living with me openly and be damned to the consequences?"

He had considered it, and the prospect was as alluring and dangerous as Eve's apple: to have her companionship in bed and out, but to be disdained by most of society; to have children who were bastards. "I've thought about it. I would prefer better for both of us."

"So would I." She sighed. "We don't always get what we want. Sometimes we have to make do with what we can get."

"That's one of life's most necessary lessons, and one of the hardest."

After a long silence, she said, "I've been thinking about my grand confrontation with my former husband at the Duchesses' Ball. Part of me wants to hurl my words like arrows into his arrogant, angry face, but I don't know if I would do that well. I might lose my temper and turn into a screaming fishwife. Even if I don't, will a woman be listened to as carefully as a man?"

He frowned. "The story is yours, and surely you're the best qualified to tell it."

"Perhaps, but I might be considered a weak, whiny woman. Would you present my case? You have a beautiful speaking voice, and as a man you'll be listened to."

He was silent for long moments. "My reputation is not unsullied. My dishonor might reflect on you."

"But who better understands my situation?" After a silence of half a dozen heartbeats, she added almost inaudibly, "Who else can I trust as much?"

Simon could be trusted with anything, but he hadn't been at Kendra's side through her difficult journey. "I suppose that could be considered an extension of my bodyguard services. But it might reinforce the idea that we're lovers."

"People will think that anyhow," she said with a slight laugh. "But they won't have proof."

"Gossips don't need proof. In fact, it gets in the way of their enjoyment." He gave his head a quick shake. "Very well, I will speak for you but you must also be there and be prepared to chime in as necessary. We can work out in advance what needs to be said, and what witnesses we'll have present. But you realize that no matter how carefully we consider the possibilities, events are likely to turn in a direction we've never considered."

"I know you're right, but considering possibilities will fill in the time while we wait."

"A fortnight of worry won't be of much aid. I intend to go to Lady Kirkland's infirmary and help as many people in pain as will hold still to let me treat them," he said firmly. "I suggest you go to Zion House and start working with small children who are eager to learn. Turning one's mind to the troubles of others is a good way to put one's own troubles into perspective."

"You're absolutely right. I'll go to Zion House," she said. "I'll also cross swords with the Fencing Females at Angelo's Academy. I'll write discreet letters to my children so they'll know they aren't forgotten. But all that begins tomorrow." She raised her face and kissed his throat. "The rest of this night belongs to us."

"Let's not waste another moment of it," he murmured.

They didn't.

—

Kendra was still feeling buoyant when they drove away from the Westerfield Academy the next morning. "I like knowing that I'll be coming back here regularly for years to come."

Lucas was guiding the horses around the turn onto the London road, but he gave her a quick glance. "The school and estate both feel warm and welcoming, don't they? It's good that Lady Agnes intends to keep the school fairly small so that all her students can receive the attention they need. If the school became too large, it would change its personality."

Kendra nodded. "I'm glad she found a place for Christopher so quickly. She was right that by this morning he'd be adjusted to the school. He was chattering so happily about his roommate Bobby and his big brother Benjamin and the other Hawks that I don't think he'll miss me at all."

Lucas smiled. "You want him to be happy and making friends and learning, but I suspect that there's a small maternal part of you that regrets the fact that he doesn't need you as much as he did."

"You're exactly right," she said ruefully. "Christopher has been the center of my life since he was born. Now

I'm trying to accept gracefully the fact that he's moving into his own life and I am less important to him."

"You're his mother and will always be important to him. Don't forget that he made his way half the length of Britain to find you," Lucas pointed out. "And remember that as he becomes more independent, you will have more freedom to move into a new life for yourself."

Yes, but what would her new life look like? She'd have a better idea after the Duchesses' Ball. She studied Lucas's calm, rather enigmatic profile and wondered uncomfortably if he would be part of her future. The first night they'd spent together she'd said she would like to have a child with him, which was true but perhaps something that shouldn't have been said at that time. And during their second splendid night just hours ago, she'd asked if he'd ever considered living with her without marriage.

In the clear light of day, she realized that she'd said too much, too soon. For all his kindness and perception, she wasn't sure what Lucas really thought of her. He seemed to enjoy her company and he was certainly attracted to her. She also knew that having committed himself to helping and protecting her, he'd stand by her no matter what the consequences to his own life.

But if she was never legally able to marry, would living with her be too high a price for him to pay? Since they had become lovers, he would probably consider himself honor bound to stay with her.

Yet doing so would mean he wouldn't have a legitimate son to inherit his title. If Camden Keep was entailed, a natural-born son wouldn't be able to inherit it.

He would also be depriving himself of the chance to find a woman whom he could love wholeheartedly, as Simon and Suzanne loved. There were many things that bound Kendra and Lucas together, but she wasn't sure that a deep and lasting mutual love was one of them.

She bit her lip, reminding herself that once more she was worrying about things that hadn't happened yet, and that might never happen. After the Duchesses' Ball, she should have a clearer sense of her future.

She hoped so. And if that meant freeing Lucas to live the life he truly wanted – well, she'd try to have the strength to do that with grace and gratitude.

In the meantime... "When we're back in London, I'll send Lady Kirkland a note to find out when it would be convenient for me to come and see if I can make myself useful."

"If you work with small children, try to teach them how not to break their bones and dislocate their joints so they need me!" Lucas said fervently.

She laughed. "I'll do my best."

Because that was the most one could ever do.

Chapter 28

Kendra and Lucas were relieved to find that there had been no dramatic events during the time they were away from London. Denshire hadn't appeared again at Thorsay House, for which the Browns were grateful, and Suzanne informed them that plans for the Duchesses' Ball were going well. Denshire had sent his acceptance immediately and was surely pleased to be invited.

A note to Lady Kirkland brought a return note suggesting the next morning as a good time for Kendra to come to Zion House for a tour and to determine where Kendra would best fit in. Because Lucas was also going there to hold a clinic for patients with bone and joint problems, they traveled over together.

Zion House had a separate entrance from the infirmary, and it also had guards with military experience to keep the peace in case an angry husband came to try to drag his wayward wife home. A brisk older woman led them to Lady Kirkland's office.

"Oh, good, Kendra!" Lady Kirkland said as she stood up from her desk. "You're just in time to save me from having to go over the month's accounts."

Kendra laughed. "I'm happy to rescue you, Laurel! Do you spend most of your days working here?"

"No, the regular staff is very capable so I'm usually here two or three mornings a week just to keep an eye on things." The countess grinned. "Shall I start with the general house tour, or shall I take you right upstairs to the children's school?"

"The children, please!"

Lucas smiled, knowing that would be Kendra's answer. "I'll leave you to learning the ways of Zion House while I go to the infirmary for a jolly morning setting bones."

Laurel chuckled. "You sound very like my brother when he has a day of surgery ahead of him. Enjoy yourself!"

"I will. Kendra, I'll see you later." Bonesetting kit in hand, Lucas headed for the infirmary, but before going to the clinic, he decided to visit the apothecary, Mrs. Simmons.

He found her whistling cheerfully as she worked on sorting dried herbs to use in one of her medications. She looked up at his entry and got to her feet, wiping her hands with a towel. "Lord Foxton! Have you come to check up on your drunken raisins? I set the gin and raisins in a warm place so the gin would evaporate quickly and I could test them."

He grinned. "I came to say hello. But since you raised the subject, have the raisins been helpful?"

"They have!" She flexed the fingers on her right hand. "With just a few days of use, the pain is in a fair way to be gone. I also tried the raisins on some of my regular patients who have bad arthritis. I gave it to six people besides me. Three had good results, two thought there was some benefit, and the last one said the raisins didn't help his joint pain, but he was willing to test different kinds of gin to see what worked best."

"That sounds similar to results I've seen. I'm glad you're one of the people who has had the best result," Lucas said.

"As for testing the gin, I've found others who volunteered to do the same thing."

"They can buy their own gin! But I'll be offering the drunken raisins to other arthritis patients, and I thank you for the remedy," the apothecary said. "Have you had time to write out your best salve recipes?"

With all that had been happening lately, he hadn't. "Not yet, I've been traveling. But I will," he promised.

"Now it's time for me to go down to the infirmary and see if any bones need rearranging."

"Because you let them know yesterday when you'd be coming in, I'm sure there will be several patients waiting for you." Dismissing Lucas, Mrs. Simmons returned to sorting her dried herbs.

Downstairs in the infirmary reception area, Lucas was welcomed by a male assistant named Reg, who escorted him to a treatment room where a woman with a broken wrist was waiting. The assistant stayed to help with the next several patients who came in with bone and joint problems. Lucas was able to help them all, which made for a satisfying morning.

They ran out of patients just before noon, and Reg left to work elsewhere. Lucas was thinking about going in search of Kendra when a tall, fair-haired man around his own age entered the room. He was dressed as a gentleman and didn't have any obvious injury, and he bore a distinct family resemblance to Lady Kirkland.

Rising, Lucas asked, "Are you Lord Romayne, Lady Kirkland's brother?"

"I am indeed." The newcomer offered a hand. "I've been away from London, but now that I'm back, I wanted to meet you, Foxton. I hear good things about your work."

Lucas shook hands, but said self-deprecatingly, "I'm pleased to meet you, but I'm a mere bonesetter. You, I understand, are a surgeon, physician, the infirmary's medical director, and I believe an ordained minister?"

Romayne laughed and sat in one of the chairs. "Guilty as charged, but credentials don't mean much when a man is in agony from a serious joint injury and it's beyond my ability to fix. I can take care of simple dislocations, but I'm told you've successfully treated more complex problems. According to my sister, you learned your trade traveling with a Belgian Franciscan friar?"

"Yes, Frère Emmanuel came from a family that had been bonesetters for generations." Lucas took his seat again. "He taught me what he knew, and I gather that some of his techniques aren't well known here."

Romayne frowned. "Personally, I think the more we share medical knowledge, the better for everyone, but bonesetting families are famously protective of their secrets. Would you consider teaching others your techniques?"

"The idea has crossed my mind," Lucas admitted, "but I haven't known quite where to start."

"I can help with that," Romayne said. "I never thought to inherit a title. I was a rather distant cousin to the heir, and when I inherited, I resented the fact that managing estates would cut into my medical practice. I've since realized the advantages of money and influence and I've founded cottage hospitals in several towns. Each also trains nurses. The program has been quite successful, so I can help you organize training for your bone work."

"I like that idea," Lucas said. "I was out of England for some years and I'm now trying to figure out how to arrange my time to take care of my responsibilities and still be able to do healing work. Working as a bonesetter and also teaching sounds very rewarding."

Romayne grinned. "I married a woman experienced in estate management. I suggest you do the same. It will leave you more time to treat those in need of your particular skills."

"I may do that," Lucas said, though it might not be possible to marry the woman he knew who had those skills. "I'm planning to arrange my work here at regular times so people who need my skills will know when to come in."

Romayne nodded. "That would be best. You're a very welcome addition to this infirmary, Lord Foxton." He pulled out his watch and checked the time, then stood. "Sorry, I have to leave now. But I look forward to talking to you more." He smiled in a way that was very like his sister's. "And to taking full advantage of your abilities."

Lucas also stood. "Easy to see that you and Lady Kirkland are brother and sister!"

"Yes, but we only exploit people for very good reasons. Until next time." Then Romayne was gone. Lucas suspected that they were going to become good friends. But now it was time to find Kendra.

—

The nursery and children's classes were on the top floor of the sprawling building. "Zion House is larger than I expected," Kendra observed as Laurel led her up the stairs and then the length of the building.

"Yes, we were fortunate to be able to buy this warehouse and modify it to suit our needs. It's built in the shape of a large hollow rectangle. Originally that was for secure storage, but we were able to put a garden inside so our residents can go outdoors in safety." She paused at a window and gestured outside. "See?"

Kendra looked down at the colorful rectangle that was surrounded on all sides by Zion House. There were paths and benches, trees and flowerbeds rioting with spring blooms. There was even a small playing field at one end where a group of children were running around. "How perfect! A safe place where everyone can get sunshine and fresh air. How many residents do you have?"

"Usually around a hundred but the number varies. Many come here in transition, often women who have left abusive men and brought their children with them. We have different kinds of classes for those who need job skills. Once they're trained, we help them find work. A few stay on and become staff members."

They stopped in front of a door. Squeals and giggles sounded on the other side. "Prepare yourself," Laurel said with a grin. "Can you tell stories? That's always popular."

"I told stories to my son," Kendra said cautiously. "I'm willing to try."

Laurel opened the door to reveal a sunny room with a dozen or so children ranging from toddlers up to about age five. The walls were painted a cheerful yellow, and shelves at the left end held toys and dolls. A large oval rag rug covered the center of the room, and small chairs and tables were clustered at the right end of the room.

A rather harried girl of fifteen or sixteen was watching over the youngsters. She looked up with relief when Laurel and Kendra entered. "I'm glad to see you, ma'am!"

"You go down to the kitchen and get a cup of tea, Emma," Laurel said. "Miss Kendra and I will be here for a while."

As the girl gratefully escaped, Laurel said to the children, "Good day! Would you like to hear a story?"

"Oh, yes!" They squealed and gathered around Laurel, clutching her skirts and demanding attention. Laurel laughed and greeted them by name. As the group settled down, Laurel said, "Say hello to Miss Kendra. She's the one who will be telling you a story today."

"*Hello, Miss Kendra!*" exclaimed the children in a ragged treble chorus as they examined the new visitor.

They were as adorable as a box full of puppies. Kendra wanted to hug them all. "Would you like to hear the story of Dick Whittington's cat?" she asked. She had told that one to Christopher so well that she knew it by heart.

A chorus of approval sounded. Laurel indicated a low chair in the center of the rag rug. "A good choice. I look forward to hearing it, too."

Knowing her ability to deal with small children was being evaluated, Kendra settled on the chair in a flurry of skirts and started in the traditional way. "Once upon a time..." The children folded onto the floor around her, entranced.

Kendra acted out the parts, including the sounds of Bow Bells summoning Dick to stay in London because some day he would become Lord Mayor. She thought her meow for the cat was quite fine – it made the children laugh.

As Kendra recounted the old tale, she studied her audience. Some were too thin. A couple had fading bruises. Many wore clothing that was clean but patched and worn.

One little redheaded girl hung shyly at the edge of the circle. Not breaking the rhythm of the story, Kendra extended an arm and beckoned her closer. When the girl approached, Kendra put an arm around her thin shoulders and drew the child to her side. The little redhead gave a small sigh and relaxed against her.

When Dick Whittington and his cat had triumphed, Kendra started another story about a princess who would rather ride her pony than dress up in princess clothes. There was some autobiography in that one!

Laurel watched from her place by the doorway, approval on her face. As Kendra finished the princess story, young Emma returned, looking fortified by her tea.

Laurel said, "It's time for your naps, my little friends. Say thank you to Miss Kendra!"

There was a chorus of *thank yous* and a number of hugs around Kendra's lower legs. Then the children pulled ragged but clean blankets from a box by the toys and curled up on the floor under Emma's watchful eye.

Kendra was smiling as Laurel guided her from the room. "You've a talent for working with the young ones," Laurel said. "I hope you have lots more stories!"

Kendra laughed. "I've always been good at making them up. Besides, in my experience, small children usually like hearing favorite stories over and over."

"Dick Whittington's cat is destined to become a favorite," Laurel said with a smile as she headed to the stairs that led to the building's middle floor. "Now it's time for the rest of the tour. After we go by the classrooms, we'll visit the kitchens and dining room on the ground floor. All meals are prepared there and aspiring cooks are trained."

The more she saw, the more impressed Kendra was. "You've really created something very special and valuable here. Have you thought of establishing other Zion Houses in other cities?"

"Actually, the first one was in Bristol, where I grew up. I set up Zion House in conjunction with my brother's free infirmary when I saw abused women who desperately needed sanctuary. It's still thriving." Laurel smiled impishly. "Once I was able to start plundering my husband's deep pockets, additional Zion Houses were established. With more on the way!"

The woman was a living saint, Kendra decided. And would surely deny the idea if Kendra said so out loud. "I'm honored to be part of this."

"I know you'll contribute a great deal, and it works both ways. You'll find great satisfaction and wonderful friends here." Laurel's tone became more businesslike when they reached the bottom of the stairs, then turned and stopped in front of a door with an elegant silhouette of a fashionable woman on the door.

"All the adult classrooms are on this floor," she explained. "Most women know basic sewing, but here we teach tailoring and professional-quality dressmaking."

Laurel opened the door a few inches. Inside, a woman standing on a platform was having a morning gown fitted to her under the supervision of a very grand older woman. Voice low, Laurel said, "We're fortunate that some of the best modistes in London volunteer their time here." Her voice turned musing. "Women who have gone through hard times are the backbone of all the Zion Houses."

Kendra was one such woman, so that made perfect sense to her. This was a place where women who had been broken could be rebuilt. "What other skills are taught here?"

"It depends on who joins our community. A milliner whose husband destroyed her business and stole all her money took refuge here, and she taught very popular millinery classes. Now she has her own shop again in another town far from her horrible husband, but one of her best students teaches millinery classes in her place.

"We also have classes for women who want to become housekeepers since that's a secure, well-respected position. Some residents take housekeeping along with lady's maid classes so they can present themselves as multitalented servants who can be employed in smaller households."

Kendra asked, "How do the women trained here do after they leave?"

"Generally they do very well. We've established relationships with several agencies that supply servants."

"There's no end to the wonderful work you do!" Kendra exclaimed.

"If someone comes up with what seems like a good idea, we give it a try if it's possible." Laurel stopped at a door marked with the image of a fashionable woman's head and shoulders and opened it partway. "This is the lady's maid classroom."

Kendra peered in and saw a slim blond woman demonstrating how to style hair. It was past time for Kendra to hire a lady's maid herself. Perhaps Laurel could suggest a suitable woman who had trained here. This woman's deft hands looked very capable.

The woman teaching the class turned so Kendra could see her face. She was slender, blond, pretty, and in her early twenties. Kendra gasped in shocked recognition.

Jerking away from the door, she pressed her back against the corridor wall, shaking. She'd just seen a woman she'd thought was dead.

Chapter 29

Swiftly Laurel closed the classroom door. "Kendra, what's wrong?"

Kendra closed her eyes and tried to stop shaking. "The woman teaching the class. She's my maid, Molly Miller. She disappeared from Denshire House the night my husband drugged me and created the false scene that painted me as a disgraceful slut."

Kendra's mind was swamped with the nightmarish memory of an increasingly frantic Molly trying to shake her awake, but Kendra couldn't move, couldn't talk. As she sank into blackness, she'd known that she was dying...

Kendra opened her eyes and drew a deep, steadying breath. "More recently, one of your husband's agents briefly joined the Denshire household and reported that Molly had run away in panic that night, but even though she wasn't murdered then, I feared that a young woman alone in London with no money or friends might be dead by now."

"She obviously found her way here," Laurel said in a soothing voice. "She calls herself Polly Miller."

"That makes sense because Molly and Polly are both nicknames for Mary, which is her real name," Kendra said as she felt her shock fade. "She must have been afraid of being found."

Laurel's brow furrowed thoughtfully. "She was certainly terrified when she arrived. She had nothing but the rather ragged clothes on her back. She barely spoke at first and she wouldn't set foot outside except in the walled garden. In the beginning, she worked in the kitchen, but after several weeks, she said that she'd been a lady's maid who fled when her mistress's husband threatened her. When I learned that, I asked if she'd teach in the lady's maid course. She's a good teacher. She's settled down here and seems content."

"I'm so glad to know that," Kendra said. "But I need to talk to her."

"Of course." Laurel cocked her head at the sound of church bells in the distance. "This class is almost over. Do you want to go in now, or wait till she comes out?"

"I'll wait." Kendra used the time to calm her nerves. She'd tried not to spend too much time worrying about Molly's likely fate since nothing could be done to help the situation. Now she felt an enormous relief, and intense curiosity. She needed to hear Molly's account of events because the girl might make a good witness at the Duchesses' Ball.

The classroom door opened and students from young to middle-aged streamed from the room, chattering happily about the lesson and speculating on what was for dinner. When the stream ended, Kendra entered the room, with Laurel behind her.

Her former maid was collecting the materials she'd used for the class. Voice under control, Kendra said, "Molly?"

Molly looked up and gasped with shock, dropping the hairbrush she'd been holding. "Your ladyship!" She backed away, looking on the verge of tears. "I'm so sorry!"

"For what?" Kendra asked. "I'm delighted to find you well! When you vanished from Denshire House, I feared you were dead."

Molly sank into a chair and began crying. "I abandoned you to those horrible men! You were unconscious and I couldn't wake you. I found Lord Denshire and told him that you were very ill and a physician must be called. He gave a nasty laugh and said it was none of my business and not to say anything or I'd regret it.

"Then he called over Brody, his big brute of a footman, and ordered that I be locked up in the cellar." Molly swallowed convulsively. "He… he said that Brody could have me later. Brody was dragging me to the cellar by my wrist. We were on the steps when I managed to yank free, then give him a shove that knocked him the rest of the way down the stairs. I bolted from the house without stopping for anything."

"Good for you!" Kendra rested a soothing hand on Molly's shoulder. "If I'd had the chance, I would have pushed that brute down the stairs myself!"

"But I abandoned you to be assaulted when you'd always been so good to me!" Her tears intensified. "Later I heard what happened. They said that three of Denshire's friends swore you'd bedded them that night, and that Denshire divorced you because of what you did. But you were unconscious! You didn't choose to let those men lie with you. And I did *nothing* to help you!"

"Molly, look at me." Kendra raised the girl's chin and looked into her tear-washed blue eyes. "What could you have done? You'd just come to London with me and didn't know anyone. Would pounding on a neighbor's door have brought help or more trouble? You did the only thing you could. You saved yourself." She gave a twisted smile. "I've been feeling dreadful because I believed I was the cause of your death. I'm so relieved that you're here and well!"

"But I abandoned you there to be ravished!"

"Actually, I wasn't ravished," Kendra said. "Denshire drugged me so I couldn't interfere with his wicked scheme. He got his friends drunk, then sent a courtesan he'd hired who looked like me to seduce them. When they swore in court that they'd bedded me, they believed they were telling the truth."

Molly blinked through her tears. "That's... very strange."

"Denshire is a very strange man. Much stranger now than when I married him," Kendra agreed. "How did you come to Zion House?"

"With no money or friends, I was afraid I'd have to turn to the streets to survive." She shuddered. "After two days sleeping in the corner of a cemetery while I looked for work, I went into the church to pray for help. I was weeping in the lady chapel when a woman who had been arranging flowers came to ask me what was wrong. When I told her, she said that I should go to Zion House and told me how to get here. So... I did." She wiped her eyes with her wrist. "The people here have been everything that is kind."

"We try our best," Laurel said quietly.

The classroom door opened and Lucas entered. "Kendra?" He halted when he saw the three women clustered together. "Is something wrong?"

Kendra straightened. "Something's very right, actually. I've found Molly Miller, my maid. She made her way here after escaping Denshire House, and she's now teaching classes on how to become a lady's maid."

After a startled moment, Lucas crossed the room with a warm smile for Molly. "What wonderful news! Kendra has worried about you."

Molly was watching him warily, so Kendra made a quick introduction. "Molly, this is Lord Foxton, an old friend of mine. He's been extremely helpful. We're trying to find a way to clear my reputation."

"You could be very helpful in that, Miss Miller," Lucas said as he took a seat, not too close since he'd seen Molly's nervousness. "We're assembling witnesses to prove that Denshire falsely accused your mistress of adultery in order to divorce her."

"Tell him what happened to you that night, Molly," Kendra asked.

The maid repeated her story as before in halting words. When she was done, Lucas said gravely, "Your evidence could be very useful. Will you describe the truth of what happened when we challenge Denshire about his vile lies?"

Molly shrank back. "A court is no place for people like me!"

"This wouldn't be a law court," Kendra said. "We've arranged a social event where we'll confront Denshire with people who will give the lie to his account of what happened. Your story would prove that I was drugged that night."

Lucas added in a steely voice, "You will be protected. You have my word on that."

Molly's uncertain gaze moved from Lucas to Kendra. Kendra said nothing, but she held Molly's gaze. If the girl felt that she had failed her mistress, here was her chance to make up for it, but Kendra would not pressure her.

Molly gave a jerky nod. "If it will bring you justice and I will be safe, then yes, I will bear witness."

"Thank you," Kendra said quietly. She rose to her feet. "Laurel, I hope you want me to come back regularly. More stories on Thursday morning?"

"You'll be most welcome," Laurel said as she also stood. "I'll show you the rest of Zion House then. Today has been most eventful for you, and for you also, Molly."

Molly gave a crooked smile. "Yes, but I feel better now."

"As do I." Kendra squeezed Molly's hand briefly, then left the room with Lucas.

"Storytelling?" Lucas asked as they headed down to the ground floor, then outside to the nearby livery stable where he'd left his horse and carriage.

"Yes, I may have found my niche," she said with a chuckle. "I told the story of Dick Whittington and his cat and enjoyed it as much as the children did."

"Stories are important because they bring a sense of wonder," Lucas said. "Even more so for children who have had a hard time of it."

"Yes, that's it exactly! In the version of the story I know, Dick Whittington started as a poor orphan, and ended as a rich, successful man."

"And the cat was treated with great respect and immortalized," Lucas said solemnly, but with his eyes twinkling.

"A good outcome for all. I'm going to prefer telling the stories with happy endings. The real world has enough grief," she said thoughtfully.

He nodded and ended the conversation since they'd reached the livery stable and he needed to retrieve his carriage. When they were inside and heading back to

Mayfair, Kendra asked, "Could you take me to Duval House? I want to tell Suzanne what happened."

"Of course. Molly is a valuable witness." He gave Kendra a wry smile. "The Duchesses' Ball is going to be very interesting."

An understatement. But despite all their good witnesses, Kendra couldn't help wondering if any of them would matter when Denshire had already won his divorce. Would she always be the loser?

Chapter 30

The next day was Wednesday, so Kendra donned her fencing costume to go to Angelo's to cross swords with other Fencing Females. She was collected by Lucas and Simon. She knew they enjoyed sparring together, but guessed that Simon made a point of going on the same days as Lucas to ensure that his almost-brother had a partner.

She was greeted warmly by the other female fencers. She'd never felt such a sense of camaraderie with another group of women. All of them were strong, kind, tolerant, and had a bit of an odd kick in their gallop. Kendra had found her tribe.

Cassie Wyndham was present and challenged her to a first bout that left them both laughing and gasping for air. "You're improving really quickly!" Cassie said. "You could have had a serious career causing mayhem."

"No, thank you. If I'm getting better, it's because I have such talented opponents," Kendra said as she pushed sweat-dampened hair from her forehead.

As Athena Masterson engaged with her sister-in-law Kiri, Kendra glanced around the large studio and saw Lucas and Simon sparring intensely. With the practice Lucas had been getting, he'd improved, and now he and Simon each won almost equal numbers of bouts.

Kendra was ready to find another opponent when the door opened and three of the Rogers brothers entered. There was Godfrey, the crippled youngest brother with lines of pain etched in his face. Behind him was his oldest brother, Patrick, the cavalry officer who had fought Lucas the first time they'd met. They were accompanied by a middle brother whose name Kendra didn't know, but who was clearly a Rogers.

Godfrey limped in on his crutches, then stopped, enraged at the sight of Lucas. "*You* again! Why does a disgraced man insist on engaging in what should be a pastime for honorable gentlemen?"

Kendra swore silently when she saw Lucas's tight expression. A pity that Henry Angelo wasn't here. He would shut this nonsense down before it spiraled out of control. But he was away this morning and his young assistant hadn't enough natural authority.

She'd always sensed that Lucas wasn't fully at peace with himself about the way he'd escaped the French prison. His head might believe he'd had no choice, but his spirit, which had been raised in the English gentleman's code of honor, still carried a burden of guilt and self-hatred for breaking his parole.

As Godfrey opened his mouth for more insults, Kendra's temper snapped and she stalked across the room to confront Godfrey, pointing her fencing foil at him. "Enough! Godfrey Rogers, I have a nine-year-old son who is more mature than you are. You aren't allowed to have tantrums and spew insults at another man without explaining your grievance. A wound uncleansed turns lethal. It's time to end this nonsense!"

Patrick Rogers took a furious step toward her. "I knew it was a mistake to allow women in here!" He cast a disapproving but fascinated glance over her black-pantalooned legs. "Don't you *dare* threaten my brother!"

"I'm not threatening him. By clinging so tightly to his pain and anger, Godfrey has become his own worst enemy, and his protective big brothers aren't helping!" Kendra retorted. "As I said, it's time this feud was explained so there is a chance of ending it. Godfrey and Patrick, come into the back room. Lucas and Simon, come also. I will attend as the referee, because any woman who has raised children knows something about settling disputes without bloodshed. Now *move!*"

She pointed her sword at the back room, and after a stunned moment, Lucas strode toward it, his expression determined. Simon followed.

Godfrey was shaking on his crutches, close to falling. In a much softer voice, Kendra said, "Believe me, painful truths are better revealed than allowed to fester inside. What is said in that room will be forever private if that is what you wish. But you owe Lucas and your brothers the full story."

Face white, Godfrey lurched toward the back room on his crutches. Patrick followed. The middle Rogers started to follow also, but she waved her blade in a blocking motion. "Unknown Rogers brother, you can stand guard outside to make sure no one tries to enter. Each of the principals has one second standing beside him, and I will ensure that the discussion stays on course."

He gaped at her. "I'm William Rogers, and how can I be sure you'll be neutral?"

She caught his gaze. "As a woman, I favor peace over bloodshed. As a mother, I know the necessity for fairness. Will you accept that?"

After a long moment, he nodded agreement and took up position in front of the door as Kendra followed the four men inside. Before the door closed she saw that Athena Masterson had come to stand beside William Rogers. No one would get past those two – and Kendra was grateful to have Athena at her back.

This spacious back room was where Henry Angelo gave private lessons, but it also held chairs and a desk and a long, narrow, padded table where injured fencers could lie down if they needed examination or treatment.

Godfrey folded into one of the chairs, with Patrick looming protectively beside him. Lucas and Simon stood side by side, their expressions calm and impenetrable.

Since none of the men seemed inclined to start the discussion, Kendra addressed herself to Godfrey. "I was present the first time you and Lord Foxton met here. You accused him of being responsible for your crippling injury. Foxton didn't understand why you were accusing him, and you refused to explain, saying he should know what he'd done. Am I remembering correctly?"

His gaze on the floor, Godfrey nodded. Not a very articulate young fellow. He must have been barely out of the schoolroom when he became a midshipman.

Guided by intuition, Kendra said, "In my experience, I've found that if someone doesn't want to discuss a fraught situation, it's because they carry some guilt over their own part in it. Is that true in this case?"

Godfrey's head jerked up. He licked dry lips before saying, "Yes. I hold Lucas Mandeville responsible for the accident that crippled me, but I… also behaved foolishly."

"Please explain why you feel the way you do," Lucas said quietly. "If there are amends I can make, give me the chance to make them."

Godfrey drew a shaky breath. "We all looked up to you so much in Bitche. No matter how threatening the situation or how dire, you were always calm, strong, and willing to speak up for other prisoners. Fearing nothing. A true English gentleman. All of us younger officers admired you so much." His mouth twisted. "Then when you were on parole in the town, you broke that parole and escaped! Hearing that news was… crushing. A betrayal of the principles of honor that we all valued. I almost didn't believe it, but you were gone, abandoning the rest of us."

"I can tell you more about why I escaped, but later," Lucas said, his searching gaze on the other man. "Tell me how my actions led to your disabling accident."

His brother Patrick was frowning down on him, but Godfrey continued to speak, his words halting. "Your betrayal made me question my own devotion to honor. I was *furious*. I wanted to be like you and escape to freedom, yet at the same time, I hated you for your dishonorable behavior. After stewing for a fortnight or two, on impulse I decided that if you could escape, so could I and be damned to the consequences."

"You were injured in your escape attempt?" Kendra asked softly.

Godfrey's gaze locked on Lucas. "You know how impregnable the Bitche fortress is. How steep the walls. How dangerous any escape attempt from the fortress would be."

"But breaking out of the prison would not be breaking parole," Lucas said. "Not like walking away from the town as I did."

Godfrey nodded. "Your walking away from the town was easy, but dishonorable. If I broke out of the fortress, I would be free in an honorable way. I was on the verge of success when my makeshift rope broke, and I crashed to the ground. It felt as if I'd broken half the bones in my body.

"The French guards came to collect me and threw me into a cell with several other prisoners. No medical treatment was provided." He drew a shuddering breath. "The pain was excruciating."

"Yet you didn't die," Lucas said. "You must have great strength of will."

"I wanted to die!" Godfrey said savagely. "But my fellow prisoners did everything they could to preserve my worthless life. They set my bones as well as they could, shared rations with me and offered words of comfort, telling me how brave I'd been to attempt the escape and how I would surely survive to go home. I hated myself for my failure and I hated you even more for being a… a false idol who had walked away from us laughing." His mouth twisted. "Spoken aloud, my words don't make much sense, do they?"

His brother rested a hand on Godfrey's thin shoulder. "I understand your anger, but perhaps it shouldn't be aimed at Foxton," he said in a comforting voice. "Surely it would have been wiser to hate the French and be grateful to your fellow prisoners."

Lucas shook his head. "Unending pain tends to warp one's thinking. Particularly when a man you've idolized seemed to have betrayed all you believed in and escaped without consequences. I don't believe I deserve to be the target of your pain and anger, but I do understand why you felt that way."

Godfrey looked away, not speaking. Lucas sharpened his voice. "Look at me, Godfrey Rogers, and I'll tell the truth of my imprisonment, escape, and the consequences!"

The younger man swallowed hard, his Adam's apple bobbing, and raised his gaze to Lucas's. When he had Godfrey's attention, Lucas continued in a flat voice, "I didn't realize that I was an inspiration to the younger officers because I was so often in pain myself and doing my best to hide it. The commander of the fort, Colonel Roux, loathed me for the same reasons you put me on a pedestal I didn't deserve. Because he was an officer of peasant origin, he despised me for being a 'damned aristo.' In his eyes I was a rich, spoiled Englishman, unworthy of respect or honor. Roux wanted me to suffer. He was a master of inflicting pain that wouldn't leave permanent marks. So… I suffered."

Wincing, Kendra pressed a hand to her mouth to keep from expressing her horror at his words. From Simon's expression, even he hadn't been told the full truth of Lucas's imprisonment. She sensed that Lucas was only speaking up now because of the need to resolve the murderous conflict between him and Godfrey.

Lucas continued, "Besides physical torture when he had time to amuse himself, Roux played cruel mental games, promising that soon I'd be sent back to England, then tellng me with obvious pleasure that the exchange had fallen through. It wasn't long before I realized that he would never exchange me. Eventually he said so in as many words."

"But the possibility of exchange is an essential part of giving and receiving a parole," Godfrey said, frowning.

"Exactly so. I was trapped between knowing that the promise of parole wasn't real, and my feeling that escaping would be dishonorable." He fell silent for half a dozen heartbeats. "You and I had more in common than simple imprisonment, Godfrey. I, too, wished I was dead."

"That's why you decided to take your chances on escape?" Godfrey asked.

Lucas nodded. "Even if I escaped the town, I knew I'd be hunted down ferociously, but I did it anyhow, not caring whether I lived or died. I was indeed hunted ferociously and was seriously wounded. Luckily I can pass as a Frenchman, which saved my life several times over.

"When I'd run as far as I could and lay dying in Belgium, a Franciscan friar, Frère Emmanuel, was called in to treat me. Like you, I managed to survive, but I was so shamed by breaking my parole that I refused to go home, refused to let the people who loved me know I was alive." He glanced at Simon. "We were raised as brothers, yet I couldn't bring myself to face Simon or my aunt and uncle. I became Frère Emmanuel's servant and companion in a bid for atonement."

Godfrey stared at him. "What persuaded you to come home?"

"Simon hunted me down." Lucas and his almost-brother exchanged a swift, intimate, very brotherly smile.

Lucas continued, "Then when he found me, his wife, the exquisite and practical Suzanne, told me not to *wallow!*" His gaze moved to Kendra. "The women in my life have pointed out that there are rules to parole and the commandant violated them when he said he'd see me dead before he would free me. There was no true bond of honor between us to be broken. Nonetheless, to this day I feel that I am unworthy to be called a gentleman."

Simon winced at that, but didn't speak. There was a long silence before Godfrey said huskily, "I have misjudged you and brought the wrath of my brothers down on you. For that I am sorry. I have no right to ask your forgiveness."

"Nor any need. We were both caught and broken in the hell of war," Lucas said with compassion. "But if you feel that you've done me an unjust injury, there is something you can do to balance the scales between us."

"I will tell my family and friends that I wronged you," Godfrey said heavily. "Is that what you want?"

"That would be appreciated, but my request is different. Frère Emmanuel, the friar I traveled with, came from a long line of highly skilled bonesetters and he taught me everything he knew. From the first time I saw you, I've felt that you might be helped by the skills I've learned. Will you allow me to examine and treat you?"

Chapter 31

Godfrey stared at Lucas, appalled. "You want to push my bones around?"

"That's an oversimplification, but yes," Lucas said, holding the younger man's gaze. "When bones are displaced, they can pinch nerves and cause excruciating pain. The whole body reacts, trying to reduce the pain, and still more misplacements occur. I can't promise that I will return you to what you were before your injury, but I feel reasonably sure I can help you at least a little."

Thinking that she should offer an endorsement, Kendra said, "I saw Lucas perform a miracle. Wouldn't it be worth a try to see what he might be able to do?"

Simon also spoke up. "I was the lucky beneficiary of one of Lucas's miracles. I would have died after Waterloo if not for him."

Godfrey looked from Kendra to Simon before saying with obvious reluctance, "It would be worth trying someday."

"Do it now, not *someday*," Kendra said firmly. "There's a good treatment table right here, and your brother will be standing by to make sure Lucas doesn't do anything you can't bear."

When Godfrey still hesitated, Patrick said fiercely, "Dammit, Godfrey, if there's a chance he can reduce your pain, for God's sake, let him try! I *hate* seeing my little brother in constant agony! All of us do. Once I was thrown from my horse in battle and was in the most shattering pain. I hoped they'd shoot me as well as my horse. I couldn't walk, could barely breathe. Then my sergeant found a local bonesetter, who was summoned and fixed me up better than I would have thought possible."

Lucas looked as if he would like to ask what Patrick's injury had been, but he refrained.

"Very well." Godfrey collected his crutches and lurched to his feet with his brother's help. Then he limped across the room to the treatment table. "Do you want me up or down?" he asked in a brittle tone.

"Take off your coat and boots, then lie facedown, please," Lucas said.

Silently Patrick helped Godfrey out of his coat and helped him to a sitting position on the edge of the table. After tugging off the boots, Patrick eased his brother onto the table, then onto his stomach. There were several painful gasps that everyone pretended not to hear.

Patrick stepped back from the table and glowered threateningly at Lucas. "You'd better not make him worse, Foxton!"

"I will do my best to improve his condition." Lucas had removed his own coat and rolled his sleeves up as he studied the thin body lying in front of him.

In deference to Godfrey's male sensitivity, Kendra withdrew to the door so that she was as far away as she could get without leaving the room. But she could see Lucas drawing into himself to that remote place of prayer and healing.

Voice calm and soothing, Lucas said, "I'll start by examining you, which means feeling the joints and bones to discover whether there are anomalies that can be readily fixed. This will probably be uncomfortable, but it's necessary."

"Go ahead," Godfrey muttered. "I've been mauled about by any number of other medical monsters."

"Were you ever treated by a trained, experienced bonesetter?" Lucas asked as his strong hands began carefully evaluating Godfrey's bones.

"Bunch of quacks!" Godfrey snarled. "Not real doctors."

"Not always," his brother said tersely. "Give Foxton a chance."

Several minutes passed in silence as Lucas performed his evaluation. As he worked, he gave a running commentary on places he'd traveled, injuries he'd healed.

When he finished the evaluation, he ran his knuckles across Godfrey's back between each pair of ribs. Godfrey jerked and gave a sharp cry before slowly relaxing. In a disbelieving voice, he said, "There's less pain! Is that your treatment?"

"This is just a beginning," Lucas said. "The worst of the pains originate in your spine and they affect your hips and knees and from there, your whole body. The force of your fall broke and misaligned the bones, and it will take strong pressure to put them into place. There will be pains, but they shouldn't last long."

Godfrey drew a shuddering breath. "Do your damnedest!"

From across the room, Kendra couldn't see exactly what Lucas was doing, but she sensed that he was pouring all his healing energy into his hands and then into Godfrey's body. Simon had moved beside him and laid what looked like a companionable hand on Lucas's shoulder, but Kendra guessed that he was adding whatever aid he could to supplement Lucas's efforts.

The next interval of time seemed interminable. Lucas worked steadily, but Kendra bit her lip at the occasional strangled sounds from Godfrey. Worse were faint, indescribable sounds that must have been a result of bones being manipulated. Patrick winced every time but made no attempt to interfere with Lucas's treatment.

Finally Lucas rested his hands on Godfrey's upper back, his head bent as if he was utterly exhausted. "I've done what I can for now," he said wearily as he straightened. "We'll see how well this holds."

Godfrey tried moving a little, then more. Tears were running down his face when he pushed himself up with his arms. "Almost all the pain is *gone*," he croaked. "How is that even possible?"

"Realignment of the bones has reduced the terrible pressures on inflamed nerves," Lucas said as he stepped away from the table. "But you'll feel sore and very weak for some time."

Eyes wide with wonder, Godfrey swung his legs over the edge of the table, and promptly crumpled like a limp suit of clothes. Swearing, Patrick caught him before he ended up on the floor. "What the devil is wrong now, Foxton?"

"Your brother's muscles have atrophied because of being used so little and so badly," Lucas explained. "It will take time to rebuild them. Godfrey, you need gentle exercise and daily hot water baths to ease the soreness. You'll be impatient about your progress, but eventually you should regain much of your strength and balance."

Godfrey nodded and gripped one of his brother's arms as he took a cautious step. "I'm weak as a babe in arms,

Patrick, but I can walk without any pain to speak of. It's... hard to imagine life without pain." As his brother led him to a chair, he gazed at Lucas. "Saying thank you doesn't seem like enough, Lord Foxton."

"I'm glad I could help," Lucas said. He was leaning against the treatment table, and Kendra guessed he was holding himself upright by sheer willpower.

"Then let me give you a piece of advice, Foxton," Patrick said gruffly. "Stop acting so damned guilty when anyone looks askance at you. If someone asks about your parole or captivity, just say that the commandant of the facility didn't uphold his end of the bargain, so you escaped. It has the advantage of being the truth. For what it's worth, my brothers and I will spread the word that we misunderstood the situation."

Lucas looked as if the other man had punched him in the stomach. Expression strained, he said, "You think that will stop gentlemen from giving me the cut direct?"

"Eventually. That, plus acting matter of fact about what you did instead of looking as if you were caught stealing a friend's wallet," Patrick said with acid humor.

He turned and helped his younger brother into his coat and boots, then collected the crutches. "Are you sure you don't need these, Godfrey?"

Godfrey stood and took another, surer step toward the door. "Not at the moment. I want to walk out of here on my own two feet." As he reached for the doorknob, he glanced at Kendra. "Are there any more like you out there?"

She shook her head. "I was an only child."

"Good," he muttered as he lurched through the door, but she heard an undertone of amusement in his voice.

He stepped outside, and his brother William cried, "Godfrey, you're walking!!"

When the door closed behind the Rogers brothers' happy reunion, Lucas asked hesitantly, "Simon, do you think he's right? That if I'm confident about what happened in France and don't look guilty, the stain of dishonor will fade?"

Simon's brow furrowed as he considered. "There will always be a few high sticklers who prefer condemnation to understanding, but I think that Major Rogers is right. If you look like you're at peace with yourself, most people will accept that. Scandals fade in time."

"Then today is the day I bury the doubts I've had about what I did," Lucas said quietly.

"It's time," Simon said simply. "I assume that now you just want to collapse into Kendra's arms?"

Lucas managed a crooked smile. "That, please!"

Simon smiled at Kendra, patted Lucas on the shoulder, then returned to the main studio. Kendra crossed the room to where Lucas was supporting himself against the table and wrapped her arms around him. "Miracles don't come cheaply, do they?"

He laughed a little. "I'll recover. I'm just glad I could help that poor devil."

"I wish he'd chosen a target other than you to lash out at!" she said.

Still leaning on the table, he draped himself over her, his arms encircling and his cheek resting against her temple. "You knew, didn't you?"

"Knew what?"

"That I'd never fully made peace with breaking my parole."

"I wouldn't use the same words as Major Rogers, but whenever the subject of your parole came up, you withdrew like a turtle into its shell," she said compassionately. "But it wasn't a true parole when your beastly Colonel Roux meant to hold you captive until you were dead, so you behaved with good sense when you escaped."

"It still *felt* as if I'd committed an act of dishonor," he said slowly. "I never really overcame that feeling. Until tonight. As you said, a wound must be cleansed if it is to heal."

"It seemed like the right time to speak up." She leaned into him, glad she could do something in return for all he'd done for her.

He ran a warm, powerful hand down her back and over her hip with slow appreciation. "Holding you helps me regain my strength." He laughed a little. "Though I'm not yet as strong as I would need to be for what I'd like to do, which is to enjoy another one of those nights that didn't really happen."

She laughed as well. "Angelo's Academy is far too public for any such thing!"

"True." He straightened and took her hand, leading her to the chairs by the side of the room. He sat her down in one and took the next chair for himself. They could hold hands but no more than that. "I'll be glad when the Duchesses' Ball is over. No matter what the outcome, at least it will be behind us."

She nodded, holding his hand tightly. "I feel as if I'm in limbo. We've invited our list of willing witnesses and know what they'll say. We've worked out how you will present the evidence."

"We might want to revise that," Lucas said. "You handled a difficult situation brilliantly tonight. Are you sure you don't want to state your own case?"

She shivered. "I'm sure. Tonight's confrontation wasn't about me, but about you and Godfrey Rogers. It was easy to keep the discussion under control."

He laughed. "You managed it all like a really good nanny. I'm impressed that you got the two Rogers brothers to come in here."

"It's my nanny voice," she said sternly before returning to her normal tone. "I've had some possibly foolish thoughts about how my case should be presented," she said hesitantly. "Not as a mock trial, but as a performance." She sketched out her idea.

"That's brilliant, Kendra!" Lucas exclaimed when she was finished. "This will take some planning and rehearsal, but I think it will be more effective than our original idea. We need to talk to your allies, particularly the Ashtons, since the ball will be at their house. And all your Fencing Females."

She smiled crookedly. "I just hope I can make it to the ball without expiring of nervousness!"

He lifted their joined hands so he could kiss her fingers where they were linked with his. "We'll go on day by day, hour by hour. We'll both continue our volunteer work at Zion House and the infirmary. We'll come here for more fencing exercise. I shall hope I won't be challenged to any more duels by any more Rogers brothers. If we think of any more ways to improve our performance at the ball, we'll add them in."

He leaned across the space between the chairs and brushed a tender kiss on her lips. "And after the ball, perhaps we will both be free."

Her breathing caught as she looked into his eyes. She was beginning to think that perhaps she did know how he really felt about her.

Chapter 32

The fateful night had arrived. Grand carriages rolled between the gates of Ashton House, home of the Duke of Ashton and the largest private home in London. The drive was lit by torches, and a scarlet carpet had been rolled down the steps to where guests would step from their carriages.

Kendra had arrived earlier, consumed by nerves but comforted by the support of the women who had become her friends. They were delighted to be part of this grand occasion and determined to see justice done. Kendra wore a sumptuous black silk gown decorated with jet beads, and she wore a necklace and earrings of black onyx. The black half mask she would don later was clenched in one nervous hand along with her black lace folding fan.

When she'd arrived at Ashton House, she'd been greeted by the official hostesses: the Duchess of Ashton; Lady Julia Randall, daughter of the late duke of Castleton; and Lady Julia's exquisite grandmother, the Duchess of Charente. Mariah studied her costume and said teasingly, "You look like a really beautiful Angel of Death!"

Kendra laughed and relaxed a little. "That was the effect I was hoping for."

Lady Julia said, "We have a whole box full of black armbands for your allies to wear when it's time for the evening's special performance."

"You don't think the idea is mad?" Kendra asked nervously.

"Not at all," the Duchess of Charente said in her charming French accent. "One must first get people's attention to persuade their minds. Stating your case in a performance will fascinate them."

"We've had a program printed for guests," Lady Julia said. "Have you seen it?"

She handed a copy to Kendra. The program described the event as "The Duchesses' Bijoux Ball & Mystery Performance." Under her breath, she said softly, "You haven't met my foster son, Benjamin Thomas, have you? He's the orphaned son of one of Alex's cousins. He goes to school at the Westerfield Academy, where Alex and Ashton and Kirkland and others became loyal friends."

Kendra's gaze shot up. "I've heard of the school."

"Benjamin loves it. If and when you regain custody of your son, you might consider sending him there." Lady Julia smiled warmly. "They have a fine big brother program where older students work with new young ones. Benjamin enjoys doing that."

Aristocratic London was a very small world. Luckily Lady Agnes could be trusted not to reveal that her son was already a Westerfield student. "I'll definitely consider it for Christopher. Do you know if the headmistress, Lady Agnes, will be here tonight? I know an invitation was sent to her."

"She declined with regret, but said we already had quite enough females of ducal blood!"

Kendra laughed. "And countesses past counting!"

A trumpet fanfare sounded from the ballroom. The three hostesses collected themselves. "Time for us to greet arriving guests," Mariah Ashton said. "We'll only have two dances before your performance. We don't want to let the guests drink too much before we start."

The women moved away, heading to the ballroom. All three were petite and exquisitely gowned. They looked like a bouquet of flowers – with spines of pure steel.

Kendra was playing with her black lace fan when Lucas joined her. He also wore black tonight, which set off his blond hair splendidly. A dark prince touched with gold.

"Everything is in readiness," he said. "The stage curtains are pale gold so our black garments will show up well in front of them. The tables are all set up in front of the stage and servants are bringing trays of delicious tidbits to each table."

She smiled a little. "How do you know the food is delicious?"

"I sampled a few pieces, of course. In the interests of ascertaining the quality." His tone was light and he took hold of her hand to calm her restless fingers. "Our special guest witnesses are dining splendidly in the break-fast room, which is small and secluded from the ball. They'll be ready when their turn comes."

She gave him an unsteady smile. "I hope they enjoy their meal. I couldn't eat a bite myself."

"Don't you want to feed those butterflies in your stomach?" he asked with mock surprise.

She laughed and her tension eased a little. "They can wait to be fed."

After that, they spoke little as they waited in the room behind the small theater. Kendra could hear the music playing in the ballroom, which was just beyond the private theater. Mariah Ashton sent a note saying that Denshire had arrived, along with the friends who'd borne witness against her in the parliamentary divorce trial. Mariah said she'd personally escort them to a table in the front row by the stage.

Then another trumpet fanfare rang out. It was the signal for their performance. In the ballroom, the hostesses were explaining that the mystery entertainment was about to begin so guests should move into the theater and find a table. Shuffling feet and light chatter were heard as people entered and found places. The number of guests at the event matched the seating in the theater, so the ball was not "a sad crush," but an exclusive entertainment.

Kendra donned her black mask with numb fingers. "Is this on straight?"

Lucas adjusted the mask slightly. "There. You look splendid and compelling."

"Mariah said that I look like the Angel of Death."

"Not the Angel of Death. The Angel of Justice." Lucas rose and moved to the slit in the back of the curtains to wait for his cue. Kendra joined him and peered out.

In the theater, the Duke of Ashton was giving the three hostesses a gentlemanly hand up the steps to the low stage. Kendra had only met him once, but she liked his obvious intelligence and quiet humor. He had been very willing to volunteer the resources of his house to the night's performance.

The trumpet players gave one last clarion call, then fell silent. As the host, Ashton joined the women on stage, then began in a voice that filled the theater as easily as it filled the House of Lords. Kendra had been told that when the Duke of Ashton spoke, others listened, and as she watched him through the curtain slit, she understood why.

"I'm glad you could all join us tonight for this very special evening," he said in his deep voice. "There will be a full supper later, after more dancing, but enjoy the refreshments on your tables in the meantime. The champagne that is arriving now will quench your thirst during the performance that is about to begin."

He paused, his gaze moving lightly across the audience. "The inspiration for tonight came from our lady hostesses and their friends." He turned and bowed to the duchesses, all of whom were now wearing black armbands as if in mourning.

Straightening, he continued, "Think of this as a mystery play called 'You Be the Judge.' A remarkable tale will be told, and you will decide whether or not you believe it. The principal narrator will be my friend Lord Foxton."

Ashton made an inviting gesture and moved toward the wings as Lucas emerged from his position onto the stage. He bowed to the audience, then began to speak.

"Ladies and gentlemen, our story is a tale of marriage and morality that reflects our society. While a love match is a beautiful thing when it occurs, it's true that even the most modest of men and women also contemplate the monetary benefits of marriage, because a love match is even more beautiful if it has a nice little fortune to go with it."

That produced a ripple of laughter as people sipped their champagne and wondered what would come next. Like Ashton, Lucas had a beautiful speaking voice, rich and flexible. She'd have to ask him to tell the tale of Dick Whittington and his cat.

Lucas continued, "For a man to marry an heiress is as timeless a pursuit as for a lady to marry a lord with a title and fortune. Our tale begins when our protagonist

– we'll call him Lord D. – is accepted by a beautiful young heiress."

This was Kendra's cue to enter in her dramatic black costume. Suddenly her nerves were gone and she was ready to give what would be literally the performance of, and for, her life.

She emerged from the curtains to glide daintily across the polished wood as if performing a minuet, demurely fluttering her fan. Lucas turned and caught her hand and they performed a graceful dance figure. As they circled each other, he whispered, "You're doing splendidly."

"As are you, my Lord Fox!"

He released her hand and turned to the audience while she took a pensive pose to his left. She saw Denshire in the middle of the front row with his friends, looking amused at the story. "The heiress's money came from trade," Lucas declaimed, "but any reasonable lord can overlook *that*!"

More laughter.

"But much harder to overlook are the stipulations of the marriage contract. What, the vastly wealthy grandfather is tying up all that lovely money in trusts controlled by his granddaughter and her trustees? Isn't it a man's God-given right to spend his wife's money? There's a reason why the Quality don't like dealing with merchants!"

That produced another ripple of laughter. Lucas's timing was excellent. "Lord D. considered withdrawing from the betrothal over the matter of the trusts, but it would make him look ungentlemanly, and besides, an heiress in the hand is worth a flock of heiresses in the bush. He didn't doubt that his manly charms would persuade her to loosen the purse strings when he desired funding."

Kendra discreetly studied the audience. All her friends were wearing black armbands in silent support of her position. Simon and Suzanne were sitting together and holding hands, looking innocent, as were the Kirklands. Rather large and dangerous-looking men were lounging by the two exit doors. She recognized the husbands of Lady Julia and Athena Masterson, both of them former army officers. Denshire would not get past them if he tried to leave.

She didn't know two of the men sitting with Denshire, but she recognized Hollowell, who had searched Thorsay House on Denshire's behalf. There was a furrow between his brows, but Denshire still looked more interested than nervous. He'd probably drunk too much champagne to recognize himself in Lucas's narrative.

Tone light, Lucas said, "The marriage started well enough. There was a measure of fondness, and a warm wife is a fine thing on a cold English night." There were more titters. "After a respectable interval, Lady D. presented her husband with a fine, healthy son. Even better, she was happy to live in the country with the child and leave her husband to indulge in the more sophisticated pleasures of the great metropolis."

His voice deepened melodramatically and he hissed, "Then once again the Sssserpent of Money entered the Garden of Matrimony!

"Lord D.'s man of business informed him that his own fortune was alarmingly depleted. It was time to charm the necessary funds from his very rich wife. He loathed going to her with hat in hand, but the first time, she reluctantly opened her very deep purse.

"But the next time he went to her, the hussy proved annoyingly stubborn. She seemed to think the money was *hers* just because her grandfather had left it entirely and legally to her."

There was a long pause before Lucas resumed speaking with a whine in his voice. "Lord D. didn't beat her very hard, and after all, he had the right to do so, as does any other husband. She was hardly bruised at all. But there was that unfortunate incident when his blow knocked her onto the burning hot grate in the fireplace."

Kendra moved to the front of the stage and lifted her skirt to show the parallel burn scars left by the grate. She had felt shy about showing her legs to so many strangers, but the gasp of shock from the audience was gratifying. Denshire sat bolt upright, staring at her. He hadn't recognized her before, but now he did.

"Lord D. left his country house and returned to London, sure that his wife would recover even though the physician had briefly despaired of Lady D.'s life. He was quite right – she did recover.

"But the incident clearly deranged Lady D. because when she could walk again, she had her lawyers send Lord D. a letter asking for a legal separation. A *ridiculous* notion! He saw no benefit to himself in a separation. Yet as he thought more, he realized there would be *great* benefit to himself if he divorced her.

"But the damned woman was absurdly chaste! There was no evidence that she ever played him false. It was easy to believe that because the icy wench had refused to perform her marital duties after the birth of his son.

"Lord D. didn't really miss her in bed because he found his London companions much warmer. But a man could only have one wife at a time, and this one was useless if she wouldn't share her wealth with him as was his right.

"Then he had a brilliant thought. What if he divorced her and blackened her reputation so thoroughly that he might be able to persuade a court to give him control of her trust funds on behalf of their son? Because he'd take the boy, of course, and send him to some school where Lady D. couldn't find him. There was nothing he could do that would hurt her more, and she *deserved* to suffer as he had!

"She wouldn't oblige him by committing adultery, but since she was now in London, it would be easy to drug her to sleep, get several of his friends drunk enough that they'd succumb when a courtesan who resembled Lady D. entered the dimly lit room and seduced them. *Voila!* He'd have witnesses to testify to her wanton adultery."

Denshire exploded out of his chair, swearing furiously. "Damn you, this is a pack of filthy lies, all lies! The bitch is trying to ruin my reputation! I got my divorce fair and square and I'm not going to stay here to listen to this calumny!"

He swept through the room – and came to a halt by the right-hand door, which was blocked by the tall, muscular figures of Major Lord William Masterson (retired) and his equally imposing half brother, Sir Damian Mackenzie. Will's mild voice said, "You really should stay for the ending of this morality play, Lord Denshire. If you wish to repeat your claims that the story is all lies, you'll have your chance."

Denshire seemed ready to attack, but as he looked at the two tall, broad, and sober gentlemen in front of the door, he backed off and looked at the other exit. Two blond men guarded it, Major Alexander Randall (retired) and the Marquess of Kingston, both of them clearly hopeful that he'd have a go at them.

"It's all bloody lies," Denshire snarled again as he returned to his seat. "You've no proof. Finish your wild talk so I can go home!"

"Interestingly, we do have proof in the form of a respectable witness." Lucas turned and beckoned stage left. "Permit me to introduce Miss Molly Miller."

Nervous but determined, Molly walked onto the stage. She wore a neat blue gown and a black armband. She bobbed her head at Kendra, then turned to face the audience.

"I'm Molly Miller and I was Lady Denshire's maid for eight years. I was the one who treated her cuts and bruises and black eyes after her husband beat her. I was the one who called the doctor after she turned feverish from her burns. I was the one who treated her with cold compresses until she was no longer in danger of dying."

Her gaze turned hard as she stared down at Denshire. "I traveled with her to London, where she planned to seek a legal separation. Then I found her unconscious in her bed. I was unable to wake her and I feared that she was dying.

"I sought out Lord Denshire and found him drinking with his friends. I begged him to call a physician for my lady. He *laughed* at me and told his most awful footman, Brody, to lock me in the basement. He told Brody that... that he could have me later."

There was an audible gasp of shock from the audience. Molly's voice broke for a moment. "As Brody dragged me to the cellar, I managed to shove him down the stairs. To my shame, I abandoned my lady and ran for my life, alone in London with no friends and no money. The kindness of strangers preserved my life and virtue. Today I am proud to speak truth in defense of my lady!"

This time there was applause, particularly from the women in the audience. Kendra felt tears stinging her eyes. As Molly stepped back to stand by the rear curtain, Kendra gave the girl a grateful nod.

Lucas said, "Naturally, Lord D. had no interest in a maid, and he never gave her another moment's thought after sending her off to be ravished. But he did think a good deal about his wife's money. As he filed for divorce and the legal proceedings moved forward, he made repeated attempts to gain control of Lady D.'s trusts. That was entirely for the benefit of his son, of course. He sent the boy off to the Scranton School so he'd be no bother."

Lucas turned stage right. "Behold, more witnesses!"

Three soberly dressed lawyers stepped onto the stage. They were Kendra's family lawyers and they detailed the repeated legal attempts Denshire had made to gain control of Kendra's money.

The senior lawyer concluded by saying, "Having worked with Kendra Douglas for years, I know what a fine brain she has for investments, and I also know her handwriting. It was easy to identify the forgeries that Lord Denshire presented two or three times." The lawyer gave a sharp smile. "He never had a chance of succeeding. The lady's grandfather was exceptionally astute, and there was no way the trusts could be broken by an ignorant amateur."

Denshire scowled at the insult, but he said defiantly, "Of course I tried to gain control of her fortune for my son's sake! In any normal marriage, I would have had control from the beginning. Nothing illegal in trying to take what was mine. But all your fancy talk doesn't cover up the fact that the slut lay with my friends. That was the basis of the divorce. They've all testified to the facts and they are honest men!"

His friends nodded uneasily, with Hollowell looking the most uneasy of all. "It's true," one of the others said. "She wanted me sure enough. I can't lie and say it didn't happen."

"It's interesting that you say that," Lucas observed with an air of innocent surprise. "Here is our final witness. Known as Aphrodite, she was hired to provide 'entertainment' for Lord D.'s friends that night."

The crucial moment had arrived. Kendra turned to the left, watching Aphrodite sweep onto the stage. She was a little shorter and rounder than Kendra, but she wore an identical gown and mask. The onlookers surely thought they were looking at twins. Shock shivered through the theater.

Aphrodite said in a ladylike voice, "Indeed he did hire me and he paid a pretty penny for my time!"

She and Kendra faced each other, then bowed politely as if they'd just been introduced. Lucas asked, "Have you two ever met or exchanged information with each other?"

"No, we have not," Kendra said.

Aphrodite shook her head. "No, there has been no exchange between us before this moment."

Lucas said, "Aphrodite, can you prove it was you who entertained these gentlemen, not Lady Denshire?"

"I certainly can!" She stepped up to the edge of the stage and looked down on Denshire and his friends. She pointed at the man on the left end. "You, sir. Naturally we were not introduced, but I remember you, of course. You have a bent Thomas, pointed west, northwest. But you knew how to use it!"

The man blushed but didn't look entirely displeased by her comment. "That is indeed something she might remember."

Aphrodite turned her attention to the next man. "You have an interesting tattoo of a lion on your left hip. Most men fancy themselves lions in such intimate situations, don't they?" She blinked at him innocently. "You called out something at the critical moment. Shall I tell the world what you said?"

"No!" He flushed violently. "I am now willing to amend my testimony to say that it must have been Aphrodite I bedded that night, not Lady Denshire."

Aphrodite gave a satisfied nod and moved her gaze to Hollowell "You, sir, said that you had always admired me, but that it was unseemly to lie with another man's wife, particularly in his own house. I did my best to change your mind, but your sense of honor was stronger than my blandishments, and my blandishments are very powerful!"

After the resulting laughter died down, she said, "We spent some time discussing the current crop of plays at the theaters until you bid me good night. I thought you were a true gentleman and friend."

Lucas asked, "Sir, do you believe that this is the woman who joined you that night?"

Looking relieved, Hollowell said, "Yes, Aphrodite is surely the woman from that night. I thought her voice was not quite as I remembered, but I'd only met Lady Denshire once and supposed I must be wrong."

"Did you go to that show at Covent Garden I recommended?" Aphrodite said.

Hollowell smiled. "Yes, and you were right. It was excellent."

Kendra had a flash of intuition then. Hollowell preferred men to women and was terrified that that fact would become known. He hadn't wanted to lie with

279

Aphrodite and he feared what she might say, but she had preserved his secret. An honorable woman.

Lucas asked, "Aphrodite, did you lie with Lord Denshire before you left that night?"

"Not bloody likely!" Aphrodite said in a much less ladylike accent. "Denshire has the French pox. I'll take his money but I won't lie with him. It's not worth my life."

The audience exploded after Aphrodite's revelation. Even Denshire's friends drew away from him, appalled at the revelation. In the shocked silence, a cool, educated voice said, "I believe the Church will feel that Lady Denshire's case should have been treated very differently."

Good God, could that have been the Archbishop of Canterbury? His opinion would surely affect a clerical court!

Denshire stood alone, his life shattered even more thoroughly than Kendra's had been. This was what he deserved, what she and her allies had worked for. She drew a shaky breath. The sight was justice, but it wasn't pleasure.

Wild-eyed, Denshire pulled a pocket pistol from his coat, cocking it in one angry gesture. "It's time to *end* this!" he spat out.

Chapter 33

Denshire's pocket pistol was double barreled, and he raised it toward Kendra as he hissed a vile insult at her. Lucas's Royal Navy battle instincts kicked in and he dived at Kendra, knocking her down and covering her with his own body.

BANG!!! A shot exploded numbingly near. Lucas felt a scorching impact across his left shoulder and the acrid scent of black powder filled the small theater.

BANG!!! The second shot was fired an instant later. Then there was paralyzed silence. Lucas rolled off Kendra. "Are you all right!" he asked urgently.

She blinked at him. "Slightly squashed, but otherwise well, I think. What about you? Did you just take a bullet for me?"

"I'm... not sure." Something had hit him, but it didn't seem like a proper bullet. He sat up and dragged off his coat. "The first bullet grazed my coat but didn't hit me. But where did the second bullet go?"

He lurched to his feet and stared down from the stage onto Denshire's blood-covered body. He must have put the second bullet into his own brain.

The audience had been enjoying the drama and titillation of the performance, and the shooting had shocked them badly. Voices rose as people began emerging from their paralysis. A grim-faced Ashton cut across the room to Denshire's body.

By the time he arrived, Hollowell had thrown his coat over the shattered remains of his old friend. He looked as ill as Lucas felt. Death in battle was expected, but not in this civilized house surrounded by civilized people. But Denshire wasn't civilized, and that had brought him to this end.

Kendra had pulled herself together, so he extended his hand and helped her to her feet. "Denshire shot the other bullet at himself," Lucas said flatly.

"Is he...?" She couldn't finish the sentence.

"Yes." He drew her shaking body into his arms. "You're safe now. You've been exonerated and your reputation restored."

"I wanted him out of my life," she whispered. "But not... like this." After a long silence, she said, "I was never madly in love with him, but I thought I loved him enough to go through life by his side. In the beginning, there were some good times."

"I'm glad of that," he said gently. "No one should be remembered only for their worst acts."

She stepped away from him. "I must thank those who have helped me."

"Of course."

She stepped to the front of the stage. Guests were still milling about, but they were recovering from their shock. By tomorrow, most would be well pleased to have attended such a newsworthy event.

Raising her voice, Kendra said, "I hoped that today's performance would bring justice. I did not expect violence, and I'm sorry for how upsetting this has been.

"But I must offer my deepest thanks to all of you who helped me to find justice, not only for myself, but I hope for other women in the future. Many of you were strangers when my campaign to restore my honor began. Now you have become friends. You are all a gift beyond imagining."

Her gaze moved around the stage, taking in Molly, her lawyers, and Aphrodite, who gave her a wink. Kendra smiled and winked back. Her gaze moved to the audience. Simon and Suzanne, the Kirklands, the Fencing Females, the men who had guarded the doors to prevent Denshire from leaving.

Mariah Ashton climbed the few steps to the stage. "You're very welcome, Kendra. I'd expected an interesting evening, but not quite this interesting!"

Mariah was known as "the Golden Duchess," and now that bright sweetness soothed away her guests' last ragged edges of shock. She continued, "I don't think it's appropriate to return to dancing tonight, but supper will be served in the dining room. Please stay and partake of the food and relax by talking with your friends."

She looked down and saw that her husband was just below her, giving quiet orders to servants to remove Denshire's body. "Most of all," Mariah said, "hug the one you love!"

She caught Ashton's hand and pulled him up a step so that he was the perfect height for hugging. Their arms went around each other in an embrace that was tender, comforting, and quietly passionate. Other couples around the room did the same.

Lucas saw that tenderness and passion among the loving couples and wanted it for himself. As guests filed out of the theater, many were arm in arm or holding hands, so Lucas caught Kendra's hand and drew her through the curtains to the room behind. Once there, he turned so they were facing each other, still holding hands.

"You're free now, Kendra. Your divorce decree forbade you to marry while your former husband still lived. Now he doesn't."

"I hadn't thought that far ahead yet," she said, a little startled.

Damning common sense, he said, "This is surely far too premature, but would you consider marrying me when you're ready? Please?"

She froze. "Are you sure this is what you want? You are my white knight who has transformed my life. I have my reputation back, freedom, amazing new friends, and justice. You are under no obligation to marry me because you feel that you should."

"Obligation has nothing to do with it, Kendra. If I have transformed your life, you have transformed mine," he said quietly. "When I met you, I was drifting and uncertain of who I was or what I wanted to do. Now I know who I am." He smiled down at her. "But there are other things I'd like to be, such as your husband and a father to your two beautiful children."

"Do you love me?" she asked softly. "Or is it more that I'm here and we get along well?"

Lucas shook his head. "That's what you had with Denshire, wasn't it? We both deserve better. I love you as I have never loved another woman and can't even imagine loving anyone else as much." He studied her lovely face, her searching eyes with their deep, compassionate warmth. "I know this is too soon. You may never be able to love me, and if so, I hope you find the man you can love." He smiled wryly. "I'm just giving a statement of intent. What you do with it is up to you."

She took their joined hands and laid them over her heart. "I thought that I loved Denshire enough, but I was wrong. I have feared that I love you too much." Her face suddenly lit up. "I hope I'm wrong again! Surely there can never be too much love."

"Never! You have so much to give, and I'm awed and grateful that you want to give some of it to me." He hesitated. "Forgive me for being somewhat dim, but does this mean you'll marry me?"

"It most certainly does!"

"When? Denshire has been dead for less than half an hour so perhaps we should wait a decent interval."

"No, we should not!" she said firmly. "I refuse to let that man rule my life again in any way." More quietly, she added, "I have been mourning the death of my marriage for a long time. Now I'm ready for my future. *Our* future."

With a deep happiness beyond words, he drew her into his arms. "With a special license, we can marry in two or three days."

She blinked. "I suppose we can, but wouldn't you like to have a little more time to be sure?"

"I'm sure now." He grinned at her. "There's a journey that we're going to want to take very soon, and I'd rather not do it in separate bedrooms."

"A journey...?" She laughed with understanding. "Of course. I hope that Simon and Suzanne have time to stand up with us in three days."

They did. Kendra's allies were also available to come to the wedding and celebrate. There wasn't a black armband in sight, and Kendra wore colors for the first time since her marriage ended. Her gown was vibrant green, the same shade as new leaves in springtime. The color of hope and rebirth.

Then it was time for the journey.

—

"Are we there yet?" Christopher was peering out the carriage window, bouncing with excitement. "I can't wait!"

"You won't have to wait much longer." Kendra couldn't resist brushing a fond hand over his hair that was so much like hers. With her other hand, she had a firm grip on Lucas. They'd only been married for three days, and she didn't want to let him get too far away.

She gave him a mischievous sidelong glance. She was definitely glad they no longer had to stay in separate bedrooms. He grinned at her, and she suspected he was reading her mind. She certainly hoped so!

The carriage turned into the driveway and rumbled to a stop. By the time Lucas had climbed out and lowered the step for Kendra and Christopher, the inhabitants of the house were pouring out into the yard. Mary Lowell, her daughter Maggie, her sister Jane.

In the lead was Caitlin, auburn haired and energetic and looking ridiculously like her brother. She slowed down and approached Christopher slowly, her wide-eyed gaze fixed on him in wonder.

Kit returned her gaze, briefly speechless now that the moment had arrived. They reminded Kendra of two cats meeting for the first time, but instead of touching noses, Christopher shyly offered his hand. "I've always wanted a sister."

Not shy at all, Katie seized his hand in both of hers. "And I've always wanted a brother!" Her absurdly colored cat had followed her out with typical feline curiosity, so she made the introductions. "This is my cat, Patches. Aunt Kendra said you have a pony with the same name?"

"Yes, he's at school with me." He laughed. "That proves we're twins, doesn't it?"

"It does! Would you like to meet my pony, Silver? I just got her. Maybe you can help teach me how to ride?"

"I'd love to!"

She caught his hand and they scampered off toward the stables. All the adults had been watching this first meeting, but now it was time for them to exchange greetings. Kendra introduced Lucas as her very new husband, then hugged Jane before moving to Maggie and Mrs. Lowell. Caitlin's family was now Kendra and Lucas's family.

And there was love enough for all.

Author's Note

Divorce in this time period was indeed as rare and draconian as depicted in *Once Dishonored*. Only a handful were granted a year and because of the cost, only the very rich could even attempt it. I didn't go into too much detail about divorce in the book because it's complicated, and boring if too detailed.

The few divorces granted were almost invariably on the grounds of adultery by the wife and there were two phases, the civil and religious. The civil issue was a "CrimCon" trial, that is, the crime of adultery, usually meaning a lengthy, flagrant affair. It was considered a matter of property; that is, the wife was the property of her husband and having an affair diminished her property value. (Pause to insert an eye roll here.)

The wife was not allowed to attend the trial nor to testify because under Anglo-Saxon common law, the husband and wife are one, and the one is the husband. If the CrimCon suit was successful, the lover generally had to pay a large fine to the husband for alienation of affection.

Then the husband sued the wife for adultery and the trial was held in an ecclesiastical court. If successful, the result would be *divortium a mensa et thoro*, that is, a separation of bed and board, and neither party could remarry.

For remarriage, a Parliamentary Private Bill of Divorcement had to be filed and a third trial was held. A successful result would be a divorce *a vinculo matrimonii*.

As I said – complicated! So divorces were very rare, very expensive, and very scandalous. I don't know of any divorce cases like the one I created for Kendra, but I think it could have happened – English law has its share of gray areas. The bottom line is that Regency divorce was particularly hard on women.

It may seem strange these days to read of men who were disdained and despised for taking the opportunity to escape imprisonment, but the code of honor was vitally important to Regency gentlemen. To give one's word was a sacred promise; to break that promise was proof of dishonesty and bad character. No wonder oath breakers were despised and considered beneath contempt!

For a prisoner to give his parole was a pledge of his sacred honor that he wouldn't escape if released from his cell and given the freedom of the local town. In return, his captors would try to exchange him for a prisoner of the same rank. A British captain could be exchanged for a French captain and so forth.

Lucas's situation was inspired by the real life Lieutenant Colonel Colquhoun Grant, Wellington's most valued intelligence officer. During the Peninsular War, Grant was captured and held prisoner by the French marshal Marmont, then sent to Paris for interrogation. When Grant saw a copy of Marmont's correspondence that made it clear the marshal would never exchange him, he decided that his parole had been invalidated so he escaped and made his way back to England. If that reasoning was good enough for Colquhoun Grant, it was good enough for Lucas!

I have no evidence that the gin soaked raisins remedy for arthritis existed then, but folk remedies weren't always well documented, and genever, the ancestor of gin, was indeed a traditional tonic in the Low Countries. So why not? The apothecary appreciated it!